Dedication: this one is for all of the school employees I have worked with over the years:  teachers, paraprofessionals, custodians, cafeteria workers, office staff, etc.  (including - of course – my mother)

Note: A FIRST GRADE FATALITY is a work of fiction. Its settings, characters, and situations exist only in my imagination and on these pages. Any similarities to existing people and places are purely coincidental.

PROLOGUE

"Miss Fallon, what's a murder?" Whaaaattt?!?! Holy Mother of the Moon! That's one question they most certainly do *not* prepare you for in any college course or student teaching experience. Nor, I can thankfully say, had I been confronted with such a query during the six years I'd been teaching first grade at the Redmond Elementary School in Arwell, Massachusetts.

What kind of a reply could I give little six year old Cody Burnett that wouldn't scar him for life and/or get me fired? I've always believed that honesty is the best policy. But, stalling a bit before revealing the truth is O.K.., isn't it? "What, honey?" I asked him, even though I had heard his question perfectly fine.

"What's a murder?" he repeated. Yeah, guess what, it didn't sound any easier to answer than when he'd asked the first time. Even the basic definition of the word was likely to be too much for a first grader to grasp. Undoubtedly, that alone would lead to a million more questions. That's the way it works with the little ones. And knowing Cody, he'd have *two* million more! "Answer the question *with* a question!" suddenly popped into my head. Yeah, that was the ticket! "Why are you asking, sweetheart?"

"'Cuz I heard that Miss Landry had a murder happen to her." Whoa! That was definitely *not* the response I'd anticipated. Where had this child overheard that kind of talk? Who else out there thought that there was something fishy about Carrie's fall down the stairs? "Well?" Cody said, with growing impatience. Oh yeah! Oops! Kinda forgot he was still expecting an answer from me. Thinking about my friend's recent demise had distracted me yet again. How could this have happened? How could my friend and colleague be dead before her twenty fifth birthday? More importantly, had she fallen to her death accidentally…or were Cody's source and I on the right track? Was there more to this tragic story than we knew about? Either way, I felt compelled to find out the truth.

# A FIRST GRADE FATALITY

## CHAPTER ONE

It was three fifteen on a particularly chilly afternoon in January. "Particularly chilly" on a wintery day in New England being a euphemism for "liable to freeze your booty off in less than ten minutes". Unfortunately for me, it was also a Wednesday, my day to do p.m. bus duty out on the playground. *Not* one of my favorite responsibilities to say the least. To those not in the know, herding lines of cute little K-2 students to their respective modes of transportation probably sounds like child's play. Yeah, right! Only if you're referring to the movie of the same name, with that heinous little doll-come-to-life terrorizing the entire town.

One would imagine that the children would be mindful when we called their bus number to begin boarding. But, between the forgotten backpacks, the students' inability to stay in single file lines, and the noise level of an Aerosmith concert, it was really nothing more than organized chaos.

"He cut me!" a freckled faced redhead whined, tugging on the sleeve of my coat as she traipsed by. "Not a valid complaint." I informed her, hustling her towards the steps of the bus. Just wait a few years, kiddo, I thought to myself. When you're at the middle school, that accusation will take on a *whole* new meaning...and maybe even earn you a trip to the emergency room!

Outside with me for this joyous task was Carrie Landry, another of the four first grade teachers at the Redmond School. This was her first year working in Arwell, but we had made an instant connection when we'd met the previous summer while we were in the building setting up our classrooms for the coming school year. (Yes, teachers *do* spend many hours off the clock toiling away in overheated classrooms!) Close in age to me and full of energy and enthusiasm, I was thrilled that she was the one hired to replace my friend Erica Talbot, who had resigned to spend more time with her new baby.

"Thank God there's only one bus left," I sighed as I made my way back to the final group of kids and she led the riders of Bus 9 to their awaiting vehicle. Dang! Why hadn't I brought my earmuffs with me today? My ears felt as if they might fall off at any second! Carrie, on the other hand, was in no danger of losing her hearing appendages any time soon. As always, she had that god awful green knit hat that her grandmother had made for her pulled snugly onto her head. Sure she'd be warm, but she wouldn't be getting any offers to appear on the cover of Vogue in the near future. Then again, neither would I, and I wasn't even sporting a frumpy evergreen doily atop my lengthy brown locks!

Mercifully, we got the last batch of students on their way and were back inside the too warm building before very long. I needed to get a few things set up for the following day's lessons and collect the papers I had to correct at home that night. "I should probably cut some white paper for those snowflake projects we're doing next week too." I remembered as we reached the top of the short set of stairs that led in from the playground.

"Well don't stay too late. You need to be at Santino's at six thirty." Carrie said as we turned down the rather dark corridor leading to the first grade classrooms.

"Shhhh…" I motioned, cupping her mouth with my still gloved hand. "Annette's going to hear you." I reminded Miss Loose Lips in a frantic whisper. Crap! The last thing I wanted was for Annette Bunting to find out that we were planning to meet some other first grade staff members, past and present, for dinner at the small casual restaurant on the outskirts of town. Needless to say, Mrs. Bunting hadn't been invited to join us. It wasn't that we didn't like the long term substitute. She just didn't quite mesh with the rest of our group.

From the first time I'd met the Redmond School's first grade "team" after I was hired, it was clear to see that they were a pretty tight trio. Admittedly, I'd been a tad leery being a newcomer on the scene initially. Fortunately, my personality was a perfect match to theirs and since then, the four of us had shared countless laughs and good times together. With the addition of Carrie to our faculty and our close knit group of friends, the fun had continued. And even though Erica no longer worked with us each day, Dale, Joan, and I always found time to socialize with her at least once or twice a month.

Without that effort, time passes by and people who were once a big part of your life could easily vanish before your very eyes without you even realizing it. We weren't about to let that happen, especially now that Joan Petrillo was out on a personal leave to take care of her ailing husband for an indeterminate amount of time. Not having her across the hall from me on a daily basis was a major adjustment for me, particularly with Erica being gone too. Since October, instead of a smiling forty something brunette seated behind the teacher's desk in Room 104, we had a forty something with a perpetually serious puss and a reddish blonde bun in her place. Yay.

Don't get me wrong, Annette Bunting and her "polygamist's wife" style hairdo was without question a very nice person. Perhaps a smidge *too* nice to mingle with our animated crowd. We're no heathens, hellions, or lawbreakers by any stretch of the imagination. But, we do enjoy a bit of gossip to liven up our days and more often than not, you'll hear a few jovially used curse words when we are around one another.

"Is Joan coming tonight?" Dale Badger asked nonchalantly as he appeared in the doorway of his classroom.

"Would you keep it down, fool!" I admonished. What was wrong with these people? We may as well just have the school secretary broadcast the details of our exclusivistic dinner outing over the P.A. system that ran throughout the building for Pete's sake! "Relax. She's already gone." the only male member of our first grade staff informed me. "The youth center asked her to come in a half an hour early to supervise the nine to twelve year olds."

"Oh, sorry. My bad."

"You need to chill out. Even if we invited her, you know she'd decline. She's got no money. With her husband out of work, she's busting her butt here and at the after school program trying to scrounge up some bucks just to live on. Mama's gotta be frugal these days."

That much was true. And being saddled with three kids and an unemployed spouse had to be hard on her. Instead of dodging the poor woman, we should have been encouraging her to join us for a night out, *our treat*. Maybe next time. After all, we aren't heartless.

Several hours later, I was enjoying a most delicious glass of Chardonnay with Dale and Erica as we waited for our other two dinner companions to arrive. We'd specifically requested a corner table to elude any Redmond parents or families who might pop in to Santino's for a bite to eat. Restaurants aren't all that plentiful in Arwell so running into a student was fairly likely, which was why we'd chosen the least "kid friendly" dining establishment in the area for our monthly outings. I love my students to death, but I also love sending them home at the end of each school day too, preferring to eat my meals in "child free" zones as often as I could. At some point in my future, I wanted children of my own…and after that happened, the phrase "child free" would be nonexistent in my world.

"Where's Carrie?" Erica wondered. "She's usually the early bird."

"This is the first time she didn't beat all of us here. " Dale realized.

"I don't know. She must have gotten sidetracked. Hopefully she didn't get snagged by a parent in the parking lot."

"Call her and see where the hell she is." I, myself, didn't really think a phone call was necessary. Yes, she was an "on the dot" type of gal, but it wasn't as if she was *hours* late. "I'll wait until Joan gets here." I told the impatient twosome.

Now Joan, on the other hand, we never knew what time she would show up. She hadn't exactly been Miss Punctuality (technically Mrs. Punctuality) even before her husband's Early Onset Alzheimer's diagnosis. Nowadays she could run five minutes late to five hours late or even wind up as a no-show. Warren Petrillo was lucky to have such a dedicated wife in his time of need. Though I knew only the basics about his devastating disease, I also understood that interacting with the victims of this awful condition on a daily basis was trying for their loved ones as well. There wasn't a whole lot anyone could do about Warren's condition, but providing his wife with a few hours of laughter and conversation was something I *could* do thankfully.

"Oh, here's Joan right now!" Erica cried out, standing up to wave her hands in the air.

"Uh, this isn't a Red Sox game, toots. " I reminded my loudmouthed pal. A rare evening away from her motherly duties always revved her up. "Park it, dearie."

By then, Joan had reached our table. "Hey, what's up?" I asked, standing to give her a hug. Our token male, Dale, remained seated. Men! Were they innately incapable of expressing their concern in physical form? Apparently so, considering he was one of the "good ones"…and yet his buttocks still appeared to be firmly attached to his chair. "How's everybody doing?" Joan asked with a slight smile. "Isn't Carrie coming?

"She is. We were just talking about where she could be. I'll give her a buzz if she doesn't show up in a few minutes. Here, sit. How's Warren doing?" The smile on her face faded. "He's okay," she replied somewhat sullenly. Taking care of him day and night had definitely taken its toll on her. "I take it Max is with him tonight?"

"Uh huh."

Thank goodness for Max Petrillo, Warren's brother. Ten years younger than Joan's husband, who was only in his mid- fifties, he had proven himself extremely dependable in helping her care for the ailing man and gladly stayed with him so that his sister-in-law could get some time away pretty much whenever she needed. Not that she took advantage of his offer all that much.

"Is he still sleeping a lot?" Dale inquired.

"Yes, thankfully. Getting him to go to bed can be a challenge at times, but once he's in there, he's typically down for the count. That's when I try to get housework and other things done." Fun, fun, fun. Laundry and doing dishes were her idea of "free time" these days. Poor thing.

"Yeah," she sighed, "He can get pretty stubborn when he doesn't want to do what I tell him. But, recently he's been watching a lot of T.V. during the day, which keeps him content and gives me an opportunity to check my email. So feel free to send me a message to keep me in the loop. But enough about my sorry life. This isn't a pity party. What's new with everyone else?"

"Well, my little Brianna peed herself again today. But that's as exciting as it gets for me."
"Spectacular."

"And Savannah's entered a delightful hair pulling phase." chuckled Erica. Savannah being her eleven month old daughter. "So I may be bald or wearing one of those huge Dolly Parton wigs the next time you see me if she keeps it up." she continued, chugging down the remainder of her Corona.

"I can't beat that one." Dale said, "I'm still trying to whip my hellish class into shape, despite the fact that we're only a few weeks away from the midpoint of the year. Oh, and lest I forget my daily dealings with my should-be-ex. Those are always pleasurable exchanges. For some unknown reason she still hasn't signed the divorce papers. She screws someone else behind my back and then doesn't get why I want a divorce! "

"Maybe there's a chance you could patch things up with her then." Joan weighed in. Had it been anyone but her to make that remark, Dale's evil eye would not only have shot daggers, but protruded from its socket and punched her in the mouth like a demented jack-in-the-box. "Yeah, *not* gonna happen." he firmly declared.

Poor Dale. He was normally such a fun person to be around. But, ever since his wife Jodi had left him out of the blue the past autumn, Mr. Badger was snippy and testy more often than not whenever the topic of his wifey came up. "Let me call Carrie!" I interjected excitedly before he could bring down the mood any further. We were supposed to be having fun dammit! "Hey, girl, what's keeping you? Hope everything's all right. I'm assuming we'll see you soon. If not, give me a call when you get this. Bye."

"Buh bye, girlfriend!" Erica felt compelled to add with a shout. I began to wonder how many beers she'd sucked down before I'd gotten there.

"No answer? Maybe she got in a head on collision" Dale carelessly suggested, earning him not one, but three, looks of disdain.

"That's terrible!"

"What would possess you to say such an awful thing?

"Jackass!"

"What?" he shrugged, "I'm just sayin'."

"Well don't say it again," I furiously commanded, "Unless you want my foot in your face. And I'm wearing boots." So much for having a jolly good time!

"Sorry, sorry. I have no idea why that even came out of my mouth. I guess I was just thinking aloud. Trouble travels in threes, ya know. My life was thrown into a tailspin when Jodi ditched me. Watching Warren deteriorate is eating away at Joan. Who's next? One of you? Carrie? Someone else?"

"Hopefully *none* of us."

"Let's put this gloom and doom to rest right now. We rarely get to see each other altogether anymore. Let's not ruin a good time." I said in my most chipper teacher voice. "With luck, Carrie will be here shortly and we can eat. I'm starving."

Unfortunately, though we didn't know it at the time, Carrie Landry would not be joining us at Santino's that night....or ever again.

## CHAPTER TWO

At ten minutes to seven, we finally got around to ordering. Having only picked at the questionable looking salad I'd bought in the school cafeteria at lunch much earlier in the day, I was hungrier than an anorexic on Prom Night by the time our meals arrived. "Hey, I just had a thought!" I said through a mouthful of mashed potatoes. Oh lord, how many times had I been on lunch duty and directed a kid to keep their mouth closed while they ate? And here I was defying the very lunch laws I laid out! *It only counts if a student witnesses your offensive etiquette and emulates it,* I convinced myself. Plus, I had an idea to share! "I wonder if Carrie blew us off for that new guy she met."

"What new guy?" Erica asked as she bit into her pizza.

"I didn't know she was seeing anyone." said Joan, "I hate being out of the loop." Dale sat silently and made no reply. "She's not really dating him or anything," I explained, "She just met him some time last week. I think she's gone out with him once, maybe twice." I pulled out my cell phone to see if I had somehow missed a message from her. Nope. No blinking yellow icon. No voice mail or unread texts. Hmm....

"Hey, ladies, I think I'm going to head home." Dale decided, laying a few bills down on the table as he got up to leave.

"That was a bit abrupt." I commented as we watcher our friend exit through the side door.

"For sure. And he barely said a word all night." observed Erica.

"You more than made up for it, Motor Mouth." Joan replied, giving Erica a mischievous grin. "And with that, I am off to the ladies' room." It was nice to see her crack a joke for a change.

She had been jittery all night, quite different than her fun loving "old self". Living her life to serve and protect her spouse was valiant, but it was certainly wearing her down. But, what more could I do for her to help keep her from becoming overwhelmed by anxiety? I'd really have to reach out to her more than I currently was. Maybe even just a quick visit to her after school might cheer her up a bit.

The next forty five minutes was reminiscent of our usual Santino's gatherings, as my remaining two companions and I gossiped and giggled like schoolgirls until Joan happened to glance down at her watch. "Oh lord, I need to get going!" she gasped. We tried to coerce her into staying a bit longer by agreeing to order *another* dessert, but met with resistance. "I *really* need to get home."

"It's still fairly early and Max is there. If there was any problem, he'd call you."

"Yes, but I don't like to take advantage of his kindness. He drives almost an hour to get down here." Joan Petrillo was hardly one to take advantage of anyone, but clearly her mind was set. After kisses and promises to talk soon, she was off, leaving just the new mom and me to finish out the night.

We rehashed the evening: Carrie's mysterious absence, how tense Joan seemed, the fact that Dale's silence was most likely due to the heartbreak he'd suffered. "He lashes out at Jodi, but he's crushed." I revealed.

"Yeah, ever since he found out that Jodi slept with her boss, he's a changed man. He used to be so energetic and witty. Now he's closer to comatose and cranky."

"He hides it well at school. I think the kids and their unpredictable antics keep him from becoming too depressed." Life sucks sometimes. It's not all rainbows and clown parades once you're out there livin' in the real world. Fortunately first graders don't know that yet. Maybe that's why I enjoyed my job so much.

"So anyway," the proud mommy relayed, "I'm going to enroll 'Vanna in swimming lessons next week." Swimming? Really? Last I'd seen, Baby Girl wasn't all that adept at walking, never mind busting out the breast stroke in the pool with Michael Phelps. But what could I say? "Cool." was all that came to mind, followed by "Savannah this…Savannah that…" and " 'Vanna blah blah blah…" and more stories about the child that I really just didn't give a flying fig about at the time. Savannah Eugenia (I know, horrific! Right? But Erica's hubby's grandmother's sister or some other long dead ancestor had that name and, now, cruelly, so did this poor child.) Talbot is one of the *cutest* toddlers you ever will lay your eyes on. But, at that moment, my thoughts were on Carrie Landry. Joan had said she would do a drive-by down Carrie's road since the house that she and her sister shared was only a mile or two away from the Petrillo's tidy little ranch on Perth Street. Still, I wondered if I shouldn't give one, or both, of them a jingle.

But, I didn't want to risk waking up Warren and seeing as I'd already left a message for Carrie, it seemed pointless. So my gal pal, Mrs. T., and I made our way to the parking lot, said our farewells in dramatic girly girl fashion, and I went home to correct phonics worksheets and math puzzles as I caught up with The Real Housewives of Somewhere on the flat screen I'd given myself for Christmas a few weeks earlier.

Six thirty a.m. came *way* too quickly for my liking. Of course, had I just done the unusually small amount of schoolwork I needed to do and hit the hay, I may have been less inclined to slam the snooze button four…okay, five….times. Instead, once I'd gotten up to speed with those trash talking housewives (some of whom reminded me oh-so-much of a certain handful of ritzy Arwell mothers), I realized that I also needed to Keep Up with the Kardashians, during which I caught wind of an upcoming Robert Pattinson story on E! News that I didn't dare miss. Team Edward all the way, baby!

Needless to say, by the time I'd showered , yanked my hair into a ponytail,  managed to pull together a remotely decent outfit, and inhaled a piece of toast, my clock was screaming, "Get moving, Snail Woman!" over and over again. Either that or I still had a mini buzz from that wine the night before and just thought the clock was giving me grief.

Flinging my book bag onto the passenger's seat, I hopped into my Toyota Corolla and quickly started the ignition, then closed my eyes for a little power nap while I waited for my trusty vehicle to warm up. Opening one eye, I could see that most of the frost was gone from the windows which meant departure was imminent.

This was pretty much my morning routine every day, not just the days after a night out, I must admit. But despite this frantic ritual, I was somehow always bright eyed and bushy tailed by the time I pulled into the small staff parking lot on the right side of the Redmond School, an imposing two story red brick building that had "elementary school" written all over it.

"Hi," I greeted the school's librarian, Fran Vespa, as I hauled my ninety two pound bag over my shoulder. She, like myself, wasn't exactly a "morning person" so we almost always arrived within mere seconds of each other.

"Tomorrow's Friday." she replied with a twinkle in her eye. Each and *every* one of the one hundred and eighty school days was measured by how close it was to that blessed day of the week by *every* school employee in *every* school in *every* town in the state, I had no doubt. And, of course, how close that given day was to the next upcoming school vacation!

"Woo hoo!" I cheered, holding the door of the faculty's entrance open for the older woman.

"Thanks, honey. Have a good day." she said, heading down the steps to her post in what I liked to call "the dungeon" due to it being on the basement level.

"You know I will." I replied enthusiastically, mentally preparing for the six hour show I'd be putting on that day for my cherubs. A parent had informed me in my first year of teaching that her son needed "to be entertained" in order to learn. I'd humorously replied, "Did you think this was America's Got Talent? Because I don't see any panel of judges and I left my tap shoes at home today." Unfortunately, she'd been dead serious. Silly me!

Coming down the first grade hallway, I hollered out my typical a.m. greeting of late, "Howdy y'all!"

"Good morning," Annette replied eloquently from inside Joan's classroom. Otherwise she would have given me that peculiar look she shot me whenever I used my "down home" welcome call. Such an old fart.

"Howdy!" a bespectacled Mr. Badger responded as I waltzed by his classroom room. Something was amiss, I realized. "Why are you wearing your glasses?"

"Lost one of my contacts," he explained.

"Ah, that bites." I said with what I presumed to be an appropriate amount of sympathy. Thus far, I'd been lucky enough to not have to rely on contacts or any other aid to assist my vision, but I was sure my day would come.

Wait a minute! Something else was off. Why weren't there any lights on in Carrie's room? Had she called in sick? In my mad dash this morning, I'd completely forgotten all about her unexplained absence the prior evening and was now more than a little worried.

"Where is she? Did she come in to drop off plans this morning?" Although it was expected that a substitute could walk into any given classroom on any given day and follow the day's lesson plans found on our desks, most of us classroom teachers were neurotic enough to type up and deliver more detailed plans and notes if we took an unexpected sick day.

"I dunno." Dale answered far more casually than I would've liked, given that he was also aware of her not showing up for dinner. "I haven't seen her, but I just got here myself and went right upstairs to make some copies. Did you ask Annette?"

Considering that in roughly two minutes, this corridor would be crawling with dozens of little bodies, I did well not freaking out completely. Carrie Landry was up at the crack of dawn daily and at school shortly thereafter. Was I the only person unnerved by the fact that she wasn't here yet?

Annette Bunting, also an early riser, didn't seem too shaken up when she informed me that Carrie hadn't been in since she, herself, had arrived at seven twenty five. But, I gave her a pass because she, at least, didn't know that my friend had been a no show the night before. Dale did.

"Did you think to ask Sylvia if Carrie was out sick while you were in the office?" I wondered aloud. Sylvia Wise was no rocket scientist. She wasn't really even a very competent secretary, truth be told. But the one thing that Mrs. Wise *was* on top of was calling the substitute's answering service to find out if anyone had called in sick that day.

"No. But, maybe she emailed you or Dale her lesson plans. Did you check yours yet?"

I hadn't and was able to breathe a temporary sigh of relief. If Miss Landry had come down with a nasty stomach bug and had been tossing her cookies and milk all night, she clearly wouldn't have been in any shape to drop of lesson plans in person. Hastily, I shuffled into my classroom, clicked on the lights, and dropped my bag onto the floor beside my desk.

In this wonderful Age of Technology, just about anything could be copied and sent virtually anywhere with little effort in the blink of an eye…or the turn of a stomach, as the case may be. It really was amazing if you stopped to think about it. Unfortunately, there was nothing on my computer screen to amaze me as the morning bell rang and the Redmond School sprang to life.

"Hi, Miss Fallon!" I heard the first shrill voice cry.

"Good morning, Mitzi," I answered vacantly. *Where the heck could she be?* "Hi, Toby," I smiled nervously as I backtracked toward the hall. Leaving the pair unattended momentarily, I rushed diagonally across to see Dale. "She's still not here. No email. No Carrie. Nothing." I filled him in tersely. "I need to call her to see what's going on. Can you send Betsy over when she gets in so I can go call from the Teacher's Room?"

"Yeah, no problem. Let me know what you find out." he replied, ***finally*** showing a trace of concern for our friend.

Several minutes later, Betsy McAllister appeared in my doorway. A paraprofessional, known to many as a "teacher's aide", Betsy worked in Dale's room for the majority of the day to assist the students on individual education plans, or IEPs. For now, she had kindly agreed to watch my class while I tracked down our missing colleague.

With no teacher, substitute or otherwise, in the room, Carrie's students had respectfully waited in the corridor until an adult arrived, as all Redmond students were instructed to do in such a circumstance. Good job, kiddos! "Miss Landry's class, thank you for waiting so patiently." I told them as I ushered them inside their classroom. Pressing down the intercom button, I awaited a reply from Sylvia in the office. "Yes?" she called down from above.

"Mrs. Wise, Miss Landry isn't in her room yet. Do you know if she's out today?"

"Who's this?" Swift Sylvia inquired. Though to be fair, people didn't always sound like themselves over the speaker system and I *was* in another teacher's classroom after all.

"It's Diana....Fallon." I added on at the last second. I was the only Diana that worked in the building, but just in case this was the day that Sylvia had lost *all* of her marbles, I figured I'd throw her a bone.

"She's not on my absentee list."

"Okay, well we need somebody to cover her class nonetheless." Just send someone, *anyone*, so I can figure out where Carrie is before I lose my breakfast on the floor. Mr. Callahan, our school's janitor, would *not* be thrilled about a clean up this early in the day!

Just then, the tardy bell rang, indicating the start of the school day. Since no one had shown up to replace me yet, I switched into Teacher Mode and began to take attendance immediately. Crisis or no crisis, the welfare of the students always came first. There was no use sending panic through the room just because their "real" teacher wasn't present.

"She's at a meeting." I told the class when asked for her whereabouts.

"Where's your class?" another curious tyke wanted to know.

"They're in my room next door, as always." I explained, running short on patience and high on anxiety.

"Alone?" a blonde who was most assuredly destined for the Airhead Hall of Fame inquired.

"Oh no, honey. Mrs. McAllister is working with my children while I keep an eye on you. Why don't you all take out your music folder and we'll sing a patriotic song after we salute the flag."

"The principal's here!" announced an unusually tall boy near the door. And so he was. In strode Mr. Welkey, walking tall and authoritatively towards me. A sudden wave of dizziness overcame me and for a split second, I was afraid I might pass out. "Good morning, Miss Fallon." George Welkey smiled as he approached.

Saying nothing, I walked in his direction. "Where's Carrie?" he inquired in a discreet whisper.

"I'm not sure. I'm a little nervous though." I relayed with a forced smile upon my face to fake out the children. "We had plans last night and she never showed up. Now, today, she's missing. I'd like to go call her if that's okay."

George Welkey knew that he had an outstanding staff. If an ideal employee like Carrie Landry hadn't shown up for work, he realized there had to be a problem. "Yes, go right ahead. Unless you'd rather I do it."

"No, that's fine. I have my cell in my pocket. I'll just phone her quickly and get right back to you."

"No hurry. I'll look after these youngsters until Sylvia rounds up a sub." Gratefully, I darted out of the classroom and around the corner into the teacher's lounge and pressed Carrie's number. It rang twice before the line was picked up. I hadn't even had a chance to express my immense relief when a *male* voice spoke.

"Hello?" I said cautiously. Had I dialed the wrong number?

"Hello," replied the man at the opposite end of the line, "To whom am I speaking?"

"To whom am *I* speaking?" I echoed, "I'm trying to reach Carrie Landry, but I must have dialed incorrectly."

"This is Deputy Frank Miller, with the Arwell Police Department. I'm afraid there's been an accident involving Miss Landry." Oh. My. God. Did Dale have ESP? Was he a regular caller to the psychic hotline? Had he foreseen Carrie's auto crash when we were at Santino's? "An accident?" I repeated, my stomach in knots and my mind chastising me for not checking on her again the previous night.

"Yes, it appears that she fell down her stairs sometime last night. Her sister discovered her when she arrived home from work this morning."

"Cassie!" I exclaimed, but was distracted by another gruff male voice in the background. "Miller, who the hell are you talkin' to? We're on the job here, man."

"It's the vic's phone. It rang while I had it in my hand and instinctively…"

"Are you friggin' kiddin' me?" roared the second voice. "Hello?" it then boomed into my ear.

"Hello. Is Mr. Miller…"

"This is Detective Paul Donovan. *I'm* the one who's in charge here. And you are?"

"Diana Fallon. I work with Carrie."

"Then I'm sorry to tell you that Miss Landry won't be reporting for work today, or any other day. She's dead."

## CHAPTER THREE

Dead? My knees weakened and I clutched the back of a nearby chair to prevent myself from collapsing. Lowering myself onto the seat, I thanked the detective and clicked off my phone. To say that I was in utter shock would be an understatement. At twenty seven, I was still young enough to have had limited exposure to death.

But because I was young, I was resilient as well. As much as I wanted to sink to the floor, bawl my eyes out, or shriek like a banshee for hours, I did my best to pull myself together. It was up to me to break this horrible news to Mr. Welkey. With luck, I'd remain composed enough to get the devastating words out of my mouth.

Mercifully, I held it together and relayed the tragic fact to him when he showed up in the Teacher's Room a few minutes later. "I'd like to…I mean, I just don't think I can…"

"Go home, Diana. Sylvia found a substitute to cover for Carrie and we can leave Betsy in your room the rest of the day. I'll go tell her and let Dale know that she won't be in his room at all today."

I nodded somewhat coherently, knowing I'd be better once I absorbed it all and my disbelief turned to realization. "Will you tell everyone that…"

"Of course." my boss declared, making hand motions to shoo me away. Geez, could he be any more eager to get rid of me? "I'll gather everyone at lunch time and make an announcement. Oh, and Sylvia will need to type up a letter to go home, I suppose. You run along, though, Diana." he directed me as he dashed off to deal with this unexpected problem.

Distraught, I had forgotten I'd need my keys in order to leave. Naturally they were tucked away in my purse, which was, I assumed, still on the floor beside my desk. "Damn it." I wasn't sure I could face the kids just yet without bursting into tears.

"What's wrong?" a gravelly voice asked from behind me.

"Holy mother of the moon!" I yelped, clutching my chest as I spun around. Oh, no. Could the day get any worse? It was Jim Callahan, the custodian, not so fondly referred to as "Creepy Jim" by the majority of the Redmond School's female faculty members. He was tall and scrawny with thinning gray hair and crooked teeth. But it wasn't his physical appearance that bothered us, it was his slithery way of moving about and his wanton stares that grossed me out. It was almost as if he viewed us as his private possessions. Even in my fragile state, I wanted to make it fully clear to him that I'd rather be possessed by a demon from the underworld than a certain semi-grimy voyeuristic janitor.

"I'm fine. " I let him know with false bravado. "I just need my pocketbook and it's down in my room."

"Yeah?" his look read. So why don't you hustle on down the hallway and get it, his narrow eyes implied. "I'm on my way out and I don't want my class to see me." I explained, at which point he offered to go fetch it for me.

"Thank you *so* much!" I said with one hundred percent sincerity. As uncomfortable as he routinely made me feel, "Creepy Jim" had come through for me and I appreciated his kindness for sure.

Minutes later, I was back in my Corolla, driving aimlessly down the road. Going home to melt down in the privacy of my apartment was an option, but being by myself at the moment didn't sound all that appealing. I made a sudden decision and swerved into a bank's parking lot to turn around. I'd go see Cassie. She was Carrie's only family in the area and surely she could use some support. On my way to the house that the sisters shared, I phoned Erica to fill her in. I figured I could stop at Joan's to break the bad news after seeing Cassie.

I guess I'd been so focused on the fact that Carrie was no longer alive that it didn't dawn on me that the police would still be at the Landry's home when I arrived. Part of me reasoned that it would be wiser to come back later in the morning, when everyone else was gone and Cassie was by herself, but I also felt an obligation to my friend to console her sibling in her time of need. Even if Cassie had had the chance to call her parents in New Jersey, it would still be quite some time before they'd be able to get up here to Massachusetts to be with their daughter.

With great trepidation, feeling as though I may pass out at any second, I emerged from my car and walked past a dark colored sedan and an Arwell police car parked in the driveway in front of the Landry's garage. I debated over which of the two doors to use. Normally I used the front door when I came for a visit. But, going through that entrance would bring me in right at the bottom of the staircase, a spot I did not want to see, be near, or even think about right now. Instead, I headed around the side of the pretty gray and white Colonial to the back door that led into the modern, though infrequently used, kitchen.

The lights were on, but no one was in the room. I knocked lightly, hoping to be greeted by Cassie, but unsurprised to see a young looking male with an olive complexion and short black hair striding towards the door. I wondered if he might be Deputy Frank Miller, the officer I'd first spoken to. "Good morning," he said in an inquiring tone. Basically he wanted to know who the heck I was and why I was there, no doubt. So, being the law abiding citizen that I am, I gave him the desired information.

After introducing himself as Deputy Miller (Aha, I was right!), he gestured me inside and had me follow him down the short carpeted corridor to Cassie's bedroom. As we passed the rear section of the living room, my gaze remained straight ahead, to avoid catching sight of anything or anyone at the front of the room, where the stairs were located.

Cassie sat silently on the edge of her still made bed as I entered the room. Crying out my name, she lunged at me and locked me into a forceful embrace. Damn! For a fairly petite blonde woman, she packed quite a punch. I felt like I'd been plopped down into the middle of a New England Patriot's game and been tackled by the entire opposing team. Once I regained my breath, I expressed my sincerest sympathy and disbelief as the surviving sister clutched onto me.

Deputy Miller made a polite escape to the front room, leaving the two of us alone. Between sobs, hers *and* mine, Cassie Landry was able to give me the basic timeline of events. Just after Carrie had gotten home from school the prior afternoon, her sister had departed for the gym and gone straight to her overnight shift at the hospital where she'd been employed as an R.N. for the last several months. She'd been surprised to see Carrie's Sentra in the garage when she returned home that morning and had, soon thereafter, discovered my friend at the bottom of the staircase and determined immediately that she was beyond reviving. Once police personnel were on the scene, they'd somehow come to the realization that Carrie's purse and keys were locked in her car. Not long afterwards, one of them had used Cassie's spare key to unlock the vehicle and retrieve Carrie's belongings, including her cell phone, which Diana had called, leading to the conversation she had had with the deputy and his superior.

"They think she was running around frantically, trying to find her things, when she tripped and fell." It was certainly a plausible scenario. There were countless times, not unlike this very morning, when I'd raced around my apartment like a madwoman, attempting to locate one misplaced (and usually quite visible!) item or another.

"But wouldn't she have thought to look in her car?" I wondered aloud.

"I don't know." Cassie replied vacantly. "Normally, she plunked all of her stuff down on the kitchen table when she came in, but only her book bag was on the chair this morning. I guess she accidentally locked herself out of her car and mustn't have noticed till after I was gone, if at all. Maybe she was in a hurry." Hurrying to meet us, I presumed. Though why wouldn't she have just called me to let me know she was running late or, if she'd known, that her keys were stuck in her car? Oh yeah…. the Landrys had no land line, only their cells. This seemed to be an increasingly common trend, though for the life of me, I couldn't understand it. Maybe because my own cellular device was a piece of crap.

Whatever the case was, it didn't really matter. The Redmond School's youngest first grade teacher had tumbled to her death and would never call me or anyone else ever again. How would the rest of the staff react when they learned that such a young life had been taken? I dreaded going into work tomorrow, but returning to our shared workplace was inevitable.

I waited until Cassie's friend, Val, arrived to replace me as a shoulder to cry on. Then, promising to stop by again very soon, I quietly let myself out through the kitchen. Today, the cold air felt refreshing, unlike the day before at bus duty. The last bus duty of Carrie Landry's too short career. The patrol car was still in the driveway. I wondered why its driver was still there or who he was waiting for as I hopped into back into my own vehicle. I didn't even bother putting the heat on for the two minute drive to the Petrillo's. By the time I'd gotten there, the heat would only be a cool breeze anyway. Why bother?

Joan's eyes were wide with curiosity as she opened up the side door of the small brown house. "What are *you* doing here in the middle of the morning?" she nervously interrogated as she took my coat and hung it on a hook behind the door. Stepping further inside the quaint cozy kitchen, I spotted a Parcheesi board on the table, where Joan's husband sat, silently watching me. "Hey, Diana," he waved. Most of the time, he recognized me, but it was always a "wait and see" moment until he addressed myself or any other visitor. Lately, Joan had confided, he was remembering faces less and less.

"Hi Warren! How's it going?" I asked casually, ignoring his wife's question for the time being. *How* was I going to tell her what had happened without breaking into tears? "Looks like I've interrupted your game."

"Yeah, we were playing Monopoly when we heard your car door slam." he nodded, turning his attention back to the game board and reaching for the dice. Awkward moment. Did I correct him by telling him it was Parcheesi and potentially embarrass him or overlook the harmless misstatement?

Joan saved me by suggesting that he watch some television while she and I chatted. "We can finish our game later. *The View* is on in a little bit anyway."

"I hate *The View*."

"No, you don't. You watch it every day."

"I do?

"Yup, you know the show with Whoopi Goldberg and Rosie O'Donnell. That's *The View*. Come on, I'll turn it on for you. Diana, just take a seat while I get him set up. I'll be right back." she told me, a hint of anxiety in her voice. Was it possible that somebody had already broken the

28

terrible news to her? Or did she just equate her colleague showing up at this hour on a weekday when she should be at work with trouble?

"So, why aren't you at school?" she asked me immediately upon her return. The poor woman was visibly shaken and I'd yet to deliver the critical message. God, poor Joan really didn't need this on top of everything else. I almost wished someone *had* beaten me to the punch. But, at least I would be able to break it to her gently, unlike a certain Detective Donovan, who'd slammed me with the cold hard facts.

"There was an accident. Involving Carrie." I began as tears filled my eyes for the umpteenth time that morning.

"What sort of accident? And how do you know about it?" she asked, wringing her hands together.

"Joan, she's gone." I told her as the floodgates let loose. Gone. Yes, that was a better way to think of it. I simply couldn't bring myself to use the "D" word. At first, she was speechless and sat in a state of catatonia. Then, her eyes, too, filled up. "Where? How? Did she suffer?"

I'd just given her the basics when Warren shuffled into the room. "I need to eat breakfast." he announced, seemingly oblivious to his wife's distress. Always the stoic one, Joan wiped away her tears with the sleeve of her cardigan, then turned to face him. "You had breakfast a few hours ago."

"No, I didn't."

"Yes, you *did*!" Joan unexpectedly snapped, startling me. Realizing she'd lost her cool, she calmly reminded him about the bacon and eggs she'd fixed him earlier. How she kept her sanity,

I didn't know. Maybe it was the patience she had mastered teaching first grade for twenty odd years that got her through these trying times. Relating to a daft six year old wasn't all that different than dealing with someone suffering from Alzheimer's at times.

"Color the clown's hat blue." I might say to the class.

"Color it *blue*?" one child would invariably ask.

"Yes, blue. Color the clown's hat *blue*."

"With a blue crayon?" someone would nearly certainly inquire.

"No, with a friggin' orange highlighter!" I'd sarcastically reply in my mind. But, naturally I would respond with a "Yes, honey. A *blue* crayon."

"I'll make you some lunch after *The View*." Joan promised, getting up from the table to escort the befuddled guy back to the couch.

"*The View* isn't on today." I overheard him telling her.

"Yes, it is. This is it right on the screen. See, there's Barbara Walters."

"Didn't she used to live down the street?"

"Nope. Not Barbara." she informed him, though he'd likely ask the same thing before the show ended in less than an hour. Joan confided, when she came back into the kitchen. "I do love him dearly, Diana. But he may drive me to drink."

We discussed potential plans for Warren once he became too much for Joan to handle on her own for a bit, before she turned the conversation back to the tragedy that had befallen our friend.

"Did she die instantly?" she wondered. Though that answer was unknown to me, I hoped that she had.

You just never knew what could happen on any given day, I realistically acknowledged. The discovery of a spouse's infidelity. A life altering diagnosis. Or a simple misstep coming downstairs that could end a life in a flash.

It wasn't until the following day, though, that I started to have concerns about the "accidental" fall that had claimed young Carrie Landry's life. But, once I did, I found it hard to quell those disturbing thoughts.

A FIRST GRADE FATALITY

CHAPTER FOUR

After spending a considerable amount of time with the Petrillos that day, I'd reluctantly gone home to grieve some more on my own. Joan had decided it was best to keep the news from Warren, as she didn't want to overload him with information he may or may not remember the following day anyway. So, as a surprisingly pleasant distraction, we'd played a few games of Parcheesi.

I spent the rest of the day thinking of ways that Joan's friends and colleagues could help ease her burden, talking on the phone with Erica and Cassie, and bawling my eyes out. That night, Dale called to give me a play by play of the school day : who'd hysterically broken down in the Teacher's Room following Mr. Welkey's shocking announcement at lunch, who'd shown little to no emotion (those heartless witches in second grade!), who'd immediately whipped out a Bible (Annette. Shocker!), and what had gone down with regards to Carrie's students.

A formal assembly was held in the cafeteria to announce the loss of Miss Landry to all of the students at 12:30. And, as George Welkey had told me before I'd left school, a letter was sent home to the parents of *all* Redmond School students. Most importantly, though, the psychologist we shared with another primary school in town had conducted and in-class discussion about death and dying in Carrie's room. Dr. Mary Wong was a consummate professional and had deftly taken all questions and comments from the now teacherless class. Miraculously, only one of the students had been inconsolable and had been sent home early.

Even so, I had a feeling that the next one would be a rough day for staff, students, and parents alike. Mary had her work cut out for her and I was oh-so-happy not to be in her shoes. (Though I willingly confess to envying a pair of dazzling red Jimmy Choos she'd worn to our last faculty meeting- Jimmy Choos on a teacher's salary? I don't think so! On a school psychologist's salary along with her private practice earnings and likely supplemented by her orthodontist husband, bring on the Choos!)

Unsurprisingly, despite crawling into my bed a good two hours earlier than my usual eleven o'clock bedtime, I barely slept a wink. By five fifteen, a full hour and fifteen minutes before my alarm clock was used to being pummeled by my fist, I was up and in the shower. Mentally, I resolved to be strong and keep the tears to a minimum. But, just to be on the safe side, I opted to go without mascara. The last thing the Redmond School needed was a tear stained first grade teacher who resembled Alice Cooper frightening the little ones today!

As any teacher will assure you, getting to school early the day after you've been out is a "must". Lord only knew what kind of a scene you'd be walking into. I always hoped for the best, but realistically expected the room to look like Times Square at three a.m. on New Year's Day.

Fortunately, Betsy McAllister was as awesome at last minute classroom coverage as she was at working with the special needs students she worked with each day. Even so, the library area and tubs of math manipulatives reminded me of the aftermath of Hurricane Katrina. Though to be fair, it had probably been Hurricanes Jackson, Daniel, and Gregory who had created *this* mess. Katrina Warner picked her nose and sampled her snot on a daily basis, but when it came to keeping the room tidy, that girl got an A+!

Although my anal retentive mind wanted *so* badly to organize and put every little thing in its appropriate place, that could wait until the children arrived. First, I needed to see how much of Thursday's planned lessons and assignments Betsy had been able to get to and, if necessary, revamp my plans for the day ahead. Thankfully I'd had everything pretty well laid out, and my plan book was meticulously filled out (unlike some teachers who wrote just a page number or one word in each subject block!). At first glance, it appeared as though things had gone very well. What a relief!

I also wanted to check my mailbox in the main office upstairs to see if anything earthshattering (besides the major news of the day, I mean) had happened in my absence. Ambling down the gloomy hall, past Carrie's room, got me misty eyed, but I forced myself to suck it up and not let myself get sidetracked. Yes, it was horrifying and stomach turning and unimaginable, but I had a job to do, and I owed it to the kids to do it properly. A devoted teacher such as Carrie would most certainly have agreed. In fact, what better way was there to help push aside your grief than spending the day with a roomful of adorable first graders?

Heading up the staircase, I could see that the lights were on in the office. Although the principal himself wasn't the earliest of birds, his longtime secretary was indeed. "Good morning, Sylvia," I said softly to her scrawny backside, which blocked my entry as she bent over to extract something from the bottom drawer of her filing cabinet. Well, Holy Hell On Wheels, I've never seen an old woman whip around so quickly in all my lifetime! Nor had I ever heard such an earsplitting shriek that early in the morning.

Sweet Mother of the Moon, was the ditzy old broad going into cardiac arrest on the spot? "What on Earth are you doing, sneaking up on me like that, and how in Heaven did *you* get yourself here at this hour?" Mrs. Wise replied in a huff. Marvelous. She wasn't having heart palpitations because she was older than Moses and had had the crap scared out of her. It was my earliest arrival in my six years at the school that had shocked her so.

"I'm sorry I frightened you."

# A FIRST GRADE FATALITY

"I'll be fine just as soon as I sit down." the stunned secretary assured me, though she was still clutching her chest.

Grabbing the small stack of envelopes and notices out of my mailbox, I asked Sylvia who would be subbing in Carrie's room. A suitable substitute was difficult to come by some days. And given the sudden loss of a classroom teacher, it was crucial to get someone that could handle the touchy situation in an appropriate manner, although I assumed that Dr. Wong would be in the room for a good portion of the day as well.

"Lucy Shinwell will be in there today."

The parent of a former student. "Oh that's good. She should be able to cope with any problems that come up." Though I didn't envy her that task. Kids at the primary level still adored their teachers. Losing their much loved Miss Landry would not be easy on them, but kids are a lot more resilient than many people would expect.

"Mr. Welkey hoped Miss Devane would be able to do it, but she's out of town until Sunday. She'll take over on Monday and, I believe, will stay on until the end of the year." I shuddered at the name. Leticia Devane was the longtime teacher I'd replaced when she had retired after eons of service to the Arwell school system. Miss Devane was reputed to be tougher than nails, but highly respected as an educator. Truth be told, she intimidated me a little, though our paths had crossed very few times.

"Mr. Welkey will be in to monitor how things are going this morning as well." Sylvia relayed. Although she was a good ten years his senior (at least!), I'd never once heard the proper old gal refer to her boss in any way than his formal title, Mr. Welkey. Many of us called our principal by his first name, though not out of lack of respect for him.

But to Sylvia Wise's generation, such an act was unacceptable. Women, and men, in her age bracket had been brought up in a far stricter environment than myself or most of my peers. Formality was expected, not optional. Perhaps if today's society took an example from that type of upbringing, our incoming student population would be more respectful of authority. Sadly, the trend was exactly the opposite.

"Did you get many calls from parents after school yesterday?"

"Oh goodness, yes! My phone was ringing off the hook by three thirty, I tell you! Mothers, fathers, even a great grandmother. Not so much worried about their child's emotional needs, though. Most of them only expressed concern over their little tyke's *safety* here at Redmond! Now, does that make any sense to you?" the cross office worker demanded.

No, it did not. But, somehow it didn't surprise me. Some parents these days were just plain *dense.* Some of the notes, emails, and telephone calls I'd received in my relatively short career (thus far) boggled my mind. How would a young woman *falling,* at her own personal residence, endanger their child? Even my pupils understood the difference between communicable and incommunicable illnesses! (Or at least they should, given the number of days we'd spent on that grade one health unit in December!) The age old adage, "The apple doesn't fall far from the tree." was oh-so-very-apt in many many cases! Though I could also pinpoint a good number of lucky youngsters who'd thankfully rolled down a hill *far far* away from the wilted "tree" they'd blossomed on as well.

Catching sight of the clock, I realized we'd been chatting for longer than I had intended. Time permitting, I wanted to straighten up the room a bit before I had to endure my final bus duty of the week at eight thirty. Of course, that plan was foiled when Annette Bunting nabbed me in the hallway and proceeded to endlessly talk my ear off. While I did appreciate her sympathetic comments and kind words about Carrie's many fine attributes, I could have done without all of the religious mumbo jumbo she tried to force down my throat.

I'm no atheist, mind you. I go to church on Easter and Christmas Eve and for other special occasions throughout the year too, but Bible toting Bunting was on a whole other ethereal level. Most days, she opted to eat lunch alone at her (really Joan's, I frequently reminded myself to improve my spirits) desk, reading the Good Book. How she had the time to sit and read for an entire hour was unfathomable. I barely had enough time to scoot my booty down to the staff rest room to relieve myself and wolf down some yogurt or a banana before the recess bell rang!

On my way out to the playground to usher in the little darlings before they could jump on a seesaw or run off and hide (which has happened to me *twice*, I might add), I chastised myself for my irritation with Annette. There were far worse things she could be carrying around with her: a Marilyn Manson CD, a copy of *Hustler*, a loaded shotgun, or a photo of *Jersey Shore's* JWoww post-Botox ! Annette busted her behind caring for her family, working two jobs all week, and even tutoring on weekends. Maybe she read the Bible to keep from losing her sanity.

Speaking of being driven mad, have you ever tried to slow down a herd of elephants about to trample you to death? Then, you can easily envision what morning bus duty is like. The doors of the long macaroni and cheese colored vehicles open, and those suckers are off like greyhounds on a racetrack. Except there *is* no racetrack, and *you*, the adult in the line of fire, are the mechanical white rabbit they're after!

Given the sadness of the previous day, though, I honestly didn't despise being out there to march the little buggers in. It was nice to see their smiles and hear their animated conversations as they passed by me on the way into the school, as my own class waited against the wall of the building until all buses had arrived and all riders had disembarked. But, alas, my happy times came to a halt when a tiny kindergartener came flying off of the bus steps onto the asphalt. I rushed to his side, relieved that the angel faced boy wasn't crying. "Are you okay, honey? You need to be careful when you're coming down the steps."

Angel Face turned satanic as he pissily told me in no uncertain terms that he had *not* fallen. "Jason pushed me!" he denounced, pointing an accusatory finger at the taller boy behind him. Looking in his direction put the accused on the defense at once. "I didn't do anything. I didn't push him. You didn't see me!" he spat out quickly. True, I hadn't seen him do it, but that didn't necessarily mean that he was blameless. More often than not, a child who so vehemently denied doing something before being questioned about it often *had* done something wrong.

As I took the boys' names down to turn in to the principal's office for further "investigation" , an unexpected and unsettling idea flashed into my mind. "No," I pooh pooed. *Why* would I even consider such a terrible notion? The police had told me flat out that it had been an accident. They were the professionals, so clearly they would know what they were talking about. So why should I think otherwise? But, what if it hadn't been? What if, like the cute little kindergartener, Carrie had been pushed?

CHAPTER FIVE

Once I was back inside and the school day had begun, I put aside the absurd idea. Carrie's death was horrible enough without adding malice into the equation.

After taking attendance and lunch count, we moved to the rug, where the children sat on the floor as we read our morning message on the easel. Per a memo from the superintendent of schools, I made no mention of Miss Landry's passing, as instructed. Unless a student brought up the topic, we teachers were to gloss over the incident. Personally, I wasn't sure that was the best approach, but I assumed he had conferred with Dr. Wong before putting out such a directive so I did as I was told. On the school system's hierarchy, who was I to make that determination? I was *only* a teacher.

At the board, I reviewed counting by fives using a number line and was pleased at how many of the kids not only remembered the previous lessons but were able to put it into practice as well. Following a fun counting game, I set them to work on two corresponding workbook pages as I started to do my lesson plans for the next week at my desk. Everything was ideal in Room 103 for a good twenty minutes, until I caught a flash of movement out of the corner of my eye.

That eye, then the other, popped to bullfrog proportions and my mouth involuntarily fell open as I took in the wildly inappropriate sight. Out of his seat, beside his best pals, the sweet role model of my group was thrusting his crotch into his buddy's face! "Oh sweet mercy," I muttered as I leapt up from my chair and speedily crossed the room to put an end to the pint sized Chippendale's routine. "*What* are you doing?" I shrieked like a madwoman.

"I'm Adam Lambert at the awards show."

"Like hell you are!" would've been my preferred reply. Thankfully I was a trained professional and was able to rephrase it as, "Oh no, you're *not!*" instead. "You *aren't* Adam Lambert and you are *not* at the American Music Awards. You're Cam Presley," No relation to Elvis in case you were wondering, given his hip moving abilities. "And you're in a first grade classroom… and first graders do not *gyrate* at their classmates."

"What does 'gyrate' mean?" asked brainy Liz Anne Bernstein. Oh crap! I'd totally set myself up for that one. Did I dare attempt to define it? Or should I ignore my star student and hope the inquisitive lass forgot about it by the time she got home? I feigned deafness and crossed my fingers that she'd mispronounce it if she went to Mommy or Daddy for clarification later on.

It was bad enough when adorable little Anni Kim was "twerking" during music class, but pelvic thrusts brought it to a whole other level! I motioned the typically well behaved Cameron up to my desk to get to the bottom of his raunchy performance. How was a cutie pie his age even aware of Lambert's risqué number at the 2009 awards show? Ah, but of course, that wonderful YouTube! "My sister watches it every night." the boy informed me. "She told me I should copy him." That made perfect sense. His sneaky sibling had perfected the skill of getting others into trouble way back when she'd been in my first class at Redmond. One had to wonder if the poor girl would wind up behind bars before graduation…or if a career with a pole and a stage was in the cards for her now.

Tossing aside my "private eye" hat for the time being, I slipped back into teacher mode and resumed penciling in lessons in my plan book. So many hats we teachers have to wear: nutritionist, therapist, interpreter, mime, doctor, squad room interrogator! We're actors and actresses right up there with Johnny Depp and Jennifer Lawrence for sure, which is why I didn't crumble to pieces when the image of Carrie in her "extra" hat, that evergreen monstrosity she loved so much, came to mind. Thankfully, I kept my composure until, in what seemed like mere minutes, it was already lunch time. Yay!

Predictably, Bookwork Bunting holed up in the classroom, leaving Dale and I to dine in relative peace in the Teacher's Room. Even better, I'd actually had the time to make myself a tasty peanut butter and banana sandwich with the excessive free time I'd had before leaving my apartment that morning. Yum, yum! No limp lettuce salad or crusty macaroni and cheese from the school cafeteria for Miss Fallon today!

If only the conversation at the round table we sat at could have been as perfect as my delicious sandwich. But, the obvious topic came up just a few minutes into our meal. "How did Carrie's class do without her this morning?" Dale asked substitute teacher, Lucy Shinwell. Carrie's class. Could that group of children still be referred to that way? Technically they'd become Leticia Devane's come Monday morning.

"Surprisingly well. Dr. Wong stayed for a while and pulled a small group of kids who seemed to need her support more than the others, but overall it's been a good day so far."

"Children can handle a lot more than people give them credit for." Dale pointed out. I nodded in agreement. It was out with the old and in with the new, I realized sadly. Life kept rolling on for the living. Any one of us could be and would be replaced once we were gone. Trying to make myself accept that grim fact, I said nothing as the pair continued to discuss the situation until a comment Mrs. Shinwell made caught my ear and slammed me out of my state of silence.

"Lauren Royal, Mark's mother, mentioned that the death has been ruled as 'suspicious'." she informed us. If so, that was news to me. I wondered if Cassie was aware of this, *if*, in fact, it was true. Having worked in Arwell for six years, I now understood how the small town's grapevine could send facts *and* rumors flying fast in just a few hours. The karate studio, the ball field, and dance classes were the hotbeds of Arwell's information highway. Mrs. So and So told Mrs. This and That, who told Mr. Man About Town, who shared what he'd heard with his wife… sometimes the parents found out about things happening at Redmond or the other schools in town before the clueless faculty had heard a peep! Then again, one misinformed mom, who got it all wrong, could send needless ripples of panic throughout the community too.

So, which was the case? Had the mommy network messed it up again? Or was my preposterous notion not so foolish after all? Dale seemed to dismiss the idea right off the bat, haughtily telling her that Carrie's house had been locked up tight when her sister came home, a fact which I'd relayed to him when we had chatted Thursday night. The validity of his argument, though, could easily be smashed to smithereens. If, by some bizarre chance, someone *had* been inside her house and pushed her to her death, all that person would have to do was lock the door before closing it behind them as they took off.

I would wait until I spoke with Cassie some more before forming my own opinion, but my nerves were racing as I delved into what Lucy Shinwell may have heard in the twenty four hours since Carrie's demise had gone public. Unfortunately, she had little more to add and, soon enough, the bell rang, and the three of us headed down to retrieve our classes.

Mercifully, the afternoon was uneventful. I got the bulk of my lesson plans finished while the kids were at physical education in the café and, by the end of the day, was packed up and ready to be on my way once the minute hand hit ten past three, our contract dictated time of departure. Poor Dale had gotten the short end of the stick this year, assigned to afternoon busy duty on Fridays. It sucked to be him today. But, it sucked worse to be Carrie, who'd never get to do or complain about the much detested duty ever again.

Having phoned Cassie while my class was out of the room that afternoon, I'd been pleased to hear that she was up for some company after school and headed directly to her place, making a quick stop at McDonald's to pick up some shakes for us. When I was little, my mom always got me a shake when I was sick, and they always put a smile on my face. Maybe the tasty treat would help cheer up Cassie too.

Her parents, she'd told me, had come up from New Jersey the prior afternoon, but were staying at a nearby Holiday Inn instead of at the house. "Mom didn't want to see the spot where...*it*...happened." Cassie had gone on to explain. The house itself was owned by the girls' parents, Arthur and Judith Landry, who had inherited it from a grandmother at some point in the not so distant past. Though Carrie had lived in one of the newer dorms on the Bridgewater State University campus her first few terms, she and two of her classmates had moved into the house, paying rent to her parents instead of the university, once it had been cleaned out and updated a bit. After graduation, Carrie had lucked out by snagging herself a job teaching in the very same town, while her roommates returned to their own hometowns. Not long afterward, Cassie searched for and obtained a nursing position in the area and the sisters had been housemates ever since. Until yesterday, that is.

The floor at the foot of the stairs was spic and span when I arrived, and I assumed that some sort of crime scene –or accident scene- cleaning crew had taken care of the matter. Yuck. "Thanks for stopping by...and for the shake." Cassie said as she led me into the living room. "My parents are a wreck. I am too, but they're making me crazy. I spent the night with them at their hotel, but came home early this afternoon for some 'alone time'." Oh. Had I intruded on her? "But, once I got here, the house felt so empty. I was actually debating going back to the hotel to help them with the arrangements for the memorial service even though I really wasn't up to it when you called. Your timing was perfect. Thanks so much for coming by. I know you must be as upset over this as we are. You were her closest friend."

Uh oh. The waterworks that had taken charge of my tear ducts over the last twenty four hours threatened to give way again. So, I fixated on something else. "A memorial service? Will there be a wake too? Or a funeral?" Somehow sipping on a delicious chocolate shake made discussing these dreadful details a bit more bearable.

"My father wants to have the funeral in Jersey since most of our relatives live down there. I don't know about a wake. We're doing a memorial service on Sunday at Beltzer's Funeral Home so that everyone up her can come. Her friends and colleagues. I suppose that's in place of the traditional wake."

"As long as there's a chance for us all to come and pay our respects and say a final farewell to her, it doesn't matter what it's called." I assured her, wiping away a runaway tear. Now, how could I bring up the primary reason for my visit without seeming ghoulish or out of my gourd? Yes, I did want to find out about the arrangements, of course. But, I also wanted to find out whether Carrie's fall had been ruled "suspicious" or not, and, if so, what exactly did that terminology imply?

Like her sister, Carrie was a very up front kind of person. I decided to come right out and ask her rather than beating around the bush. For a moment she didn't say anything and I was afraid I'd pushed past the limits of decency. But, then I saw that she seemed to be pondering the question.

"That detective, the brusque one, he did comment on a few things, but I can't recall exactly what he said. I do remember overhearing him talking to some other guy, not that young cop that was here when you came yesterday, about lost blood or the lack of blood. Maybe that's why the case was labeled that way."

"That could be." So, naturally, I wanted to get to the specifics regarding that issue ASAP. Then another, much different, idea sprang to mind. "Perhaps it was just because her belongings were all locked in the car." I suggested. "Weird circumstances."

"Possibly, but why would that be considered 'suspicious' rather than 'stupid' or 'careless'? The only time that's happened to me, I was running late on my way to take an exam in nursing school. In my haste, I locked the car doors, but neglected to grab my purse first, which I didn't even realize until after the test was over and I went to go home."

"Yeah, I suppose. But, Carrie should've had plenty of time to spare before coming to meet us for supper."

"Unless she was going somewhere else on her way.

I hadn't thought of that possibility. "Maybe someone called her between the time she left school and the time she got home. Did the police listen to her messages by any chance?"

"I don't think so, but they could have, I guess. They left her stuff on the kitchen table. Let me go get her phone and we can check her messages and voicemail."

So, we did just that, to no avail. There were no texts and just two voice mail recordings from two days prior on it. The first one was from me, calling from Santino's. The second one, received at 11:14 p.m. that same night, was Joan. "Hi, Carrie. It's Joan. Sorry to call so late. I was going to stop by on my way home from dinner, but your lights were off so I thought that maybe you weren't feeling well and had gone to bed. Just wanted to check on you. Call me tomorrow." Another dead end.

"Have your parents talked to the police at all?" I wondered.

"I don't think so. Why?"

"Come on, let's go." I told her, grabbing my purple purse and taking my keys out before she could resist my abrupt directive. "We're going to the police station."

"What? Why?"

"Because you want answers."

"I do?" Well, maybe not. But *I* did! Only I wasn't a blood relative and she was. Ever since I'd learned that word on the street was labeling this death "suspicious", I'd wanted to know why. And factoring in little Angel Face's tumble down those steps made me even more curious.

Turns out I was right to keep asking questions.

## CHAPTER SIX

My stomach was in knots by the time we pulled into the small lot in front of the white rectangular building that housed the Arwell police department. I'd put on a brave front to persuade Cassie that we needed to hear what the cops were *officially* thinking, but by then I *officially* wanted to puke up that chocolate shake and delectable sandwich I'd had at lunch. Approaching the gray haired officer behind the glass window in the miniscule lobby caused an unwelcome shift of my stomach contents.

Luck wasn't on our side, as Detective Donovan wasn't in. On second thought, I surmised, that could totally work in our favor if Deputy Frank Miller *was* in. He'd been much nicer to deal with than the gruff detective. Shockingly, good fortune had finally found its way to us. Not only was the "bad cop" out. But, the "good cop" was in! As we watched him come out from an office behind the gentleman at the window, he waved and I realized how cute he was. Stunned by the horrible turn of events and nervous about going into the Landry's house, I had apparently overlooked his killer smile and tight bod.

A door on the right side of the bland beige lobby opened up. "Ladies, come right in." he invited, chivalrously holding the door for us as we entered and equally bland gray corridor. We followed him into a small room that was slightly more cheerful looking and took seats in the chairs that Miller moved in front of the desk. "What can I do for you Miss Landry?" he politely inquired. Just call me Chopped Liver. Screw him. I wasn't here shopping for a man anyway.

"Cassie and I have heard from several sources that her sister's case may not be as cut and dry as we were originally led to believe." I let him know, getting right down to business. "Basically, we, rather *she*, wants to know if you, or rather your *boss*, feels as though there might be reason to believe that Carrie's fall wasn't a simple accident."

"Well, Miss Fallon," So he *did* know my name after all! Now I felt a teensy bit bad for diminishing his rank that way. "I'll tell you what I can for the time being."

Deputy Miller and his keen eye had found the positioning of the body a bit odd. Having (mercifully!) not seen my friend splayed out on the floor, I was unable to comment. But apparently it was the back of Carrie's head that had made contact with the floor and been damaged to a fatal degree. "I, personally, found that difficult to envision. Most often when someone stumbles while coming down stairs, they fall headfirst, with the front of the head taking the impact. Contrarily, one who trips going up, falls forwards, not backwards."

Whether or not the information he'd presented was correct or not, I couldn't say. But, it sounded quite logical. "That was my observation," he continued. "However, I can't say with a hundred percent certainty that it would be impossible for her to land in that manner. We can't refute that as *not* having happened." He was very good at covering the department, rightfully so. Litigation seemed to be the newest form of entertainment for this millennium.

"What did Detective Donovan think?" I quizzed him.

Miller seemed to take his time answering, carefully choosing his words perhaps. "I can't speak for Detective Donovan." he finally replied. Another example of the professional hierarchy? Right or wrong, his theory appeared to have been dismissed by the guy in charge. Not all that unusual. Authority figures disliked having their power challenged or being proven wrong by those on the lower rungs. I'd seen it happen plenty of times at school wide in-service workshops and curriculum committee meetings.

"What about the blood?" Cassie asked in a hushed tone.

Directing his gaze at Cassie, he said, "As for the blood that had pooled up under your sister's head wound, there didn't seem to be a whole lot of it. Head traumas and injuries are funny though. You can have very little bleeding with fatal results *or* a gaping gash with what looks like buckets of blood and the victim walks away from the scene unassisted. The medical examiner did note the lack of blood, but it didn't seem to go any further than that, unless he included something more in his report."

"Carrie's family, Cassie and her parents, would like a copy of that report if possible." I told the dashing deputy. Cassie obediently nodded her head in agreement.

How I was able to hear such gruesome details about my friend's tragic end and respond in such a detached manner bewildered me. Yes, I read plenty of mystery and suspense novels whenever I could find the time, some of them exceedingly gory, but that was fiction. This was real life. Friendly law abiding elementary school teachers didn't get murdered in the real world, did they?

"What do you think happened, Deputy Miller?" I wanted to know. "Are you confident that it was an accident?"

"Based on the facts we have thus far, it certainly could have been a freak accident." he stated.

"But…?"

"Let's just say, anything is possible." A fine noncommittal way to make me believe that my worries were not irrational? That's what I took it as.

"Thanks very much for your time and assistance, Deputy Miller. We very much appreciate it." I told him, nudging Cassie to get up.

"Yes, thank you." she repeated quietly. Unlike me and my unusually unemotional reaction to the information we'd gathered, Cassie appeared to be worse for the wear. Perhaps bringing her along hadn't been the best idea after all. But, without her present, I wasn't sure, legally, how much the police could or would tell me. At least now I was armed with a bit more knowledge than I had been when my suspicions were initially aroused. But, now what?

I took Cassie back to the house and hung out with her awhile longer, until she was ready to leave for the Holiday Inn, where she'd promised to spend the night with her folks. By that hour, it was dark out, it being the middle of winter and all.

When I finally returned to my apartment, some twelve or so hours after leaving that morning, the bitter chill in the air had intensified greatly. "Hopefully it isn't going to snow." I mumbled as I made my way up the stairs. Not over the weekend, that is. Come Monday morning, I'd be saying, "Bring on a blizzard, Mother Nature!" wishing for a "snow day". As of yet, we hadn't had any days off due to the weather, but there were still a good two and a half months left before we'd be snowless for sure.

I nuked a frozen lasagna entrée and dined on it in front of my precious flat screen. Though I yearned for a dose of reality T.V., I put on the local news instead, wondering if Cassie's passing would be relevant enough to make the broadcast. Apparently, it wasn't. Vowing I'd be back later on (yes, to the *T.V.*, which for some inexplicable reason didn't reply- imagine that!) to watch something more scandalous and brain numbing, I headed to the kitchen, where I tossed the remnants of my fine Italian dinner into the trash and washed my fork.

# A FIRST GRADE FATALITY

Changing out of my work clothes into my snug Smurf covered flannel pajamas, I did a belly flop onto my bed and lay there for several minutes in ecstasy until the shrill ringing of the phone startled me right out of my Happy Place. It was Erica. "Yay, girl! I was going to call you in a few, but you beat me to it. Boy, do I have a boatload to tell you…" So tell I did, beginning with Big Boy pushing Little Boy. (Unbeknownst to primary school students, who genuinely believe teachers tuck their names away into some sort of mental Naughty Files when they reprimand them one time, their names are actually only retained for about forty five seconds before the files disappear like Amelia Earhart and her airplane, never to be seen again.)

I went on to cover the *American Idol* runner up's impersonation, Lucy Shinwell's tidbit, and everything that followed. I finished my rambling with "So now I'm fearing that her fall wasn't an accident even more than I was before!"

Erica was not convinced. "Diana, I think you should accept that it was. No good is going to come from fretting over it. Besides, who in their right mind would want to kill Carrie?"

I fought the urge to point out that anyone who kills another human being *isn't* in their right mind, though I did concede that no one had motive to do away with our friend. "But, what about her purse and keys and phone being locked in her car? I'm questioning whether somebody else locked her stuff in there."

Only a true friend isn't afraid to hold back. "Have you lost your freakin' mind?" she asked, "Why on earth would anyone do such a thing? That makes no sense. Are you sure that *you* didn't fall down some stairs and hit *your* head? Maybe that's why you're so paranoid."

"First off, that was one sick comment. Secondly, don't mock me. I'm not saying somebody *did* push her, just that it *could* have happened." When my reluctant "sounding board" didn't

51

reply, I took that as a sign to continue on. "Two scenarios come to mind. One is that some mystery person, whoever that might be, shoved Carrie down the stairs for whatever reason they had and then planted her things in the car to make it look like she'd been stranded at the house.

"*Or*, if you don't like that theory, how about this one? The person deliberately locked all of her belonging in her car to *trap* Carrie at the house with no means of escaping or calling for help."

"Except for her two legs, that she could use to run away from this imaginary madman, and her vocal chords, with which she could produce screams as she hauled ass down the street." my naysaying friend countered, her voice dripping with sarcasm. Thankfully she was a good friend most of the time. Otherwise, Girlfriend would've been talking to the dial tone by that time.

"Point taken," I accepted, "But…"

"But, nothing. Yet again, let me ask you why someone would lock her keys in her car either before or after tossing her to her death? To prevent her from dining with her colleagues? I don't think so."

"To keep her from telling us something?"

"This isn't *Desperate Housewives*, Diana, and we don't live on Wisteria Lane. I hate to burst your imaginative bubble, but we're all pretty boring."

"I suppose we are." Perhaps I was letting my love of murder mysteries and T.V. crime dramas get the best of me. "I simply want to be one hundred percent certain about what happened. Let's say, *hypothetically,* that something did happen to Carrie, that somebody else was responsible. Wouldn't you want to make damned sure that the guilty party paid for taking her away from us?"

"You know I would." That's all I needed to hear her say to make me a happy camper for the time being. Friends didn't have to be in complete agreement every second of every day. And, although I was frustrated as all hell not knowing if we knew the whole truth yet, I was also woman enough to admit that I could be acting like a total nutcase for no reason whatsoever. My intuition, fueled by Deputy Miller's skepticism, really had my mind working overtime, but it could be that I was blowing things way out of proportion to mask the tremendous sense of loss I was feeling. "I'll call you tomorrow." I told my gal pal to end the night on a peaceful note.

"Sleep tight, my friend." she replied as I put down the receiver. But, if you think that actually happened, you're easier to fool than a first grader…and I've got a bridge to sell you.

True to my word, I returned to my lonely flat screen, curled up on the couch wrapped in a raggedy old comforter, and watched three full hours of my favorite shows on Bravo before channel surfing for at least another hour. Finally, I decided to head to my bed, for what I anticipated would be a very long night.

I tossed and turned for God knows how long. Eventually, sometime around two thirty I later estimated, I must have nodded off to sleep. "Why me?" I heard a familiar voice cry out from somewhere in the darkness that surrounded me. Huh? What? "Why me?" the voice called out a second time.

Looking around aimlessly, a shadowy figure appeared under a dim light nearby. She was on the ground clutching her knee, repeating that same phrase over and over. I found myself moving in her direction. "Are you all right?" I inquired. "Can I do anything for you?" Just then, I saw the blade gleaming brightly. "Oh no!" I yelped, nearing the helpless victim. Her leg was positioned at an unnatural angle and the glare from the blade on her ice skate caused me to shield my eyes, which were clearly deceiving me. "Nancy Kerrigan?" I asked, spotting the form fitting USA bodysuit she wore. "What the...?"

Suddenly, Nancy's trim body collapsed into a flattened heap, mangled limbs protruding from beneath her. "Why me?" she whimpered one final time. Only this time when I looked down at her, it was the ghostly white face of Carrie Landry that stared back!

With a swift jerk, I awoke, breathing in frantic gasps and scared out of my mind. Evidently watching that *Scandalous Olympic Moments* countdown special so close to bedtime had *not* been a wise move. And, truthfully, I could understand why my deceased coworker would be confused if she'd been attacked by someone as vile as that piece of trash, Tonya Harding or her despicable husband. Like our home state's skating sweetheart, Carrie Landry had never done anything to warrant such violence against her.

"Why me?" I could hear the beloved teacher innocently inquire. Why indeed? Why not some low life wife beater or a disgusting child molester like Jerry Sandusky? Why not a terrorist or a savage beast who plundered African villages and brutally ravaged its girls and women? Why not a corrupt politician or a deranged serial killer?

With all of these viable candidates available, how was it that a young vibrant woman had come to such and unexpected and tragic end, either accidentally or otherwise?

CHAPTER SEVEN

Quite understandably, I slept well into Saturday morning. Finally, shortly before noon, I threw on some clothes and headed over to the Petrillo's house to bring Joan her plan book so that she could complete her lesson plans for the upcoming week. In the past, because she lived so much closer to Joan, Carrie had been the one to deliver it to her and then pick it up on her way to school each Monday to give to Annette. As of this week, it looked like the task was now mine. Although Mrs. Petrillo was not expected to do the plans for a long term sub (who probably would have liked to be allowed to fill in the daily plans herself, truth be told), she was always ecstatic to have something "normal" to do for a few hours each weekend. "That way I'll know exactly what's been done when I come back. It'll make for a much easier transition." she'd say.

Personally, I thought that was wishful thinking on her part. Warren's condition, sadly, was only going to get worse with the passage of time. Despite his deterioration, though, I knew that Joan desperately wanted to keep him at their longtime home until circumstances became drastic enough for that to no longer be an option. At that point, I supposed, she could potentially resume her teaching duties.

Warren's devoted wife looked particularly haggard and more frazzled than usual when she answered the door, still clad in her nightgown. I had a feeling that sleep had eluded her the night before, as it had me. "Oh, Diana, I'd forgotten that you were coming by." she sighed, allowing me entrance. "Rough morning," she explained in a voice soft enough that her husband, who was once again parked in a chair at the kitchen table, would not overhear.

"Good morning, Warren." I smiled, realizing as I said it that morning had passed and it was now early afternoon.

"How do you know my name?" he asked warily. Uh oh. Evidently he was in a confused state today.

"Oh, I've met you before, Warren. I'm Diana Fallon. I work with Joan."

"At the hospital?"

"No, at the Redmond Elementary School. I teach there."

"Oh," he curtly replied, continuing to eye me suspiciously. Joan merely shook her head and shrugged slightly, indicating that it would likely be a waste of time to continue on with the conversation. The poor guy. Only a small percent of Alzheimer's patients were diagnosed with the disease before age sixty. Warren Petrillo, who was younger than my own father, just happened to be one of the unlucky ones in that sad minority.

With regards to Joan, she looked like a hot mess today, not that I would tell her so. And Warren was now gazing blankly across the room at the wall. Having ascertained that he did not want to eat, watch T.V. or nap, Joan informed him that she and I would be in the living room for a bit. "Call for me if you need me."

Sagging onto the green mosaic patterned sofa beside me, tongue hanging goofily out of her mouth, the harried caregiver let out a moan. "I am *so* happy you stopped by. Thank you, thank you, thank you."

"Not a problem. Any time you need me to come keep you company, just say the word. It's one of the few things I can actually do for you. I wish there was more."

"You are a dear friend, indeed. So brighten up my day. Any fun stories? Hot gossip? Whatever you've got, lay it on me."

"You know my darling Cam Presley, yes? *Wait* until you hear what he did yesterday!" I teased, going on to relay every crotch grinding detail.

"Oh my word!" she roared with laughter. "That is hilarious!" Hooray! First grader tales always improved people's moods. Unfortunately, that was the only one I had to share. The last two days hadn't been all that much fun overall.

"What about the Phantom Farter?" she inquired with grand enthusiasm, referring to the currently anonymous gas passer in my class.

"No gaseous eruptions this week. I'm hoping that a gastroenterologist has intervened and come to my rescue!"

"No! Not until you identify the culprit. I'm dying to know who it is. My guess is Tameka. Have you seen how much crap she eats at lunch? That can't be good for her system. Five bucks says I'm right."

The jovial mood had been broken when I heard the word "dying". Even used in an alternate context, it spun my thoughts back to Carrie. "What's wrong?" Joan asked, having detected my change of expression. I tried to brush it off, but we'd been friends for too long for the anguish which had overcome me so suddenly to escape her attention. Rather embarrassed by my ridiculous obsession with Carrie's death, I closed my eyes and rubbed my temples.

Finally deciding that treating Joan with kid gloves might disturb her more than a frank discussion about our mutual friend and her demise, I filled her in on my suspicions, citing each of the bits of "evidence" that had persuaded me that Carrie *might* have been pushed.

Joan sat in silence, incredulously watching me while nervously picking at her fingers. When my long winded spiel wrapped up, she stated, quite simply, "No."

"But, what *if…*"

"No, Diana. You're making this far more difficult on yourself by entertaining this crazy premise. What happened to Carrie is ***dreadful.*** It breaks my heart. But, by stringing it out without a shred of solid proof is not good for you. It's preposterous to believe that ***anyone*** would intentionally harm that sweet girl. You must realize that."

"Well, don't hold back or anything." Clearly the kid gloves had not been necessary.

"I'm sorry, honey. I don't mean to hurt your feelings or belittle your ideas. It's just that we need to move on and let Carrie rest in peace."

"You're probably right." I replied, more so to appease her than because I actually agreed. Just then, the doorbell rang. Saved by the bell. (Not only a fitting figure of speech, but also one of my very favorite shows growing up…in reruns of course. That A.C. Slater was a major hottie!)

"I bet it's Dale. He called earlier to see if we were up for a visit. As if I wouldn't be!"

Sure enough, in came Dale Badger, looking pretty darned spiffy, it being a non-school day and all. "Hi there," I waved, having followed my hostess out of the room.

"I thought that was your car in the driveway." Dale observed.

"Seeing as you've seen it practically every day for the past five and a half years, you ***should*** be able to recognize it." Then again, if he paid as little attention to makes and models of automobiles as me, maybe not.

"Oh, and here's your newspaper by the way." He said, holding out the coiled up parcel. "It was sticking out from under one of your bushes."

"That damned paper guy! He drives his fat ass right behind my parked car to throw it, and it still doesn't land remotely close to the door half the time." Taking the paper from Dale, Joan led us back into the living room at the front of the house. Oddly, Warren, who hadn't made so much as a peep since my arrival, trailed after us. With Joan in the rocking chair and Dale seated on the blue recliner, I playfully invited Warren to join me on the couch. "Hey, Hot Stuff," I winked, "Come sit over here with me."

"Hot Stuff? Who the hell are you? Donna Summer?" I wasn't quite sure if he was making a joke or if he'd honestly confused me, a diminutive white girl, with the bigger boned black singing sensation. Either way, he took a seat beside me and smiled.

"Joan, can I see the paper for a minute?" Dale asked, extending his hand. "I wanna see if Carrie's obituary is in today's edition or not. It should be." Flipping through the pages once he had the newspaper in his possession, he summarized the obit for us. "Pretty short, says 'died unexpectedly' on Wednesday. Oh, memorial service is at two tomorrow. Should we meet at the funeral home at like ten of so we can sit together?"

Both of us were in agreement, and I made a mental note to call Erica to see if she wanted to join us. Hopefully she'd be able to find someone to watch Savannah. Even a well behaved child like hers might not be welcome at the solemn service if she was having an off day. I made another mental note to myself: Put off kids as long as you can.

"This is a crying shame," Dale lamented as he poked through the paper some more. "Not even a sidebar about a hard working teacher, dead before twenty five. Yet half the front page is covered with an article about the Branson Boys' concert at the Orpheum Theatre Wednesday night. Photos and all."

"That does suck." I seconded. "Especially since I haven't the foggiest clue as to who they are or what they sing. Never heard of 'em."

"The Branson Boys? You've heard them on the radio, I bet. They're an up and coming country/rock group. Gaining popularity very quickly it seems." Badger informed me.

"Actually," I remembered, having heard Dale's description of the "Boys", "I think Carrie and Cassie had tickets to see them down in Providence next week." Yet another experience that Carrie would miss out on.

"Yeah, we saw that concert." Warren interjected from his own little world.

"No, we didn't." Joan patiently clarified. "Max did. Remember he was telling you about it yesterday?"

"Oh yeah," he seemed to recall. "But, we saw Fleetwood Mac at Great Woods."

"Yes, we did." his wife replied with a smile on her face. "We went with Greg and Donna a number of years ago. We had such a fun time."

"We sure did! And then we went parasailing with them afterwards." Joan, parasailing? With her fear of heights, I very much doubted that.

"Warren, hon, you've never been parasailing." she confirmed.

His dementia was intensifying, Joan told Dale and me later that afternoon while Warren napped. "At least he hasn't reached the incontinent stage." Though apparently, he would at some point. So sad. Losing your dignity in addition to your memory. How very horrible. I prayed that I'd never have to endure a similar fate down the line.

"I'll get in touch with Max to find out if he can come stay here tomorrow so I can go to the service." Joan told me as Dale and I were on our way out. "If you don't hear from me before then, I'll see you there at the designated time."

So, a little less than twenty four hours later, our trio reconvened, alongside Erica and Betsy McAllister, who'd called Dale to see if she could meet up with us beforehand. As I'd imagined, the place was packed with people. George Welkey and his wife were seated toward the front of the large room, not far from a tearful Cassie and an elegant looking couple who had to be her parents. Sylvia was there, as were Annette and "Creepy Jim", who stood awkwardly against the wall at the back of the crowd. It was freaky to see his gangly form in a sports jacket and slacks instead of his custodian's uniform.

I nosily searched the rows for Redmond School's team of second grade teachers and spotted the pack of not so cordial coworkers off to our far right, along with another attendee, whose presence took me by surprise. Nudging Dale, I pointed her out. "Jodi?" he asked, a look of confusion or irritation – or maybe both – upon his face.

Jodi Badger, his soon-to-be ex-wife, picked that precise moment to turn in our direction. With my index finger still aimed at the young woman, I lifted the rest of my fingers and attempted to smoothly transition my ignorant pointing into a friendly wave. Smiling, she returned the gesture. The wave, not the ignorant pointing, that is. Jodi and I had always gotten along well. Just a few years older than me, she, like her husband, was fun loving and very sociable. She was well liked by all of Dale's first grade colleagues and many a time, we'd hung out together at staff Christmas parties and had a blast.

Regrettably, I hadn't spoken with her in several months. It was one of those awkward situations where friends of the couple sort of had to choose a side after Jodi made it known, out of the wild blue yonder, that (a) she'd been cheating on Dale for a lengthy period of time and (b) she was leaving him. Given that I worked with the mister and had only come to know her through him, my allegiance was clearly to her brokenhearted hubby.

But it wasn't my place to judge her actions or the reasoning behind what she'd done. If my phone rang tomorrow and Jodi Badger was on the other end of the line, I would gladly chat away. That happy scene of us rekindling our friendship, however, was quite likely a long way off. Recent communication between the Badgers typically involved arguing, name calling, and someone storming off or slamming down the telephone. *Not* a pretty picture.

Not long after I'd caught sight of Mrs. Badger, my people watching was brought to a temporary halt when the funeral home director stepped up to the microphone to begin the afternoon's unpleasant event. Although the speeches were all quite poignant and kind words flowed endlessly, I found my eyes passing over the mass of mourners once again, in an attempt to avoid the harsh truth that Carrie Landry was gone forever. As my thoughts wandered back to my discussion with Deputy Miller and my twisted dream two nights earlier, hostility began to swell up inside of me. As much as I wanted to shake this feeling of doubt, it just wasn't happening. Each mourner's face was also the face of a potential suspect as far as I was concerned. But, Joan Petrillo had made me realize that there was no hard evidence to back up my gut feeling. So, I'd keep my mouth shut until I had something concrete to support what my intuition was telling me.

## CHAPTER EIGHT

Because my mind had been roaming, the service was over in what felt like minutes, although, obviously, it had been much longer. Some people, maybe half of those in attendance, departed immediately, while the remainder of us lined up to express our condolences to Mr. and Mrs. Landry and their remaining daughter at the front of the expansive room. As we made our way in their direction, shoulder to shoulder with a multitude of others, Dale, being a man, showed little visible emotion. Likewise, Erica, who some would consider a hard ass, trudged ahead in silence. Joan, on the other hand, was at the opposite end of the spectrum, wailing incessantly as I tried to console her. "I'm not sure I can face her parents," she wept. "How could I have allowed this to happen?"

"Allowed what to happen? Carrie's death is most certainly not your fault. There's nothing you could have done to prevent her fall." I assured her, hoping to ease her apparent guilt. I had a feeling that in her already fragile emotional state, her frustration over being able to keep Warren well was now carrying over to our communal grief and sorrow over our lost colleague. "There's nothing any of us could have done." I said, truthfully.

"But, we were all out having a good time as she was dying. We should have gone to *find* her when she didn't show up. We should have known that something was wrong." she declared adamantly.

Blessedly, Erica attempted to lend a hand in calming her down. "Diana *did* call her, Joan. At the time, we had no reason to think that Carrie was in trouble."

"You called her too," I reminded her. Replaying her late night message in my head, I then understood why she was such a basket case. She'd planned to stop at Carrie's house on the way

63

by, but hadn't because no lights were on. She had to be wondering if she could have gotten help for our fallen friend, medical assistance that could have saved her life. Oh my God, the poor woman. Despite being a wonderful caretaker for her husband, she was essentially helpless in stopping the progression of his disease. Now, she had this new additional burden.

I hugged her tightly and by the time our turn to speak to the grieving family was upon us, we were both blubbery messes. What I said to Carrie's family members, I honestly don't recall. But once we'd spoken to them, the four of us made our way out of the too warm building and went our separate ways.

At home that evening, I tried to keep my spirits as "up" as I could following such a grim afternoon. After killing several hours on Facebook, reading a hundred pages of the latest Tamar Myers mystery, and doing away with some brain cells by watching a Real World marathon on MTV, it was time to call it a night. Which, of course, gave me nothing but time to rehash a few feasible scenarios that could have led to Carrie's much-too-early date with the Grim Reaper as I lay sleeplessly in my bed.

*If* someone else did have a hand in causing Carrie to tumble down those stairs, there were a couple of ways it could have gone down. Either Person X deliberately shoved her, with the intent to seriously injure or kill her, *or* Person X had struggled with or pushed her near the top of the stairs, inadvertently sending Carrie down the staircase. Horrified (or satisfied, depending on the circumstances) at having caused her to fall, Person X then panicked and ran. Another, more gruesome possibility was that Person X had bashed her head in, then staged the scene to make it appear as though she'd tripped coming down the stairs to cover up his/her malevolent deed. Or, what I truly hoped for, she simply slipped and fell. A tragic accident. Which meant I was on a wild goose chase.

Perhaps I should just leave it alone. Yes, I resolved, why initiate a witch hunt when it wasn't necessary? I was done playing C.S.I. Arwell. And with that firm oath, I nodded off into a peaceful slumber.

But, it seemed Fate had other plans for me, life altering plans, as I would find out the very next day. Monday's early morning routine was the same as every other weekday, with me scurrying about like a chicken with its head cut off, yet miraculously arriving on time for work nonetheless. "Good morning." I greeted Fran Vespa, the librarian, who, of course, had pulled in just a few seconds ahead of me today. Per usual, we walked inside together and, as she went down, I went up. That's when the regular routine started to swerve off course.

The lights in Carrie's classroom, as I still thought of it, were on, meaning that Leticia Devane had returned to her old stomping grounds. Much as I dreaded it, good manners forced me to pop in to welcome her. "Good morning, Miss Fallon." she said crisply as I entered the room.

"Hello, Leticia, uh Miss Devane." I threw in when she glared at me. Evidently we would *not* be on a first name basis, I inferred. Now what? Did I dare offer her assistance if she needed help finding anything? One glimpse at the seventy three year old sourpuss made me think that would not be a wise move. With her ghostly white hair pulled back into a tight bun, she was clad in a mustard yellow dress with a calico print that was almost floor length. She was the epitome of an old fashioned schoolmarm…or a "sister wife" living on a polygamy compound!

"Have a good day," I managed to spit out before retreating to my own classroom.

A few minutes later, the a.m. bell rang and, just moments after that, pudgy little Cody Burnett was in my face. "Miss Fallon, what's a murder?" he sweetly inquired, sending me into a tailspin!

"What, honey?" I replied, hoping I had misheard the boy.

"What's a murder?" he repeated. Nope, no need for a hearing exam.

"Why are you asking, sweetheart?"

"Cuz I heard Miss Landry had a murder happen to her." OMG! Maybe there really *was* something to my foul play theory after all! Clearly someone else thought so, as I highly doubted that the child had reached that conclusion on his own. He was a good student and all, but I didn't envision him as the Doogie Howser of the criminal justice system.

"Well?" he prodded. Damned kid! Mommy had probably denied him the word's meaning so now he was hitting *me* up. *Or*, even more likely, his wench of a mother had eagerly told him to "Ask your teacher."! I'd been down that road plenty of times, including a father who expected me to fill his daughter in on how her soon to be sibling wound up inside her stepmother's tummy! Yeah, right, Daddy O.! Try again.

Searching my mind for a student friendly definition for such an adult word, I came up with nothing. Nada. Zilch. So, although I would never in a million years promote lying to my students, I had no choice. "A murder is when someone dies." I told Cody, unwilling to teach him about violence and malice at his tender age. Keeping kids innocent in today's society is no easy feat, but I try my best. "Remember last week when Mr. Welkey met with all of the students in the cafeteria? He told you that Miss Landry had gone to Heaven. That's what that word means." With luck, that explanation would suffice. And if his parents even *thought* about objecting to my use of the word "Heaven" during our chat, they had better prepare to wind up in that very same place when I came to their house with my personally recruited firing squad!

"Go hang your things up in the coat room," I directed him. Thankfully, he actually went. All seemed to be back in order as I recorded the names of the two absentees and counted hands for each of the mouthwatering (insert barfing sound here) lunch options for the day. I was just about to have my Leader of the Day start us off with the Pledge of Allegiance when I heard an urgent "Pssst!" off to my side.

There, in the doorway, stood one of the most attractive and most likable parents I'd had the pleasure of becoming acquainted with at the Redmond School, Daylona Sanchez. She was a mother known by practically every teacher in the building, old timers and newcomers alike, since she'd been around "forever". That's what happens when you've got like twenty eight kids! O.K., so that may be a slight exaggeration, but Daylona popped 'em out left and right, and there had yet to be a year when she didn't have at least one of her offspring attending Redmond since I had been there. Given her exotic beauty, it was no wonder that her equally hot hubby would want to procreate with her…and practice lots more in between deliveries. Hell, if I was a straight guy, I'd go at it like rabbits with her too!

Daylona was both sweet and good humored too. When I'd seen her daughter Lola's name on my class list for this year, I'd been thrilled, having had her son Antonio two years earlier. She and her husband, Alberto, were what we in the world of public education call "Dream Parents", couples whose progeny we all yearned for, unlike certain other sets of parents, who we wished upon a falling star would *never ever* reproduce again, for varying reasons.

"Class, I'll be with you in just a moment. I just need to speak to Mrs. Sanchez for a minute." I explained, leaving my position in front of the white board and walking to the door.

"Sorry she's late," Daylona apologized placing her hands on Lola's shoulders. "I was on the phone gabbing and lost track of the time so she missed the bus. I hate to disrupt your morning like this."

"Not to worry. We were just getting started. Lola, honey, why don't you go put your stuff away and take your seat." Without hesitation, the youngest Sanchez girl (for the time being at least!) obeyed. Daylona's eyes seemed to widen as her daughter walked off. "So, is it *true*?" the Dream Mom asked with a sense of great urgency.

"Is what true?"

"That Miss Landry was murdered?" Well, knock me down with a feather! Had the planet gone topsy-turvy overnight? Just as I had begun to accept that Carrie's fall had been purely accidental, everyone else in the world seemed to have jumped on the bandwagon I'd just leapt off of. What the hell?

There was a fine line between personal beliefs and professional conduct. I didn't want to tell tales out of turn, especially to a parent, even a Dream Parent. So, I kept my comment short and sweet. "I believe that the police had some concerns. But, as far as I know, it isn't being investigated as a criminal matter."

The disappointed look on Mrs. Sanchez's face lost her a point or two in my book. Granted, Arwell isn't exactly a hotbed of homicide, and perhaps the soccer moms and other residents of the town found this bit of gossip exciting, but I couldn't take pleasure in the uncertainty that surrounded my friend's passing. Always a lady, Daylona apologized if she had upset me and wished me a great day before we parted and I resumed my place at the head of the class.

By lunchtime, both Dale and Miss Devane had both been privy to the local grapevine's hot new topic of the week also. "Such a sordid world we live in." the elderly substitute spat. "Speaking about the dearly departed in such a cavalier manner is an abomination!"

"I agree wholeheartedly, Leticia." Dale observed. *Leticia*? Apparently Mr. Badger *did* get the privilege of addressing her by her first name.  Though, to be fair, he had worked across the hall from her for a good many years before I came aboard. "But," he added, "I have my reservations. On a scale of one to ten, designating one's likelihood of being murdered, Carrie Landry would rate a negative twelve."

"True," I replied, "But, that's based on her actions and her ability to win people over with her personality without even trying. There are other motives for doing away with someone. Maybe she stumbled across some kind of secret or information that someone was willing to kill over. Totally random and nearly impossible, I grant you. I'm simply throwing it out there since it's obvious she had no enemies."

"All this talk has made me lose my appetite." the newest (though chronologically oldest) member of our lunch trio complained, packing up the rest of her meal, and bustling out of the lounge. No disrespect to the woman, but a sense of relief washed over me once she was gone. "I feel like I have to act all prim and proper around that old maid." I confessed to Dale once I thought she was out of earshot. With my luck, she was probably hiding behind the door keeping a tally of every curse word or inappropriate topic that came out of my mouth!

"Speaking of 'prim and proper'," he began, "Wait until you hear what Annette had the gall to say to me this morning!"

"Spill it."

"So I'm in my room before school, trying to sort out that box of leveled readers that the kids shoved in every which way, and she glides in like Jesus walking on water with a smug expression on her face to tell me she's made an appointment to meet with George this afternoon."

A meeting with the principal? "Why?"

"Hold on. I'm getting there. She had the balls to give me an *in depth* explanation as to why, if Joan comes back before the end of the school year, *she* should then be moved into Carrie's room and Leticia should be sent packing."

"Are you freakin' kidding me? Who the frig does she think she is?" Leticia Devane wasn't exactly Miss Personality, but from what I'd heard, she was a very capable teacher.

"She claims that Leticia is too *old* to work with children at this age level."

"Old? The chick with the antiquated hairdo that went out of style like forty years ago had the nerve to call someone else old! I mean, Leticia *is* older than Moses himself, but still…"

"Exactly. And Leticia's been teaching elementary school since before Annette *entered* elementary school, I'm guessing. She's so drab, it's kind of hard to pinpoint her age. Oh, and she's fully expecting to be hired to permanently replace Carrie in the fall."

That heartless viper! I don't think she'd bothered to ask herself, "What would Jesus do?" in that situation. Campaigning for someone else's job less than a week after that person died *didn't* sound like something he would do. However, it *did* sound like a first rate motive for murder to me!

## CHAPTER NINE

While my class was downstairs in the library that afternoon, I emailed Joan to give her the lowdown on her job snatching long term sub:

*Hope Warren is having a good day cuz that means U will 2. Your greedy sub is having a spectacular day. She's meeting w/ George today to submit her resume for Carrie's job. Can't even believe she went there! She hasn't even been buried yet! Oh yeah, she wants to replace Leticia if you come back before June. What a wench! I know her family needs the $ but come on! I'm wondering if she bonked Carrie over the head with her Bible and then threw her down the stairs so she could steal her job. It makes sense. TTYL    Diana*

With just a few minutes left until my prep period was over, I checked my computer to see if Joan had replied. Indeed, she had. *That's crazy*! was the first line, followed by *Annette is the last person on Earth who would kill somebody! It was an ACCIDENT. Stop with this foolishness!*

True, the selfish substitute would make for an improbable murderess. But, likewise, Carrie Landry made for an unthinkable murder victim. Sadly, these days, anything could happen. I mean even wholesome Martha Stewart's been to the clink!

On my way down to retrieve the kids, I vaguely recalled our librarian having some relative on the Arwell police force. Could she get me some inside info per chance? It wouldn't hurt to ask her. Which is exactly what I did as Fran Vespa called each table to push in their chairs and line up at the front entrance of the long boxy room.

"Yeah, my brother-in-law has worked for the Arwell P.D. for ages."

"Would he be able to tell you the status of the investigation into Carrie's fall? Open or closed case? Accident vs. foul play?"

"You've heard the rumors too, eh?"

"I have. And what's even odder is that I've been inclined to think the same way, for no logical reason. Just a lingering feeling."

"I hope your hunch is wrong." Mrs. Vespa grimaced.

"Me too. Oh gosh, I've got to get these kids out of here before you next class gets here," I realized as I glanced at the clock on the wall. "Thanks for any assistance you can give me."

"My pleasure. But, don't get your hopes up. I can't guarantee anything."

"See you in the morning!" I called out as I herded my single file line of young ones past the second grade class coming from the opposite direction. But, unbeknownst to me at that time, I wouldn't see Fran Vespa the following day, due to another unforeseen situation that would be thrown my way that night.

My digital clock had just clicked onto 6:34 p.m. (which I only recall because I was lounging lazily on my bed trying to summon up some energy to go do a load of laundry) when I got the jolting call from my kindly landlady, Rose Gort. "Uh huh…I see…okay…all right, buh bye." Dumbfounded by the news that I was being unceremoniously evicted from the apartment I'd called home for the last four years of my life, I sunk back down onto my bed and cried like a first grader who'd lost her lunch money.

Despite the fact that I had been, in Rose's own words, "the best tenant she'd ever had" and that I had never *once* been late with my rent, she was giving me the heave ho so that her nineteen year old granddaughter could move in, rent free no less! Worse yet, Granny's little lovebug would be arriving in three freakin' weeks! What if I couldn't find suitable living quarters before then? I'd have to take up residence in a discarded cardboard box underneath an overpass alongside Route 495!

Once I came out of my stupor, I did what any other levelheaded American would do: posted the catastrophic news on Facebook! *I just got ****ing evicted!* My fingers furiously typed. As much as I wanted to include the actual four letter word, my common sense thankfully took charge. Teachers, the bright ones at least, knew to be extra cautious when posting comments and photos. Educators had been known to be suspended, even terminated, for inane reasons like being shown holding a glass of wine at a party or complaining about "a horrid day at work" on social media sites. Losing my living quarters so suddenly was devastating enough. I sure as hell couldn't afford to lose my job on top of it!

Following my astonishment came fury! I was livid that Rose would drop such serious news on me so last minute. At least if she had given me some advance notice, I could have started apartment hunting and possibly found somewhere decent. As it stood, I might have to take whatever place I could get at this point, even if it meant trading in my current pristine fully furnished piece of Heaven for some tiny flea ridden pit from Hell.

Damn that nasty old bag! If she wanted me out, then out it would be. In fact, the sooner, the better. Then Rose would have to refund me part of this month's rent in addition to my security deposit and I could treat myself to a night or two at a nice hotel to recuperate from this unpleasant predicament if need be.

Why I decided to phone my mother to whine about my situation escapes me. Ever since she retired to sunny Florida, the woman has become sue happy, I tell you. That's the result of being able to lounge around all day watching consecutive episodes of Judge Judy, Judge Mathis, The People's Court, and countless other litigation inspired programs. "Haul that bitch into court!" Mom demanded, never one to mince words. But after I explained to her that I hadn't signed a lease after my first year was up (in good faith- yeah, look where that had gotten me!), she backed off. In hindsight, I now realized that had been an error on my part. But Rose was a doll and repeatedly expressed her gratitude to me for being an ideal renter. Never in a million years had I seen this coming.

As my chat with the maternal unit was nearing an end, my other line beeped, giving me the perfect excuse to bid her a hasty farewell and click over to my incoming caller, Joan Petrillo. "Perfect timing!" I commended her. "I wasn't sure my mother would let me hang up any time soon."

"Your *mother*?" Joan replied, sounding perplexed. Mom and I aren't exactly "close". She does her thing, and I do mine, just like the rest of my fiercely independent family does. So, of course, I then had to relay the grim news to her as a means of explaining the call I'd made. "Come stay with us until you find a place. That way you can wait to find someplace nice." she graciously offered.

"Thank you so much, but the last thing you need on your plate right now is a houseguest."

"I'd love the company. Really. Having someone to talk to that can maintain a sensible conversation would be wonderful."

I did contemplate it, but had to decline. If worse came to worse, I could always take her up on it at the end of the month if I needed to. "But, I do want out of here ASAP." I admitted. "I'm so mad at Rose. I'd pack my stuff up and hightail it out of here tonight if I could." Which, unfortunately, wasn't a feasible option.

However, a new option presented itself just minutes later. After finishing my conversation with Joan, I beelined it back to my computer to read all of the sympathetic comments I anticipated would be there to greet me. Sure enough, everyone from coworkers to college friends and childhood neighbors I hadn't seen in over a decade had expressed their thoughts, which ran the gamut from concerned to violent (against Rancid Rose that is). As I was reading a message toward the end of the lengthy list, a message from Cassie Landry popped up at the bottom of the screen.

"Come stay at my house." I read aloud. Hmm…now *that* might not be a bad solution, I thought, staring at the monitor as I decided how to reply. A few more messages back and forth between us had me feeling pretty good about it, in fact. Cassie didn't like being by herself at the house and was practically begging me to do *her* the favor of moving into the Landry sisters' home. Looking up to the ceiling, I wondered if my pal Carrie had been looking down upon us tonight and had somehow intervened to help out both her sister and her soon to be homeless friend.

"It wouldn't be permanent." I later apprised Cassie on the telephone. Based upon past experiences, I wasn't too fond of living with roommates.

"That's fine. Stay for as long or as little time as you want."

The more we discussed it, the better it sounded, killing two birds with one stone. "When can I move in?" I finally shrieked with unexpected excitement.

"Whenever you want."

"Is tomorrow too soon?"

"Not at all. After school gets out?"

"Will you be around in the morning?" I asked, now eager to hit the road and leave my Loser Landlady inhaling my dust. Since Cassie had no plans to return to work until after the funeral in New Jersey, she could be available anytime that next day to let me stop by and pick up a key.

My next call was to the answering service that took "sick" calls for all of Arwell's school personnel and booked substitutes to fill in for them. That way I could make an early morning stop at school to type out more detailed lesson plans if needed and lay out any materials or worksheets the day's plans called for. Then I could bop home and start packing. My miserable night had done a three sixty and, although I honestly had to admit that I would *totally* miss this fantastic apartment, my newfound worries had been alleviated in just a few short hours. Unfortunately, those worries would be replaced by new concerns the very next day.

Tuesday at dawn, I hauled myself out of bed, flew over to school, and was back at the apartment to start packing in no time. Though I was eager to be done and out as soon as possible, feelings of unease and guilt were also present. The day before, I had lambasted Annette Bunting for targeting Carrie's job, and yet here I was moving into her house, her bedroom, for Heaven's sake! What a hypocrite I was!

With a few small boxes of books and knickknacks and a large box of pots, pans, and other assorted rarely used kitchen supplies, I drove back to Arwell for the second time that morning. Cassie was in very good spirits when I arrived at the house. After we carried my boxes inside and deposited them on the living room floor, she handed me a key to my new digs. "I couldn't find a spare key so I'll just give you the one off Carrie's key chain." she informed me.

Accepting the key, the whole scene took on a sense of morbidity. Moving had not been in my plans for the immediate future. Moving into the room of a recently deceased colleague and friend was not on my life's agenda *at all.* But, logically, I understood that life has to go on for the living after any loss, no matter how great. And Cassie seemed legitimately joyous to have me here, which did make it a bit easier to swallow.

When I'd phoned Joan on a break from boxing up my belongings, she volunteered to help me clean the apartment. Yeah, I was still pretty pissed that Rose was giving me the boot, but even though I was making an early escape didn't mean that I would leave the place in anything but immaculate condition upon my departure. My initial polite refusal of her assistance had been trumped by the pleading tone in her voice. "Please? It will give me a chance to get out of the house for a little while."

So after Cassie and I moved the bulk of her sister's miniscule wardrobe to one end of the bedroom closet, I told her that I would be back later and headed around the corner to pick up Joan. Pulling in behind the white Eclipse I knew belonged to Max Petrillo, I left the car running and went to the door. From inside, I heard raised voices and hesitated to knock. Should I retreat to my vehicle and honk the horn to alert them that I was there? Too late. Max spotted me and opened the door, looking less than pleased. "Hey," was his grand welcome.

"Hi, Max. How are you?"

"Not bad, Diana. I hear you're moving, huh?"

"Yup. Not really by choice, but it is what it is."

Mrs. Petrillo yanked on her coat and pushed her way past her brother-in-law. "I'll be back in a few hours." she sniffed, stepping outside. "He shouldn't give you any problems as long as the television is on." she continued quickly.

"*I'm* here. There won't be any problems." Max Petrillo sniped. Very out of character for him. I assumed that the pair of caregivers had been having a tiff when I showed up. "Bye, Diana."

"Bye now. Tell Warren I said hello."

"Will do," he replied, closing the door behind us.

"What was that all about?" I just had to ask once my passenger's seatbelt was fastened and we were backing down the small driveway.

"Oh, ummm…" Avoidance tactics.

"Sorry. I was being way too nosy. You do *not* need to tell me a thing."

"No, no, it's nothing. Warren dumped the entire contents of our fish tank into the toilet. Just as Max was pulling into the driveway, of course."

"And Max was mad? It's not *your* fault."

"Yeah, it *was*. I was washing the breakfast dishes and didn't pay close enough attention to what he was up to. Max has a right to be angry. It's fine. Don't fret over it."

"Okay," I said, dropping the topic somewhat reluctantly. Warren's two relatives relied heavily on one another. Sparring and laying blame wasn't good.

But, since Joan's idea of fun these days was mopping and vacuuming, I said, "Bring on the fun!" By early afternoon, we (or should I say *she*) had that place looking spic and span for Rose's lucky granddaughter. Once we had thrown the last couple of boxes into my trunk and stacked a heap of clothes on the backseat, off we went. I estimated one more trip to collect the remainder of my (not so miniscule) wardrobe should do it. Then I'd be completely cleared out and surprise my soon to be ex-landlady with the key and make arrangements to get my security deposit and rent reimbursement, some of which I would give to Cassie for letting me stay at her house.

When we got back to my residence-for- the-time, Cassie appeared to be out of sorts. "What's wrong?" I asked.

"Nothing, really. Just something weird. Did you happen to hang up Carrie's coat on the coatrack when you were here earlier by any chance?" Oh great. I hadn't even spent a night there yet and she was already quizzing me about misplaced items. Was Cassie Landry going to be a Roommate from Hell?

But, since I hadn't touched the garment, it shouldn't become a problem, I reasoned and let her know that I had not moved the coat. "Why? Was it elsewhere before I came?"

"I don't know. I've been out of it these past few days and it didn't really register that her coat wasn't with her book bag."

"Why is that weird?" Joan inquired, obviously as lost as I was.

"Carrie *never* hung her coat on the rack. She'd leave her bag and whatever else she might have on the kitchen table and hang her jacket on the chair, where it would remain until she went out again."

"Maybe she was trying to be more tidy than usual. Lord knows I should be." Joan chuckled. This, coming from the woman who had just single handedly cleaned my entire apartment!

"No, she *always* left it on that chair. I'm surprised I didn't notice it before now."

"Could one of the policemen put it over there?" I posed.

"I doubt it. Other than retrieving her purse from the car, they pretty much left everything as it was, as far as I can recall."

Joan glanced out the window and announced that she had to get home to Warren so that Max could get home. "I'll walk so you ladies can get organized over here."

"Don't be crazy. It's cold out. I'll drive you."

"Oh, thanks. But, I don't mind. I'm not some decrepit old woman…yet." she smiled. "And I've got my mittens." she assured me, waving her black and white checkered hands in the air. "Cassie, honey, you take care. Diana, I'll talk to you later."

"Okey dokey." I replied, walking her to the front door. "Thank you *so* much for all that cleaning you did. You are a timesaver extraordinaire!" Giving her a brief hug, I let her out and made my way back to the kitchen, where Cassie stood, looking intently at the oak coatrack in the corner of the room.

It then dawned on me that the dreadful green knit hat was nowhere in sight. "Where's Carrie's hat?" I wondered out loud as my eyes began to scan the area by the table.

"That's a good question. Normally it would be on the table or chair too. Unless it's in the pocket of her coat?" Sticking her hand into both sides of the hanging coat, Cassie came up empty. "Nope, not in there either. That's doubly weird."

# A FIRST GRADE FATALITY

On any other day, I probably would have overlooked a missing hat and a coat that was out of place. But, coupled with the fact that the owner of both pieces of winter wear had just met an untimely demise, it was indeed odd, and made me curious as to what else of Carrie's might have gone missing.

## CHAPTER TEN

When we weren't able to locate the unfashionable, yet sentimental, headwear, I logged onto my school email account using Cassie's laptop. Maybe Carrie had left the hat at school that Wednesday afternoon. I'd ask Dale to look in her classroom before he left at the end of the day.

No luck on his end either, Mr. Badger notified me via cell phone while his class was attending their weekly art class. "*But*," he announced quite enthusiastically, "I do have quite the tale to relay! My Darrin Parker mooned half my class today when we took a bathroom break!"

"What?" I screeched, "Where? In the boy's room, I'm hoping."

"Yup. Three of my other boys came rushing out with looks of horror on their faces. And, when I called his mother at lunch to let her know about it, she wanted to know if it could have been an *accident*!" Naturally. No parent wanted to believe that their precious Johnny or sweet Susie was capable of doing anything inappropriate.

"So what did you say to her?

"Told her what the three kids had reported to me and that jeans *and* Fruit of the Looms around your ankle, bent over with your ass aimed at others was *not* unintentional." Leave it to Dale to have that conversation! "Oh, and your not- so- secret admirer was asking for you this morning." Ugh. Creepy Jim.

"What did he say?"

"Just wanted to know why you weren't at school today." Okay. Harmless enough, I guess.

"Yeah, well I'll probably pop in after school to pick up papers to correct and whatnot on my way back from giving Rose her key back."

"I'll be sure to let him know." Mr. B. kidded.

"And I'll be sure to slash all four of your tires tomorrow if you do!" was my speedy retort. On that witty note, we ended our call, leaving me free to terminate my tenancy even earlier than my landlady was expecting.

Rose Gort, an older woman who had to be close in age to- dare I say it- *Leticia* , really was a nice person. Although ambushing me to give me the heave ho a night earlier didn't exactly give me reason to sing her praises at the present moment. When I phoned ahead to let her know I was on my way over, Rose was taken aback by my insistence that I evacuate her premises immediately. Whatever.

Even after I had returned the key and written down the Landry's address for her to mail me my due, the sweet old lady still tried to pacify me. "It's nothing personal, dear." she assured me, "If it wasn't for my granddaughter coming, I'd keep you in that apartment *forever.*" she told me with such sincerity that I actually believed her. Our relationship had always been a pleasant one, and she was looking out for her family. I could hardly fault her for that. "Feel free to stop by for a visit anytime you like."

"Yeah, okay. Maybe." was my polite response, knowing full well that that was about as likely as one of my students whipping out a copy of *Hamlet* and reciting a soliloquy for their upcoming book report. Bidding old Rose a final farewell, my next stop was school.

By the time I'd gotten there, nearly all of the vehicles were gone from the staff lot. That was fine by me. With nobody else around, I could tend to what needed to be done and be on my way.

The room didn't resemble a scene out of *Twister*, which was a good sign. Nevertheless, there had to be some bad along with the good. The Phantom Farter had perpetrated yet another silent but deadly attack, the sub had so thoughtfully filled me in on the "How the Day Went Today" pad I always left out for a substitute. An attack so offensive, in fact, that it had led to hands over noses, finger pointing galore, and further dramatics. I dare say, had I been present, those little suckers would've held their breath in silence instead of causing such an uproar. But those are the breaks of working as a substitute teacher unfortunately. Children never viewed you as a "real teacher". Still, I didn't blame her for the commotion. Nor could I really blame the class either. I'd been around more than enough of those gaseous assaults…and the stench was vile. I really needed to sniff out the culprit ASAP. Something to look forward to. Hooray!

I spent the next half hour counting out sets of gingerbread man manipulatives for the next day's math lesson, writing up my morning message on the easel, and other necessary- if less than thrilling- chores. When my cell phone rang, it startled me, and I let out a short squeak. The caller was Fran Vespa, imparting what her sister's cop husband had told her.

"I came up to your room at lunchtime, but Annette told me you were out sick. I hope you're feeling better."

"Oh, I'm fine. Something came up suddenly that I needed to take care of, so I had to take the day off."

"You've earned one with all that's gone on lately. Speaking of which, I spoke with Vince last night. He says that Carrie's case is 'open', meaning there could be something that doesn't sit well with whoever is in charge of it."

"Interesting. Thanks."

"I tried pumping him for more details, but either he didn't know or couldn't say any more."

"Not a problem. Thanks so much, Fran. That's really all I wanted to know."

"My pleasure. I'm happy to help. I'll see you in the morning."

"See you then."

Hmmm…given what Deputy Miller had relayed to me and Cassie, it made sense that those "in the know" hadn't yet closed the case. I sat down at my desk to ponder everything I knew, anxious to figure this matter out. From behind me, I heard a sound. "Who are you talkin' to?" a male voice inquired, scaring the daylight out of me and leading me to spew off several words a first grade teacher would *never* utter in front of her students.

"Oh, it's only you." I exhaled after I spun around and found Creepy Jim standing just a few steps inside my classroom. Not my favorite person, but not a psycho killer out to get me at least. At least I *hoped* he wasn't.

"Sorry. Didn't mean to scare you." I knew that he spoke the truth, but was still unnerved and a little ticked off at him for sneaking in like that.

"Whatever," I replied rather testily. I'd no idea he was even in the building since his beat up Buick hadn't been in the lot when I came in. "Did you need me for something?" I asked curtly, not wanting to encourage a lengthy tete-a-tete. I'd made the mistake of entering into a friendly conversation with him late one afternoon when I was a newbie and didn't know any better, leading him to believe I'd be up for a lengthy chat *every* day thereafter. "You've lured him in." Erica had taunted me the following morning. "Once is all it takes and then you've got yourself a brand new BFF."

Right she was. Lucky me. From then on, Jim Callahan showed up like clockwork for a daily gab session unless I managed to elude him. I tried not to be rude when he stopped in, but even on days when I had a zillion and one things to do, he wouldn't take the hint to buzz off so I could work. Yes, Creepy Jim was my very own school day stalker…well, semi-stalker at least. And for someone so boring, dang, he could talk your ear off about nothing for (what seemed like) hours on end!

"You were talking to yourself." he stated. "Heard you say something about Miss Landry."

"Really?" I hadn't realized that I was musing out loud.

"Something about her being pushed down the stairs…?"

"Yeah," I admitted freely for some unknown reason. Maybe because he wasn't likely to disagree with me (over anything), unlike certain other people were doing. "I don't have any concrete evidence, but there have been a few things that have come up that make me speculate."

"You should leave that sort of thinking to the cops. What if Miss Landry *was* pushed? If her killer found out you were stirring things up, he might come after *you*."

Possibly, but unlikely, I thought. Whoever had killed Carrie, *if* anyone had, would want people to keep believing it had been an accident. Attacking me, or anyone else close to her, would only spark further suspicion and cause the police to investigate more intently. "I doubt it, but thanks for your concern." I told the custodian. At least my semi-stalker was looking out for my well- being instead of invading my home to steal a pair of my well- worn panties. "I've actually got to get going. I need to pick up some groceries. Have a good night." I smiled, shoving papers into my tote bag and putting on my coat. Jim didn't quite take the suggestion to leave, remaining in the same spot.

"Miss Landry probably just tripped. Don't worry yourself over it." he urged. Sweet as he was trying to be, I had no recourse but to waltz by him into the hallway, leaving him to do his work so that I could get home to do mine.

Although I felt like I'd known Carrie Landry for ages, the truth was, our friendship had existed for less than a calendar year. Perhaps someone from her past had reentered her life, or had – unknown to me – been part of her life these past months. Because she had grown up in an entirely different state, there could be dozens of potential suspects out there for all I, or the Arwell police department, knew.

As I pulled in to a space in the large Stop and Shop lot, I dialed Cassie's cell, but reached only her voicemail. "Damn," I mumbled, thankfully before the recording ended and the beeping tone signaled me to leave a message. How could I phrase what I wanted to ask her gently? BEEP. "Hi, Cassie. It's Diana. Um…can you…is there…well, did Carrie have any enemies that might have wanted to see her dead?" I finally blurted out, instantly wishing I could retract the blunt inquiry, hang up, and try it again in a more sensitive manner. She was going to think I was nuts!

Worrying about the potential damage my tactless message might do to my relationship with my housemate of less than a day consumed my thoughts on the way to the house. Hopefully she hadn't been infuriated by my recorded question and changed the locks on me. Otherwise, I would've been ejected from two separate residences in under twenty four hours. Even those uneducated drunken hot messes on Jersey Shore couldn't list that on their list of unhappy life experiences I was fairly certain.

But, the house was dark when I pulled into the driveway and began lifting my bundles out of the trunk. Foolishly, I didn't request that my bagger use paper, so my bottle of Diet Pepsi ripped through the plastic bag, fell to the ground, and rolled between my legs into the street. Could anything *else* in my world go wrong? Before I could find out, a smooth baritone voice spoke to me from somewhere in the growing darkness. Mother of Glory! What was it with guys popping up out of nowhere to spook me today?

"I think this is yours," said the shadowy figure I heard approaching. A few seconds later, a good looking young man with a dark moustache stepped into the yard, his handsome face illuminated by the streetlight a little way down the road. In his hands was the bottle of soda that had escaped from my clutches. Who was this fine specimen?

"I'm Miles Kendrick." he answered in response. Sweet kangaroos! Was this hunk a mind reader too? Clad in a tan sports jacket, striped button down shirt, and a pair of dress pants, he looked like some sort of businessman. "I live across the street." Miles explained, pointing to his house. "Are you another sister?"

"Oh, no. Not me. I'm Diana…Fallon. I'm staying with Cassie for a while."

"I see. Terrible about her sister, isn't it? I was away on business when it happened. Just found out about it yesterday when I returned." I nodded my head in agreement. "Do you need some help getting your bags inside?"

"If you don' mind. That would be great. Thank you so much." *Easy on the eyes, seemingly well employed, and chivalrous to boot* I thought to myself as I fumbled with the keys. Opening the front door, I flipped the lights on with my shoulder and plunked the torn bag and another one by the bottom of the stairs.

"Where would you like these?" my dashing new neighbor asked, stepping inside.

Suddenly, an overwhelming sense of unease took over. What in bloody hell was I thinking, allowing this complete stranger into the house? I only had his own word that he was nowhere in the vicinity the night that Carrie had died. And that he was a neighbor, for that matter. For all I knew, he could be some serial rapist who'd charmed his way in, chased my desperate friend throughout her home, and flung her down the stairs to her death! "I'm all set. Thank you." I hurriedly replied, snatching the bags out of his grip.

"O…kay." he drawled, probably as freaked out by my weird reaction as I was by his mere presence. "Good night then," he said, backing away from me towards the door. I returned the sentiment, then slammed the door shut and locked it at once.

In the kitchen several minutes later, I reflected upon the batty behavior I'd just displayed. If Mr. Kendrick was completely innocent of any wrongdoings (which he probably was, I had to admit now that my nerves had been calmed), and he was simply a nice neighbor who'd gone out of his way to help me, then I was nothing but a jittery fool who'd made an ass out of herself in front of an attractive guy. On the other hand, if Miles Kendrick was, by some remote chance, the person who had murdered Carrie, had I unwittingly led him to believe that I knew what he'd done and set myself up in his line of fire? Oh lordy!

## CHAPTER ELEVEN

"You do know that you're off your frickin' rocker, don't you?" Erica asked after I'd given her a play by play of the Good Samaritan's offer to assist me and my frantic urge to get rid of him. "You need to hang up this phone and call the funny farm, fool…because you are going bonkers obsessing over a death that may or may not have been intentional."

"This isn't funny, Erica! I realize that my panic was probably a tad irrational, but there I was inside the very house where Carrie died with some man that showed up out of the blue!"

"I agree that letting a stranger in, particularly when you're alone, at night no less, was not your wisest move. But, you can't let fear control your life." She was right. But, until I found out whether or not something shady had happened that horrible night, a life filled with paranoia and uncertainty was likely to be my future.

"Blame Rose." my friend declared, "If you were still living in your apartment, this whole incident would never have transpired. And while we're on the topic of your temporary digs, I clearly recall you vowing to *never* live in the town where you teach."

As a teacher, living and working in the same town could be problematic at times, particularly when shopping in public. Kiss your privacy good bye! I'd once been approached by an irritating mother as I perused the cold and flu section in CVS. The nuisance mom wanted to conduct a parent conference right there in aisle eight while I wiped runny snot from my nose for Heaven's sake! Buying a bra under the scrutiny of a watchful mom had proven awkward for a friend of mine. Would she go for the basic white matronly style or opt for the slutty black lace number with nipple zippers? And Joan had once been busted by a student while buying some Hostess cupcakes the very day she'd banned sugary snacks in her classroom.

'This isn't a permanent arrangement." I reminded Erica. "When I start apartment hunting, it'll be outside of Arwell for sure." Landing Rose's furnished apartment on the outskirts of town had been a stroke of luck. It was close enough to school to avoid a lengthy commute, yet far enough away to retain my privacy, and I'd been able to pay off my graduate school loans due to the inexpensive rent as well.

"Yeah, yeah, yeah, enough about Saint Rose. Let's not forget that she tossed you out faster than a used tampon."

"Ewww! That is nasty! You are a *mother*." Leticia Devane would have washed her mouth out with a bar of Ivory if she'd heard such a disgusting comment.

"Oh, please!"

Attempting to change the subject, I said, "At least while I'm staying with Cassie I'll get a few extra minutes of sleep in the morning."

"Yeah, until you start hitting the snooze button an extra time or two." True.

"And being right around the corner from Joan's house is a nice benefit too." Erica agreed with me on that one. We chatted awhile longer, then I yanked my schoolwork out of my book bag and settled in for an evening of correcting while I caught up on a few episodes of *Modern Family*.

Believe it or not, I slept soundly that night. I'd been nervous about being alone in Carrie's former home overnight when Cassie had called to let me know that she was staying with her parents at their hotel, but it had been a long tiring day and I most definitely needed the sleep.

Arriving at school a few minutes earlier than usual the next day, it dawned on me that it was already Wednesday again. Bus duty day with Leticia Devane. Woo hoo!

Despite that less than lovely prospect, I was determined to make it a great day nonetheless. Tameka Jones started things off just right when she arrived carrying a tray of chocolate cupcakes. "Yum yum!" I said to the birthday girl. Could this adorable little child, the spitting image of her mom, who hailed from Jamaica, actually be the Phantom Farter as Joan suspected? Maybe I should do some sniffing around after those cupcakes were consumed after lunch.

Even after I'd securely tucked the girl's special treat on top of my filing cabinet, Tameka remained at my desk. "Is that a D.K. bag?' she asked, ogling my purse. How the heck did an almost seven year old know about Donna Karan?

"No, honey." I smiled sweetly. "It's a WM bag."

"WM?" she replied quizzically.

"Yes, Walmart." Frugal *and* quick witted. Dang, I'm good! "It's just as pretty as a D.K. bag, but costs a lot less…which leaves me money to buy candy for the prize jar!" Nodding her head in approval, she wandered off toward the coat room. Little did she know that I filled the prize jar with Dollar Store candy and kept the good stuff on the top shelf of the closet for myself and any other teacher in need of a chocolate boost throughout the workweek. First graders were too young to be aficionados yet. Let's face it, you could roll a cat turd in sugar and they'd love every bite if you told them it was candy!

The morning passed in a flash, and before I knew it, recess time was upon us. Yahoo! Thankful that Arwell teachers were not assigned to recess duty like some other towns' teaching staff, I sent the kids on their way with a smile. Except for tiny Mitzi, who had to stay in to finish her math since she worked slower than a dying tortoise. Waiting for her to complete the simple worksheet, I puttered around the room, tidying up a bit. After she turned in her work, I sent her outside and went upstairs to the office to get my mail. Since Dale was on lunch duty, leaving Leticia as my only lunch mate, I decided to pull an "Annette" and eat in my room by myself.

Sampling a new brand of blackberry yogurt, I flipped through the pile of papers I'd retrieved, tossing most of them into the recycling tub. Near the bottom of the stack, I came across a white sheet of paper folded in half. Opening it to find out what it was, I read the message typed in large bold print. **DON'T GET INVOLVED OR YOU MIGHT GET HURT TOO.** "Fiddlesticks!" I exclaimed, dropping the note from my slightly trembling hand. Okay, so that wasn't exactly the word that slipped out of my mouth. But, it did start with "F". It just had a lot fewer letters. Four, to be precise.

Who had put this threatening note into my mailbox? Not just anyone had access to the school's office, and Sylvia's desk was right next to the wall of built in cubbies where our copy work, notes to be sent home, and other things were left for us. Whoever it was had to be someone with a reason to be in there, a staff member or parent most likely.

Without setting off any panic alarms, I returned to the office to interrogate Sylvia Wise. The woman's mind was nowhere as sharp as Freddy Krueger's fingertips, but one would think she'd be able to tell me who'd been in the office that morning. Then again…

"People are in and out of her all the time, Diana. I can't recall exactly who was in here this morning," the secretary whined.

"Who *do* you remember seeing by the mailboxes today?"

"Well, Dale was in just before you, I think." Wonderful. Dale Badger was clearly not the one who'd dropped the anonymous warning in my box. He had no reason to. He'd tell me to butt out right to my face.

"Who else?" I demanded as politely as I could manage.

"Well, Mr. Welkey, of course…" the bird brain thought aloud, finger on her chin, looking into the air above for a clue. "And Betsy was in here midmorning. Why is it that you want to know anyway?"

"I'm just trying to figure out who left a note for me. It was unsigned." I explained, deliberately vague as to what was printed on the page. "Can you think of anybody else? Maybe somebody who isn't in the office on a regular basis." I suggested.

"Oh! Mrs. Carson was in to do the laminating today. She had to get the key from me to unlock the closet."

Mrs. Carson? "The heavyset woman with a bad perm?"

"That's her. Very nice gal. Her son is in Miss Landry's class, well Miss Devane's class now."

Interesting. The parent volunteer who laminated for the staff once a week did have a connection to Carrie, albeit a weak one. But, it seemed doubtful that she'd risk dropping such an incriminating message in my mailbox, knowing that her presence at the school wasn't an everyday occurrence and that she could be a prime suspect given it was the one day she was present. Plus, I couldn't believe that a parent was responsible for Carrie's fall. Even if she had let one of her student's mom or dad into her home for some reason, why would she have taken them upstairs with her? That didn't make any sense.

I flagged down Dale as the lines of children stomped back to their classrooms. "We need to talk!"

"During our specialists," he nodded, obviously spotting the crazed look of bewilderment in my eyes.

Our prep times were during the same block of time that afternoon. While my class was having art, his had music, and we were able to meet up in the Teacher's Room so I could show him the note that had me so freaked out. "Seems like someone is trying to prevent you from exploring your theory that Carrie didn't die by accident." he observed rather calmly.

"Right. And if that's the case, then evidently there *is* something to be found out. Otherwise, why would this mystery person warn me off?"

Dale did not reply, seeming to collect his thoughts. Mr. B. wasn't a great supporter of my hunch from what I could tell. "You need to be careful." he finally said. "It could be someone's idea of a prank, but if foul play *was* involved, which now appears to be a possibility if this *is* meant as a direct threat, it stands to reason that the guilty party wants the truth to stay hidden."

"Well, by letting me know that there are answers out there, all they've done is egg me on! We *need* to find out what happened to Carrie. "

"I understand where you're coming from, Diana. But, let the cops deal with it. That way you stay out of harm's way and Carrie's killer can still be brought to justice. *If* there even is a killer involved." Dale was right, of course. Much as I hated to admit it.

So, yet again, I found myself inside the Arwell police station after school got out for the day. I'd had more dealings with the police in the past week than in the first twenty six years of my life combined! Unluckily for me, the head honcho, Detective Donovan, was on the premises this time around and, unlike the friendly Deputy Miller, this guy was all business. By the time he finished grilling me, I was ready to bawl. But, at least he had seemed to take my worries seriously and held onto the typed note to run it for fingerprints. Then again, maybe he just wanted to get me off his back.

Rather than send Joan into a tizzy over the threatening note, I drove right past her house and went straight home, well to the Landry's home, technically. "Home" for me was still my newly vacated apartment. Their house was only a place I was staying until I could find myself a new "home".

Cassie was there when I arrived, seemingly eager to talk to me. "Oh good, you're home!" she said before I had both feet in the door. Did she have information to share? Had a new suspect come to mind? Or perhaps she had received a note similar to the one I'd gotten!

No such luck. She wanted me to go to some stupid concert with her that night. The Branson Boys concert that she and Carrie had planned to see together. Swell. Watching some lame country dudes performing songs I didn't know wasn't at the top of my bucket list....or even at the bottom of it. Country music bites.

I found it a little odd that Cassie was so amped to attend when her sister had died less than a week earlier. But, after listening to her rationale, that Carrie wouldn't want us all to stop living our lives and enjoying ourselves just because she was no longer with us, I felt a tad guilty about my quickness to judge. Cassie had been kind enough to let me move into her house. The least I could do was accompany her to the show.

So, although I was less than enthusiastic about it, there I was at the Providence Performing Arts Center listening to the "Boys" singing about chugging whiskey to cure a heartache a few hours later. The newspaper critics had been right. The Branson Boys were quite good, even to a non-country fan like me. Unfortunately, my mind kept wandering, and I found it difficult to focus on the show.

On the ride down, as we sat in stop-and-go traffic on Route 95, Cassie reminded me about the message I'd left her the previous day. "I can't think of anyone who would've wanted to harm Carrie." she told me, which was no surprise. Most of us "everyday joes" live our entire lives without making even one enemy. It would take a *lot* to make most people end another human's life.

So, then who had taken Carrie's life away from her and for what reason? I pondered those questions in bed for most of the hours that I should have been sleeping after we returned home from the Bronson Boys concert and, again, in the shower the following morning as I readied myself for work. The movie *Groundhog Day* came to mind as I blew my hair dry. How many times had I asked myself these questions in the last week, always coming up empty? Now I knew how poor Bill Murray felt in that film, doing and saying the very same things over and over again. The simple fact was that no one had motive to kill Carrie Landry. There had to be something that I was overlooking.

At school, just over an hour later, I realized what that missing piece could be. As the kids came streaming down the hallway after being dropped off, I spotted the sibling of a former pupil headed towards Joan's classroom. The cute little peanut with her rosy red cheeks gave me a shy smile and wave as she approached. "Hi, Nicole. How are you, honey?" I greeted the adorable munchkin.

"I'm not Nicole!" she cheerfully reminded me.

"Oh gosh, sorry, Nina!" I smiled. "You look so much like your sister that I always confuse you two, don't I?" Little Nina shook her head before filing into her classroom with several of her classmates. It was at that moment that it dawned on me: not only were Carrie and Cassie's name similar, but they looked very much alike also. In fact, even Joan and I had mistaken Cassie for her sister one afternoon when she'd been walking down the school's corridor on her way to Carrie's classroom.

Perhaps Carrie had not been the intended victim…and Cassie had!

## CHAPTER TWELVE

I had to wait until my class had music late in the morning to call Cassie and let her in on my lookalikes theory. "I don't think so." were her first words on my newest idea.

"But, it *is* possible. You need to be careful in case you were the true target."

"Maybe she really did fall down the stairs accidentally. It makes more sense than someone doing something like that to her...or me." she rebutted.

"What about the missing hat?"

"Okay, that is a little weird, I'll grant you. But, it may turn up at some random time down the line and we'll be like, 'Oh, *that's* where it was all this time!' Besides, there's nobody out there that would want to see me dead. I'm pretty boring."

Frustrated that she was shunning what I believed to be a monumental revelation, we wrapped up our chat fairly quickly. I then used the remainder of my time without students in the room to get some real work done. The truth of it was that I was just an ordinary first grade teacher, not a super sleuth. Lesson plans, lunch duty, and read alouds were my specialty. Not hunting for a despicable murderer who might not even exist. Deciphering the written ramblings of six year olds was the only mystery I should be concerned with, I resolved.

Miraculously, the rest of my workday continued smoothly with nary a thought of killers, dead bodies, mistaken identities, or the ominous note I'd been given the day before. Likewise, I was able to keep focused on things like doing errands, organizing my clothes, and working on report card grades for the remainder of the day and night.

In what seemed like the blink of an eye, Dale was announcing with glee, "It's Friday!" as I made my way down the corridor to start another day in grade one.

"Yay!" I cheered, shaking invisible pompoms in the air. Things finally appeared to be going back to normal. We'd miss Carrie forever, but we also had to keep on truckin'. Just then, Leticia Devane rounded the corner with a hefty stack of worksheets in her arms. "I thought some children had entered the building already when I heard you two carrying on down here." she felt the need to inform us as she bustled into the Teacher's Room. Ugh! Between her and Bunting the Bible Queen, we were losing our fun faculty to downers one by one.

Dale and I exchanged looks of irritation. "Piss off, you old biddy," he replied, quietly enough that said biddy wouldn't hear.

"Who is *she* to admonish *us*?" I threw out there.

"She needs to lighten up." Mr. Badger agreed, "We should ply her with alcohol and let her grind it out on a stripper pole. Let down that gray hair, granny. Your bun's wrapped a little too tightly." The image of the snippy schoolmarm's fragile frame slithering around such a pole, whipping her long locks free from their constraints was too much to take. For the first time in days, I found myself laughing out loud.

At lunchtime, I retrieved the lone voicemail message on my cell phone. It was Cassie, letting me know she was planning to spend the evening with her parents and wouldn't be home. A night at home catching up on some correcting and working on report card comments sounded good at first. But, as I mulled it over, a night alone in the house where Carrie may or may not have been murdered by person or persons unknown had a lot less appeal.

To remedy the situation, I called Erica with an invitation to hang out together if she could find a sitter on such short notice, if her husband wasn't going to be home. Unsure as to whether or not the new mom would be available to "babysit" her scaredy cat pal (me!), I decided to include Dale and Joan on the guest list as well.

Dale was game, naturally. Since the Badgers had split, his Friday nights were apparently as rip roaring as mine from what I'd ascertained. I called Joan, too, but got the machine. So, I shot her a quick email instead of leaving a message.

Joan got back to me late that afternoon to decline my offer. "I wish I could," she lamented, "but I don't have anyone to keep an eye on Warren."

"What about Max? He can't come down for a little bit?"

"No. He's been really busy lately. I hate to impose on him."

"You can bring Warren with you if you want. Or we could come to your house instead." Nothing like inviting myself over!

"No, I'm good. Thanks anyway. Warren went to bed right after he had an early supper and I'd rather leave him to sleep. Over at Carrie's...well, Cassie's, I guess, you guys can get as loud as you want."

"Oh yes, I'm certain all of the neighbors will be calling the cops to complain about our rowdiness! If you hear sirens, you'll know where they're coming to."

"Well, have some fun for sure. We all need some." She needed some more than the rest of us, I wanted to remark. But, if she felt better staying at home with her husband, I wasn't going to strong arm her into coming over. Having to decline social engagements had to be hard enough for her without resistance or bullying from her friends.

As a last ditch effort, I told her, "If you change your mind or Warren wakes up yearning for a night out, we're right around the corner."

"Thanks, Diana. Tell the others I said hello and that we'll definitely all get together soon."

I did just that when Erica knocked on the door half an hour after we'd ended our call. "Oh, that's too bad," Erica agreed. "Poor Joanie needs a break from playing nursemaid more regularly. Being cooped up in the house with Warren all day every day can't be good for her spirits. I don't know how she does it, especially when he's rambling on about nothing." But, that was Joan Petrillo for you. Devoted to her husband till death did they part. If only more married couples believed and lived up to that philosophy these days.

Sadly, Dale and Jodi Badger were not one of those pairs. A fact we were reminded of when the typically chipper Mr. B. showed up ten minutes after Erica, armed with two six packs of Budweiser, a bottle of wine, some vodka, and a smaller brown bottle with, as of yet, unknown contents. "To toast Carrie." my colleague said by way of explanation.

"Aha, okay…though I'm thinking a glass of wine apiece would've been sufficient. No need for you to knock over B.T. Liquors on your way over. You know I don't drink, Dale."

"I do!" my other guest cheerfully reminded us.

"You also have to drive home, as does Dale." I wisely pointed out. "And you have a child to care of when you arrive home. Who's watching Savannah by the way?"

"Her daddy, of course. And don't think for a hot second that I would drive while intoxicated."

"I know. I know." Unfortunately, Dale might be another story. On a typical day, I wouldn't have had any doubts, but he seemed to be in a sour mood *and* had shown up with enough alcohol for every apostle at the Last Supper to have his fill. That could mean only one thing. "Jodi called." I presumed aloud.

"Even better. She was at the house when I got home from work. Needed to pick up some fancy-ass pair of shoes she'd left behind because she's going out to dinner in *Boston* tonight. Goody for her."

"That sucks." was Erica's blunt assessment.

"Oh, by the way, do you think you could maybe leave a light on when you're expecting guests? I almost took a nose dive off of the steps."

"What? The front light *is* on. Maybe you just missed it in your rushed attempt to get inside and drink yourself into oblivion."

"Uh, no, smartass. Look for yourself!" he instructed, opening the front door and motioning with his hand at the now darkened bulb which had been glowing with electricity when Erica had come in. Flipping the light switch yielded no results. "That's strange." Reaching up and touching the warm bulb confirmed what I knew to be fact. I jiggled it and saw a flicker of light appear. Turning it some more brought back the full illumination. "The bulb was loose, I guess."

"Will you close the frickin' door please! It's *winter*." I did as Erica requested, still wondering about the unscrewed light bulb. Had the wind shaken it out of place? Or had it been twisted by someone? And, if so, who? And why?

After working with me for several years, Dale Badger could read me like a book. "What's bugging you?" he finally inquired as the three of us took our seats around the bowls of munchies atop the coffee table.

"Nothing. It's stupid. I'm just being paranoid, speculating about how the light went out so suddenly.

"Well, given that warning you got yesterday, it's no wonder you're on edge." he consoled, which led to a rehashing of the mysterious note that had appeared in my mailbox at school.

"Clearly someone doesn't like me asking questions and voicing my opinion about the doubts I have regarding Carrie's fall."

"And, if somebody's scared that you'll find something out, there must *be* something to be found out." Erica concluded.

"Whether Carrie was mistakenly or purposefully killed," Dale added, resting his first empty beer can down on the table, "or Cassie was the one that particular fate was meant for, somebody is definitely spooked. Otherwise, why not leave well enough alone and let you try to piece together exactly what went down that night?"

Excellent point, Badger. "Maybe I *will* have a drink after all." I decided, heading to the kitchen to track down a corkscrew. *Not* a swift move on my part, I realized much later in the evening. After several hours of discussing, whining, questioning, laughing, complaining, gossiping, and- yes- plenty of drinking, my somewhat fuzzy brain had a surprisingly solid thought. "I'm living in my dead friend's house. How morbid is that?"

"Pretty damned morbid." Erica replied.

"Yeah, it kinda is, isn't it?" Dale agreed with a freaky looking grin.

Talk about a buzzkill. "So my close friend dies and my warped self decides to do what? Move into the place where she fell to her death, or was pushed to her death, or was accidentally knocked down the stairs to her death, or possibly tripped over her own foot and was sent flying…"

"Enough already!" shrieked my bestest BFF, the lovely and in-your-face Erica Talbot.

"We get the point, Di." Dale sweetly informed me. *Di? No one calls me Di. What the hell was that about?*

"Was I rambling?" The look on my tipsy pals' faces provided the answer I sought.

"But, honey, don't forget. You **needed** somewhere else to stay after that wicked wencheroo evicted your rump."

"Rump?" Dale repeated with a chuckle.

"Rump." Erica said again, eliciting more giggling from Mr. B., which in turn caused her to break into some wild cackling. Seeing them behave so sillily over a simple word brought me a case of the giggles too.

Mother of the Moon! We were acting like the first graders we taught! I can't count the number of times the innocent usage of the word "but" has sent my students into a fit of the funnies. Moments later, my mood turned nostalgic.

My eyes got watery as I remembered how lucky I'd felt when I'd first set eyes on the adorable four room apartment and been accepted as a tenant by the sweet little old lady who owned it. "Mrs. Gort isn't a wencheroo," *Wench-a- what?* my working brain cells queried. "She's just **old**."

"Old people can still be mean." one of my visitors (or maybe the disembodied voice of the dearly departed Amy Winehouse) reminded me.

But I wasn't quite done strolling down Memory Lane just yet. "I can't complain too much," I said weepily. "I *loved* that place and the rent was ridiculously cheap the entire time I lived there. Rose was so nice to keep it that low. I think she took pity on me since I'm a teacher who won't be raking in the big bucks any time soon." I suddenly felt the need to defend my former landlady. "Besides, she only gave me the boot to help out a family member. Who can fault her for that? It's not like she sent me packing so she can open a brothel or turn the place into a crack house. Well, unless her perfect little granddaughter is a voracious slut and an insatiable coke hound…" Was I rambling again? "How funny would *that* be? Not 'ha ha' funny, I mean, but 'superbly ironic and vindication for the responsible tenant who was unceremoniously kicked to the curb' funny!"

I must admit that I did have a good laugh thinking about that malicious scenario. Okay, so I actually cackled like a hyperactive hyena and nearly wet myself in the process (but, that is most certainly a case of T.M.I. !). Soon my two fellow hyenas joined in and we roared together for a few minutes.

When I finished laughing, though, I broke down into tears without warning, shooting me from hilarity to sadness in mere seconds. What did we have to laugh about, really, I chided. Dale's wife had cheated on him. Joan's husband had been stricken with a life changing illness. Rose Gort had evicted me out of the blue. And, Carrie. Poor Carrie Landry was gone forever.

That grim thought caused a sudden shift in my stomach, and my quote from earlier that night,

"You know I don't drink." Resonated through my mind. I then lowered my head and proceeded to vomit all over myself.

Party night was *over.*

## CHAPTER THIRTEEN

Needless to say, I felt like I'd been run over by a fleet of gaudy macaroni and cheese colored school buses when I awoke the next day. Dale was asleep on the couch in the living room, and since Erica (a drinking "pro" who rarely exhibited the side effects of it) was nowhere to be seen, I assumed she'd felt well enough to drive home after graciously helping me remove my puked on garments.

That, people, is why Diana Fallon *doesn't* drink…usually. There's just too much unpleasantness involved afterwards. Though, I could now understand how individuals living in less than ideal circumstances could be lured into escaping their woes by the temptation of alcohol, I, for one, would never allow myself to fall into that trap. I did, however, allow myself the priceless joy of crawling back into my bed for many many hours.

When I finally emerged from beneath the covers in a state of Hangover Hell, I actually felt way better than I'd assumed I would. Even in college, I'd never been a drinker. Thus, the previous night had been the first and *last* time I'd officially gotten drunk.

Dale had evacuated the sofa (presumably for his own), and Cassie had taken his spot by the time I made my way downstairs following a glorious thirty minute shower. I no longer felt like I'd chowed down a half dozen lunches from the Redmond School cafeteria, and, in fact, was quite lucid. Despite my foray into the world of frat party foolishness a night earlier, my belief that Cassie might have been on a killer's hit list was still front and center.

The living Landry sister, however, wasn't buying it. And, seeing as I had no proof to the contrary, I let it go. "At least be cautious when you're alone." I told her, "*Just in case* I'm right." True, I was the only one with strong suspicions about Carrie's death. But, I was also the only one who'd been given a written warning. I wasn't a complete moron. (Was I?) I needed to watch my step as much as Cassie did. But that threat had achieved the opposite of what its author had intended. My desire to learn exactly how Carrie Landry had met her maker had been strengthened by it.

There was one question I'd been meaning to ask Cassie about the night in question, as a matter of fact. "Was the door to the house locked or unlocked when you came home the morning you found Carrie?"

"Locked, I think. Why?"

"If the door had been unlocked that Wednesday night, anyone could have entered the house. If it was locked, just those of you with a key could get it, without being admitted by Carrie, which also could be the case, of course. Are there only two keys to the house?"

"I'm not sure. I think so."

"No neighbors have an extra copy?"

"Not to my knowledge, no. Unless she gave out a copy before I moved in."
Hmmm….something that we may want to look into.

Another bit of information that I hoped to obtain was whether or not Carrie's sister was on the up and up when she'd told me that she had no enemies. There really was no reason for me not to believe her statement, but if there *was* someone with a vendetta against her, she may not want the reason behind it broadcast to anyone or everyone she knew.

So, although I had put my detecting on the back burner a couple of days ago, and despite the fact that I hadn't corrected any papers or written a word in my plan book for the following week yet (yes, that's the excitement that the weekend brings for most teachers!), off I went to follow up on this "lead". And by "lead", I mean "crazy notion possessing my every thought". Granted, I could be a complete lunatic wasting my time, but at least I would be *doing* something, rather than sitting on my rear end imagining even more outlandish theories. Plus, after staying in bed for the better part of the day, I could use an excursion.

My first stop was the hospital where Cassie worked. There, I heard nothing but complimentary comments about her professionalism, excellent work ethic, and cheery personality. Both the duty nurse and the head nurse on Cassie's floor were positive that their colleague was held in the highest regard by everyone at the hospital. Then again, my distrustful mind reminded me, if one of them had it out for Cassie, would they really come clean about it to a complete stranger? Probably not.

Hoping that someone at the gym Cassie worked out at might know something that could confirm or refute my "enemy" theory, I headed to the Gold's down the street from Nurse Landry's workplace. "Friendly", "respectful", and "polite" were the words that the staff member at Gold's used to describe my new housemate. Another dead end. Though, on a personal note, I was happy to hear that about the woman I was currently residing with.

Apparently I was much better suited to teach youngsters than to track down murderers. Police officers, detectives, and private eyes surely deserved props.

One would assume that my lack of success on my recent sleuthing endeavors would dampen my confidence. Not so. As I lay in Carrie's bed the following morning, summoning up the fortitude to brave a particularly cold winter day, I mentally planned out my next step: go house to house in the immediate vicinity of the Landry's home to speak with the neighbors. Detective

Donovan, cute Deputy Miller, and/or other police personnel had undoubtedly spoken to all of my soon to be interviewees, but maybe, just maybe, I'd uncover some tiny tidbit that would help break the case!

I began my queries directly across the street with Miles Kendrick. With any luck, he'd have forgotten that I'd accepted his kindness then shooed him out of the house two seconds later like a crazy loon. Optimistic, but unrealistic, I know.

Evidently, he'd forgiven *and* forgotten my bipolar antics because his front door was opened before I could even knock. "Hey there, what's up? It's Diana, right?" he greeted me with a smile of bright white teeth. Dang, he was even hotter in the daylight, and the tight tee shirt and jeans he had on showcased his athletic build way better than his business suit had. His moustache was immaculately groomed, and his eyes were crystal blue. "To what do I owe this visit from a beautiful woman on my very own doorstep?"

I wondered if, perhaps, his contacts weren't in. I like to think of myself as an attractive gal, but I most definitely had not glamorized myself to interrogate the residents of Tremaine Road. In fact, my hair was thrown back in a shabby looking ponytail, I hadn't a stitch of makeup on, and was in an old gray parka and some baggy red sweatpants. Either this dude had been brought up well enough to compliment a lady even when she looked like a hot mess, he was trying to butter me up for some reason (which was kind of working), or was vision impaired. Suspicious woman that I am, I voted for option number two. "Just a few questions I wanted to ask you."

"Sure. Well, I'm a Virgo, I love pasta, and, yes, I am single." Wink.

Whaaaat? Did he use that line on all the girls or just the pale faced ones with chapped lips that showed up at his house unexpectedly on a Sunday morning?

With looks like his, I normally would have swooned. But, I was on a mission. "No, no, no," I stammered, clarifying my reason for showing up uninvited out of the blue. "Some questions about Carrie…Landry…from across the street. Do you happen to know if any of the neighbors have an extra key to her house?"

"Would you like to come inside? It's awfully chilly out here." I noticed that he didn't answer my question.

"No, thank you." I politely declined in the sweetest voice I could muster. If he wasn't going to give me any info, there was no reason to stick around.

"That's too bad." he replied, sounding quite sincere. "As for the key, I don't have one, but I'm away on business so often that I probably wouldn't be first pick to keep a spare. Not sure about anyone else though. I really only know the neighbors well enough to wave and say hello."

Strike One. "All righty, thanks anyway."

"You do know that the Yeagers, the yellow house right next door, are in Florida for the winter, right?"

"I do now." No use going there then. "Thanks for the tip."

"No problem. Come again sometime when you can stay for a bit." the could-be-supermodel suggested before giving me a quick wave and closing his door. Hmm….Miles Kendrick, a rare handsome *and* nice guy…or a sleazy sex addict attempting to lure me into his S&M lair? I couldn't quite decide as I walked past the empty Yeager residence to the beige raised ranch on the opposite side of it. Unfortunately, the young couple I spoke to there had no more information than Miles did. Ditto for the next house on that side of the road.

# A FIRST GRADE FATALITY

At that point, I opted to double back to check with people on the other side of the street. The first place I stopped, I was greeted by a young mom and her three screaming kids. Blessedly, she had nothing to offer and I got the heck out of there as quickly as I could, crossing my fingers that the trio of shriekers mellowed out by the time they hit first grade!

Nobody answered at the next two homes, and I started to get ticked off at having foolishly wasted so much of a Sunday morning. Thankfully I had just one more stop, the small white house with maroon shutters that was separated from the Landry's yard by an extremely tall wooden fence. The mailbox, too, was white with a black cat painted on one side and the name Charm on the other. Though I'd never met her, I did recall Carrie mentioning Mrs. Charm, the crabby widow who lived next door to her, on more than one occasion. Maybe *she* would be the one to assist me, which would be par for the course since I'd been to every house *but* hers already!

After ringing the bell, I could distinctly hear movement inside, yet nobody came to the door. So I rang it again, twice. Still no reply, but the pink paisley curtain in the window to the left of the door moved ever so slightly. "I know you're in there, lady." I whispered, banging on the door in frustration. This time, the occupant wasn't fast enough and I got a glimpse of her face in the window before she could let go of the curtain.

The poor thing looked terrified. No wonder. Her neighbor had recently died suddenly and tragically and Arwell's finest had, no doubt, come a knockin' less than a week ago. And here I was rapping on her door like an overzealous trick-or-treater who'd missed her morning dose of Ritalin! Clearly I needed to try a calmer and less abrasive approach.

Stepping back from the door a bit so that elderly Dorothy Charm could see me, I put on my friendliest smile (not quite as white as hunky Miles Kendrick, I was pretty certain) and waved at the eyes peering out at me. "Hello, Mrs. Charm!" I shouted, in case the white haired widow was hard of hearing. "My name is Diana Fallon. I'm living next door to you for the next few weeks." Or months, or years, depending on how difficult it would be to find an acceptable apartment that wouldn't eat up my minimal teacher's salary…or have rats and roaches as my new roomies!

"I'm a friend of Carrie's. I taught with her at the Redmond School." I continued, senselessly pointing off to my right as if the woman could see the actual school building. But, hey, wouldn't you know, it worked! I'm not sure if it was Carrie's name or her presumption that an elementary schoolteacher was no threat, but frizzy haired Dorothy opened the door slightly and took me in with her beady little eyes. She was, as Carrie had described her, a cranky looking being whose last name did *not* fit her in the least. If the spooked septuagenarian silently surveying me was full of *charm*, then I was full of…well, never mind. "Whatta ya want?" the charmless one inquired, quickly resuming her scowl.

"I'm so sorry to bother you. I hope that I didn't frighten you by knocking so loudly. I wasn't sure if you heard me." I lied.

"Just 'cause I'm old don't mean I'm deaf, girlie." Oops. Foot in mouth!

"No, of course not. In fact, I came to see you because Carrie told me that you're as sharp as a tack and I'm in need of some information." Deadpan Dorothy said nothing, evidently waiting for me to get to the point.

Stepping forward, I inhaled a whiff of cat urine and tried not to gag. That black cat on the mailbox either had an abnormally overactive bladder issue or lots of feline company inside.

Could the less than charming Mrs. Charm be an animal hoarder? "*Back on track*!" I mentally snapped at myself, much like we teachers have to do on a daily basis to avoid hearing two hours of personal stories about going to the zoo during a lesson on fire safety. So often, a six year old's desired topic of discussion has ***nothing*** *t*o do with the subject matter being taught, much like my own random distraction of the moment.

Crazy cat lady or not, I was willing to throw myself down on my knees if it meant finally getting some facts. Haplessly, the wary woman had none to share, so I thanked her and turned to depart. "Wait a second," Mrs. Charm commanded, causing me to look back at her. There is something that you might want to know about. Last night, early this morning really, probably around four o'clock, I saw a car stop out in front of your house. It stayed there a good few minutes. Not sure why."

That was odd. "What was the driver doing? And how did you see all this?" I was fairly sure that fence would've blocked her view.

"Don't know what he did. Seemed to be just sitting in the car, looking at the house. I only saw him because Esmerelda, my calico, ran out the door at dinnertime and wouldn't come back in." Maybe even the cat was overwhelmed by the smell of cat pee! "And when I got up to get a drink of water, I spotted her on the front lawn and went out to lure her back in with some tuna."

Marvelous. Not only had I learned zilch about Carrie's "accident", but whoever had left me that ominous note was apparently keeping tabs on me at home too. Could things get any worse?

## CHAPTER FOURTEEN

The existence of a spare key meant absolutely nothing, my wise friend Joan Petrillo made me realize as we talked on the phone that Sunday afternoon. "Yes, if someone had an extra key, they could've gotten inside on their own. But, Carrie could have let someone in or the door might even have been unlocked. Either way, a person without a key could've gained admittance and then locked the door behind them on their way out." Why, then, had I been so convinced that an extra key was so vital in solving this mystery? Perhaps I was just a birdbrain with farfetched notions!

"I really do think it was an accident." Joan declared. "It's terrible. Awful. Unfair. But, we should just accept it and move on, Diana. You're driving yourself crazy over this, yet you haven't unearthed even one bit of evidence that would indicate any sort of foul play."

"You're probably right." I conceded. "If only there were some way to be positive about what happened."

"But, there isn't. And we *know* for a fact that nobody would want to intentionally hurt Carrie. There are no suspects, no motives, no anything."

Erica, too, hoped I would give up my wild suspicions. "Joan's right. The likelihood that Carrie didn't just slip or trip on the stairs is slim to none. This is Arwell, Massachusetts. We're schoolteachers. It's not like we're all high priced call girls in L.A. or Sin City."

Rationally speaking, I knew that my friends were right. Accepting the tragedy was what I needed to do. Nevertheless, there was that one bothersome tidbit that was hard to ignore. "What about the missing hat?" I wanted to know. "She had it on that Wednesday afternoon, yet it was

116

gone as of Thursday morning. It isn't at school. It's not in her car or at the house. Where did it disappear to?" I asked Dale via instant messaging online awhile after I'd talked to Erica.

He was also of the consensus that my "investigating" had gone on for long enough. Strengthening his argument was the explanation he'd come up with to satisfy my curiosity about Carrie's sentimental headwear. We (or at least I) had been going on the assumption that Carrie had come right after school and not realized that her keys were locked in the car until she was leaving to meet us for dinner at Santino's. Dale's theory was that our friend had come home and then gone out again – maybe to the post office or Rite Aid, during which time she'd lost her hat. Returning home *that* time was when she'd mistakenly left the keys in the car. It made sense and eased my one final concern.

With the trio of Petrilo, Badger, and Talbot urging me to put an end to my inquiries, thereby regaining my sanity, I reasoned that it was time to let it go. Hadn't I made a similar promise to myself just a few days earlier though? Hopefully I would demonstrate an increase in willpower this time around. And, trust me, I totally *would* have…if only I hadn't remembered one more potentially enlightening avenue I'd yet to explore!

It wasn't until early Sunday night that I finally got a chance to relax and let my mind wander. Most of the afternoon had been spent preparing lessons for the upcoming week and determining what other concepts I had to cover in class over the next few weeks before report cards were issued. That task alone took up the majority of my day, coupled with the correcting and logging grades for a three part grade level math assessment I'd been avoiding for four days.

Cassie was watching an old episode of *Law and Order* when I plunked myself down onto the couch beside her, so I blame her for challenging (inadvertently, of course) the investigative instincts I'd so recently denounced. Had she been watching *Here Comes Honey Boo Boo* , my mental state would then have been one of bewilderment and disbelief. Instead, as the pair of T.V. detectives ran through a list of motives for the gruesome crime they'd been assigned to, I could hardly help myself from applying that same type of reasoning to the "highly unlikely criminal act" I was "no longer looking into".

Greed was a no-go for sure. Like most first year teachers, Carrie's salary was nothing to applaud, and she was still paying off student loans to Bridgewater State. Anyone, most likely Cassie or her parents, who'd inherit Carrie's "estate" would be sorely disappointed if they'd done away with her in the hopes of receiving a plentitude of cash.

Revenge? Unthinkable. As Erica had pointed out, we common folk hardly ran the risk of wronging someone or pissing them off to the extent that murder became a viable solution. Primary school teachers, as a rule, are pretty outgoing and easy to get along with, at least on a personal level. (Staff meetings, on the other hand, could get a little intense from time to time.) Wicked acts and scandalous improprieties weren't exactly part of our daily routine.

Stumbling upon and/or keeping an explosive secret couldn't be ruled out completely, I supposed. But, if Carrie had been keeping a secret, though, who would have known about it? It was a secret! Duh. Still, hiding the truth about something earth shattering enough to force a person to kill didn't' seem all that plausible even to me, Miss Suspicious.

Romantic entanglements? "Had she been seeing anyone lately?" the detective with the bushy moustache asked his informant on the screen. OMG! How stupid of me! How had I forgotten about the new man in Carrie's life? Was the mysterious male, who we knew virtually nothing about, involved in whatever had transpired that fatal night?

"Brian!" I shrieked, startling poor Cassie enough that she, too, yelped. I could practically see the letters WTF on her face as she jerked away from me and looked at me with confusion.

"Sorry. But something just came to me." I explained, filling Carrie's sister in on what little I knew about this Brian guy and bombarding her with questions she evidently was unable to answer.

"All I know," Cassie replied, once I finally gave her a chance to speak, "is that she met some guy, I guess by now it'd be a few weeks ago. She thought he was nice and they went out once or twice. Why such a sudden interest in him?"

In a garbled mishmash of sentences and ideas, I relayed my latest suspicion. "Didn't you give up this line of thinking earlier today?" she asked.

"I did. I was. I had." For a full four and a half hours that is. "Just humor me this one last time." I implored, clicking the pause button on the remote so that Cassie could continue her viewing in a few minutes.

Had this Brian been at her memorial service the previous weekend? Was he even aware that Carrie was no longer among the living? Who else might have info on this guy?

"You were her closest friend at work. What she told you is pretty much what she told me." As Joan, herself, had said, she was "out of the loop" these days. Anything she or Erica had been told about this guy had come from my lips. What about Dale, though? His friendship with Carrie did not include exchanges about her love life, I had to assume. Dale put up with a gang of estrogen filled co-workers better than most straight men in his spot would have. However, dating was one topic he and I did not share intimate details about. Not that there were any intimate details for me to share. But that was beside the point.

119

Calling Mr. B. at this hour would alert him to the fact that I'd not completely given up on my quest, which would likely sour his mood. A casual text would have to suffice.

"Is there anyone else Carrie may have mentioned Brian to?" I asked.

Cassie doubted it. "The only friends from college that she keeps in touch with semi-regularly are Lara and Misty. Both of them came to the service. Neither one lives around here, but they chat on Facebook a lot, I think."

Facebook, the modern way to snoop into someone's personal life without them ever catching on! Perhaps Brian was on her list of FB "friends". With Cassie's permission, I beelined it upstairs to Carrie's, temporarily *my*, bedroom and revved up my laptop. With a few punches of the keys, I was on.

First off, I found posts from both Misty and Lara and sent them a join message to inquire about "the guy Carrie went out with recently". Playing dumb rather than implying anything about him was probably my best bet. Especially since this was almost guaranteed to be another irrelevant piece of the pie.

Next, I scoured Carrie's list of "friends" on the site, a vastly assorted crew that could be anyone from a long lost childhood neighbor to a friend's brother-in-law to her gynecologist! Bingo! There was one "Brian". Clicking onto his profile, I could see only his basic info, which was enough to bum me out. Brian Slater currently resided in Topeka, Kansas. Somehow I had a feeling that Mr. Slater hadn't flown halfway across the country to take my now deceased friend out to dinner a couple of times. Just to rule it out, though, I sent him a vague message. After all, as I'd learned from the MTV program *Catfish*, profiles could be very deceptive and this fellow could very well be living in or temporarily here in Massachusetts.

After an extremely restless night, spent wondering if any of the messages I'd sent had gotten a reply, I managed to crawl out of bed and stagger into the bathroom when my alarm clock went off for the third time. With only about two hours of sleep, the reflection that greeted me was not a pretty sight. I worried that my class might confuse me with Miss Viola Swamp, a hideous looking substitute teacher in the popular children's story, *Miss Nelson Is Missing*, which I'd read aloud a few weeks earlier.

Running even later than usual, checking Facebook for responses to my inquiries about Brian should have been at the bottom of my "to do" list. But, naturally, I couldn't wait to see what kind of answers awaited me. Only Misty had replied, stating that she did not know that Carrie had been seeing anyone new and that she hoped I was doing well. Short and polite. Pretty much what I had expected so my hopes were not dashed completely, although a feeling of defeat began to creep over me yet again.

By the time my laptop was shut down and I'd managed to transform myself into something slightly less horrifying than Miss Swamp, it was nearly time for me to leave. Desperate for a quick pick me up, I had no choice but to start the coffee maker and wait for it to brew if I was to get a shot of caffeine into my system. As popular as places like Dunkin Donuts and Starbucks are, my taste buds had never taken a liking to their offered beverages, meaning I might be arriving at the classroom door just as my students did, something understandably frowned upon by the higher ups. It had yet to happen, even with my lack of a.m. time management, and I hoped that today would not be any different.

As I waited for my coffee, about as patiently as my first graders in line for our morning bathroom break, my mind began roaming back to Brian. He must have heard about Carrie's passing. Otherwise, he surely would have called her, and as far as I could tell he had not. Then again, he wouldn't be the first guy in the world *not* to call when he'd said that he would!

Actually, the ringtone on her phone, the Backstreet Boys' *I Want It That Way*, hadn't sounded off since my arrival as a houseguest, nor had the more-than-annoying beeping sound which indicated a voicemail. "Where is her phone anyway?" I wondered, scanning the kitchen counters and table. Spotting it beside the toaster, a burst of excitement came over me. Brian and Carrie had obviously made arrangements to get together when they went out so Brian's number would be stored on the phone, unless by some chance Carrie had deleted it. "Yes!" I exclaimed like an overzealous soccer mom, grabbing the cellular device and playing around with it to locate its contact list. Flipping to the "B"s, I was dismayed not to find his name among the index of names. Crap! I scanned the list again, in case my "morning sight" was playing tricks on me. Wait a second! My eyes stopped on the entry "BF".

"BF?" The commonly used abbreviation for "boyfriend". Was she labeling him that way after having gone out with him so few times? Or had things progressed more rapidly than we knew? I clicked on it anyway, figuring I could call the number, ask for Brian, and then feign misdialing if it wasn't him. My dismal detecting skills were improving at long last! Yahoo!

Scribbling down the digits onto a napkin, a number that began with a local area code I happily noted, I was ready to rest my inquiring mind and rejoin the real world, scooting my booty to school as fast as possible.

Too bad "as fast as possible" wound up being "not fast enough". Not only had the morning bell rung by the time I whipped into the very last parking space in the staff lot, but almost all of the walkers, drop-offs, *and* bus riders were inside the building before me. Cursing at myself for getting too wrapped up in snooping, I flew out of my car, across the pavement, and up the stairs faster than a caffeine infused Boston marathoner. Mortified by my tardiness, I regained my composure to the best of my ability before rounding the corner, marching down the hall as if nothing was out of the ordinary, and ushering my students into the classroom. Slipping directly into teacher mode, I hastily unpacked my bag. "Good morning, boys and girls!" I said with a smile.

I pride myself on being a hard worker and a dedicated teacher, so that morning, to compensate for showing up late, I worked more diligently than ever. I checked in with all four math groups to determine who knew what and recorded what I learned on sticky notes, which I would transfer into each child's individual assessment folder later on. I dug through a twelve gallon plastic tub and successfully located the oaktag houses and buildings for the afternoon's map skills lesson. I even corrected two entire stacks of the children's independent assignments as they continued to work quietly at their desks. I was back in business!

As the hands of the clock tediously ticked their way towards noon, however, nervous energy began pulsating through my body. What the heck would I say to Brian if the number I planned to dial once the kids headed off to lunch did, in fact, lead me to him? Mentally rehearsing a few lines didn't help whatsoever. Everything that came to mind sounded wicked lame. Maybe winging it would be a better course of action. Hell, the number probably wouldn't pan out as it was. Chances were I wouldn't even get to talk to this "Brian" guy who'd gone out with Carrie.

Well, I was right about that much. When I let my fingers do the dialing a few minutes later, hidden away in the A.V. room so I wouldn't be overheard, I *didn't* reach Brian. Instead, I reached his *wife*!

## CHAPTER FIFTEEN

"Have a good lunch, everyone." I'd told the kids as I sent them off to what was (much to every teacher's chagrin) their favorite part of the day. Then, like a frightened baby antelope being pursued by a ravenous cheetah, I darted down to the audio visual closet before any of my colleagues could spot me or stop me from following my newest hunch. One colleague, in particular, that is… my good friend, Dale Badger.

His email reply to my nonchalant inquiry about Carrie's recent dating status made his disapproval abundantly clear. *I thought you were refraining from playing cops and robbers* was all that he had written back.

Not so easily dissuaded, I'd gone to retrieve my cell phone from my coat at eleven fifty five, only to realize it wasn't in either pocket. In my rush to get out of the house that morning, I must have left it behind. Undaunted, I concluded that the telephone in the tiny audio visual room would offer me the most privacy of the few phones we had access to. It was the one I always used when calling a parent, to provide confidentiality when discussing their little one.

Moving aside the two (heavy!) television carts, I wedged my body between a shelf of CD players and the life sized stuffed kangaroo that had been shoved in there after being used on "Australian Night" several years back. Who'd imagine it would be such a workout to make a simple telephone call? Probably just about every employee at an elementary school!

As I listened to the ringing at the other end of the line, I felt a little bit sick to my stomach, unsure of what words might spout from my lips if someone picked up. Brian answering, a voice mail greeting, or no answer at all had seemed the only options when I'd considered calling this number. So I was completely unprepared for the female voice that said, "Hello?"

"Oh, um…hi. Could I speak to…uh…Brian…please?" Silence on her end was all the reply I got at first. "Hello? Are you there?"

"Who is this?" the woman hostilely demanded.

"Who is *this*?" I echoed back.

"You listen to me, whoever you are. Don't call this number again! Understand?"

"Is this Brian's phone?"

"You damned well know it is if you're calling him. Now leave my husband alone!"

*Husband* !!! Before I could ask anything more, the woman claiming to be his spouse terminated the call, leaving me sitting in a closet, alone, with more questions than I'd had before. Stunned by both the unexpected revelation and the fury in her voice, I flipped the lights off and scurried back to my room to take it all in.

I was deep in thought when Sylvia Wise's voice came over the P.A. system. "Miss Fallon?"

"Yes?

"Mr. Welkey would like to speak to you in his office before the end of your lunch hour." the witless secretary informed me.

"Okay, thank you." Thank you? Why the heck was I thanking her? It wasn't like I was yearning for a one on one chat with my principal and had been given permission to approach his royal throne. My nerves were frayed enough at the present moment. Being beckoned by my boss was something I could definitely do without.

Nine times out of ten when George Welkey summoned a staff member into his inner sanctum, there was no need to worry. A question about the grade level's supplies or a personal request to join a curriculum committee or do some other unwanted school related task was typically the reason for the invite. But, there were always those occasional times when he was following up on a parent complaint against you. Perhaps I'd been accused of unjustly keeping a student in at recess or assigning too much homework.

Whatever the cause, I preferred to get this meeting over and done with prior to grabbing a bite to eat. "Knock knock." I said to let Mr. Welkey know I had arrived.

"Come right in, Diana." he welcomed me. "Close the door behind you." Uh oh. A closed door seemed a likely indicator that what he needed to say was probably not something I'd be thrilled to hear.

Taking a seat across from him, I put on a phony smile. "Sylvia told me that you wanted to see me."

"Yes, I did. I just wanted to check in with you, see how you're doing. I've heard that you've been having a difficult time dealing with Carrie's accident."

He had? From who? Somebody at the Redmond School obviously needed to mind their own business. (This coming from the chick who'd been poking her own nose every which way but Sunday lately. Yeah, I know. Total hypocrite!)

"Oh no, I'm fine. I appreciate your concern though." The man just looked at me, yet said nothing. Did he expect me to keep speaking? "I mean, it's an absolute tragedy and it still feels weird not seeing her here each day. But, I'm good."

"Are you? I've been told that you believe her fall wasn't accidental, that you have some cock and bull notion that someone pushed her down those stairs to her death."

Normally George Welkey did not intimidate me. Today was different. I felt like I was being reprimanded for not sticking with the pack and accepting my colleague's sudden death without question as they'd all done. True, my theory could be as far off as the now non-planet, Pluto, but nobody had provided me with any solid proof of that yet. And until such evidence was produced, a shadow of a doubt would continue to linger.

The way he'd studied my reaction and the tone of his voice led me to think that he viewed me as an over imaginative fool. However, he *was* my boss so I didn't want to appear *too* oppositional. "I'm not sure exactly what happened." I admitted.

"Well, I do. She fell." he stated bluntly, "You really can't be running all over town implying otherwise." *Keep your mouth* shut was his implied message.

"I understand," was my simple reply. What I understood was that he didn't want me making such bold speculations in public. Notice, though, that I never actually agreed not to make these observations again in the future.

"Oh, and I was also concerned because you were late this morning." Welkey threw in. "Nothing too problematic, I hope. Annette was worried when you weren't in your classroom when the bell rang, which is so unlike you." Annette Bunting! Why did I have a feeling that she was more concerned about making me look bad than my personal well-being? Oh, I know. Because she'd not even had the human decency to wait until Carrie Landry was buried before she went after her job! So much for all that Bible reading she did. It didn't seem to be helping mold her into a better person.

"No, nothing major." I informed him as I stood up to leave. "Just a way crazy morning. I assure you, it will *never* happen again." This time I was stating the truth and nothing but.

Running around playing private eye on my own time was one thing. Having it affect my career was another thing altogether.

Our tete-a-tete left me with, literally, three minutes to eat lunch. Abandoning the idea of obtaining nutrition, I instead raced down to the Teacher's Room to tell Dale about my call and near heart failure when Brian's *legal* mate answered. I accepted the fact that Dale would have preferred me to write off Carrie's death as an accident and let the event fade into a distant memory, but how would he not find the fact that Brian was married as mind blowing as I did?

Finding only Leticia Devane in the teacher's lounge, I promptly left without even saying "Hello" (rude, yes, but my time was severely limited don't forget!). Had this horrifying tidbit been about anyone but a friend, I would undoubtedly have treated it as a juicy piece of gossip and spread the word to even the prim retiree. Knowing Carrie, though, and believing her to be a person of good values, my lips remained sealed.

Dale was in his classroom at his desk when I arrived there. "Where were you? I couldn't find you the entire lunch period." That'd have to wait. Ignoring his query, I blurted out the news immediately. "That guy Carrie was seeing, Brian….he's married!" Dale's expression was unreadable and he said nothing.

"Dating someone who is in a wedded relationship is a *sin*." I heard from behind me. There was no need to turn around since her voice and preachy sentiment were clearly recognizable, but I did so anyway.

Apparently I'd been so hell bent on filling Dale in on what I'd learned that I hadn't noticed her, kneeling down on Mr. Badger's "reading rug" with several children's titles in her lap. Ugh. What a complete moron I was! My plan had been to keep this potentially damaging fact under wraps, letting just Dale and Joan in on my discovery. Well, that plan had gone up in smoke faster than one of the Phantom Farter's silent attacks. And Annette Bunting was the very *last* person in the universe I'd ever want to be privy to this information!

"I'm certain that she wasn't aware of his marital status!" I snapped back, despite the fact that I possessed no such knowledge at all. It was entirely *my* fault that the self-appointed Sister Bunting was laying down judgment on our former colleague so obviously I felt obligated to defend her good name, regardless of what she may or may not have known. And, though I could have used some back up, Dale had still yet to say a word.

"It doesn't matter. Conducting oneself in such a manner is unbecoming and immoral. It's vile!"

Suddenly remembering that I was face to face with the tattletale who'd ratted me out for being late one time in *six* freakin' years got my blood boiling even more. If the stress of that overly dramatic day hadn't momentarily claimed my soul like poor little Linda Blair in *The Exorcist*, the next words out of my mouth would *not* have been quite so obscene, I promise. "Oh, Annette," I smirked, "Why don't you just shut the…"

No, that is *not* my retort in its entirety. But, I'm pretty certain that anyone, including some of my first graders with siblings in middle or high school, could supply the four letter word which preceded the word "up" in my not-so-nice reply.

Well, you would have thought I'd *shot* Mrs. Holier than Thou with a harpoon given the zombie like expression on her plump puss. Her mouth hung open wide, the eyes rolled up in her head, and all the usual color in her cheeks had been drained. *Please don't let her pass out*, I silently pleaded. Tardiness once in a blue moon might be overlooked easily enough, but rendering a coworker unconscious was bound to have some severe repercussions!

Hopefully Dale would come to the rescue if need be. Performing mouth to mouth on the preachy pest *wasn't* written on the daily agenda on my white board…and I *am* a stickler for following it to a "T". One look in his direction, however, led me to believe that his body had frozen in horror in response to the vulgarities I'd spewed at the sin slamming substitute. Like he had a mouth of virtue on him!

What could have happened next, we'll never know. Because, at that very fortunate moment in time, recess came to its end and streams of children started filing down the hallway. Ah, saved by the bell!

## CHAPTER SIXTEEN

"Miss Fallon!" screeched an anonymous voice from the tangled mass of small bodies stripping off their winter gear in the coat room. Ryan Wilby, I identified using my innate teacher's super power to recognize any and all students' voices, even when said student was well out of my vision, a handy ability that could be utilized while searching a closet for misplaced flash cards, scanning a teacher's manual during instructional time, or while writing on the white board with my back to the class. "Yes, Ryan?" I replied, my magnificent voice recognition instincts going sadly unnoticed by everyone seven and under in the vicinity.

"Gregory said..." Of course he did. That *darling* Gregory. "that if a girl kisses you, you get an infection." Oh, these poor innocent little minds.

"Gregory is mistaken. You don't get infected by girls who kiss you." Technically this wasn't the exact truth, I knew. But those types of girls had graduated from first grade long ago, and most of them now worked on a city corner somewhere. The boys on the Redmond School playground were safe for now.

"My father told me!" grueling Gregory objected. Naturally.

"That's hogwash." I told him.

"But, why would you wash a hog?" asked Victoria Overton, looking more befuddled than usual. "It's just gonna roll in the mud again." I couldn't deny her that. In fact, it was the most astute observation she'd made since being plunked in my class in mid-November, having moved to Arwell from "elsewhere" ("elsewhere" typically synonymous with "someplace-whose-school-system-is-inferior-to-Arwell's-high-standards-so-get-ready-to-catch-her-up-to-first-grade-level-the-best-you-can-by-the-end-of-the-year") .

"You're right, Victoria." I praised the buck toothed blonde. "But 'hogwash' is actually another way of saying that something is ridiculous or silly. I was pointing out how silly it is to think that if a boy is kissed by a girl, he'll get an infection."

"Ahhh," she nodded blankly.

"But that *doesn't* mean I want any of you girls trying to kiss any of the boys!" I made sure to throw in. All I needed was a phone call or email from a distressed mother complaining about the six year old siren who'd "seduced" her son!

"Ewwwwww…." My band of mini cootie catchers groaned in unison.

The afternoon moved along quickly and, in what seemed like mere minutes, it was time to drop the kiddos off to Fran Vespa in the library. My stomach grumbled on my way back upstairs, an audible reminder that I hadn't eaten a thing all day. You'd think I'd have been famished by then, but, honestly, I was too amped up for my appetite to be intact.

Dying to hear Joan's thoughts about the whole "Brian's wife" situation, I logged onto the classroom computer. Sending this info via school email would not have been my first option, but with my cell phone at home, it was either that or use the school line to call. At least if I typed it out, no one could overhear me. And hopefully the superintendent didn't really monitor staff emails, as had been rumored more than once.

Having just begun what I knew would turn out to be a long winded narrative, I was interrupted by Betsy McAllister, who worked in Dale's room. As she walked across the room, I speedily scrolled down to hide the few words I'd typed thus far. "Hey," was my attempt at a casual greeting. "What are you doing on this side of the hall?"

"Oh, I'll be quick!" Betsy whispered nervously as she scurried over to me. "I just wanted to see if you knew what's up with Dale. He is in a ***mood*** like I've never seen." Oh, Maniacal Muskrats! Was he that pissed at me for telling off Annette? Or maybe it was the fact that I'd run off like a wimp after hurling expletives at her and left him in there alone to settle her down.

"I asked him what was wrong, but he just mumbled something about 'another cheater' and said 'How could she do that?' so I have no clue what's going on." Obviously I did, but I didn't intend to besmirch Carrie's good name.

"I don't know the specifics," I lied. "All I know is that he found out that some friend of his was supposedly cheated on and got angry."

"Ah, gotcha. Obviously that would be a sore spot since…"

"Yeah,"

"Okay, thanks. I've gotta get back over there. I told him I was running to the ladies' room. I'll talk to you later." Not about ***that*** subject, I hoped, now wondering if Dale was furious over the news that Carrie had been seeing a married man or at my carelessness in divulging it to Annette. Either would give him good reason to be upset. In fact, I'd rather have his anger directed at me since I just couldn't believe that Cassie would knowingly get involved with another woman's significant other. Especially since Betsy made it sound like he was still fuming a good hour and a half after my bungled revelation.

A sickening thought entered my mind, one that I dismissed almost immediately. Clearly I was going off the deep end to even imagine something so horrible. There was no way on Earth that one of my closest friends could be responsible for murdering another of them!

Dale *obviously* didn't know the deal with Brian before today. Otherwise his reaction would not have been so intense. Even if he *had* found out, would he have confronted Carrie about it? Under normal circumstances, no. But, Jodi's cheating had really done a number on him. Was it remotely possible that he'd gone to see our friend, "the other woman", to give her a piece of his mind?

Never in ten trillion years would he have gone to her house with malice in mind, intending to punish our colleague for becoming involved with someone else's spouse. Unfortunately, tragic *accident*s happen all the time, and I couldn't seem to block the mental images my mind was repeatedly conjuring up. Images of Dale and Carrie at the top of the staircase, arguing. Images of Carrie turning to go downstairs, her arm being grabbed by Mr. Badger. Images of Carrie twisting out of his grasp, losing her footing, and plummeting down the stairs.

Then I pictured cute little Victoria Overton and her hog washing quandary. *This* was a prime example of hogwash: envisioning Dale Badger as an accidental killer! My level of absurdity had risen to new heights.

Regaining my sensibility, I returned to the task at hand, emailing Joan. Just a day before she'd pointed out my failure to turn up any suspects or motive. Today, I'd unearthed both. Granted, I didn't yet know the details of Carrie's relationship with Brian. But, I did know that a woman scorned was not someone to mess with. Having been brusquely commanded to not even *call* her husband, one could only imagine what the furious wifey might do to anyone of the female persuasion who spent actual time with her dog of a man.

Brian, on the other hand, remained an enigma, a situation I hoped to remedy as soon as possible. Depending on the circumstances of his involvement with Carrie, he, too, could have had reason to want her out of the way. Or, he might just turn out to be a nice guy. Well, a nice guy who goes out with other women despite the fact that he's legally and morally bound to another, that is.

When I talked to Joan and Erica after I'd gotten home from work that afternoon, I neglected to mention that I planned to call Brian's number again that evening in the hopes of reaching him instead of his disgruntled bride. I had wanted to speak with Dale also, about the lunch time showdown, but he had apparently left just after the afternoon bell had rung, and he wasn't picking up when I called. Clearly the guy was trying to avoid me. Rightfully so, I might add. Putting him in the middle of two catty chicks (although Annette was more of a grumpy goose really) going at it and dashing away like a gutless chicken wasn't exactly a shining moment on the timeline of my life. Tomorrow was *not* a day I looked forward to.

Similarly, making a repeat call to Brian's number was also causing my stomach to churn a bit. What if the Mrs. answered again? Hanging up on her didn't seem right. I didn't want to taunt or harass the poor woman. It wasn't her fault that her husband had been seeing someone else behind her back, at least as far as I knew.

Anticipating the worst, but mentally begging for *him* to answer this time, I flipped on Carrie's cell phone and entered the digits with a trembling finger. One ring. Two rings. "Hello?" a male voice answered.

Oh shoot! What the heck was I going to say now that I actually had him on the line? Whatever words I'd prepared in advance had flown the coop the second he spoke, leaving me as mute as the mime who'd performed at the Redmond School's last enrichment program! "Hello?" the man I presumed to be Brian repeated tentatively.

"Hi, um, Brian? How are you?"

"Carrie?" the man asked warily.

Carrie? Did he really think that she was still alive? Or maybe he was just trying to fake me out. Should I pretend to be her and bluff my way through the conversation? Was I even capable of pulling off such a charade?

There was no way in hell that ploy would be successful, I conceded before I spoke again. "No, this isn't Carrie."

"Oh, because her number came up on my phone, but I thought that she…"

"Was dead because you and/or your irate wife pushed her down the stairs?" I wanted very badly to inquire.

"Who is this then?" he inquired.

"A friend of hers. I'm using her cell."

"And why are you calling *me*?"

"Uh, well, um…"

"And who is this again?" he asked a second time, clearly puzzled – or possibly spooked- by my call.

"My name is Diana. I worked with Carrie. She mentioned you to me a few weeks before her 'accident', and I wanted to ask you a couple of things."

"Such as?"

Think before speaking, my brain reminded me. How was I supposed to casually include the fact that he was a cheater without sounding judgmental, preachy, or like a nosy interfering pain in the ass? "I was just wondering if the police had spoken with you in regards to Carrie's fall."

"No. Why would they?" He was starting to get annoyed.

"There's some question about what may have happened the night she died."

"I don't know anything about that. The last time I spoke to Carrie was a few days before that. Do you work for the police?"

"No, I'm a teacher. I'm just trying to figure out some things."

"I'm afraid I can't help you. That's all I know. I really need to go now."

"Oh no, you don't! Not before you give me some answers, buddy." So much for good manners and playing nice. "You're married. I know it and you know it. Did your wife know about Carrie? And did Carrie know about your wife?"

Evidently those last few statements rendered him speechless because dead air was all I got for a good sixty seconds or more. "You don't have any idea what you're talking about." he finally replied.

"Oh, but I *do*. As a matter of fact, I spoke to your wife this morning."

"You did *what*? You talked to Gwen? When? How?"

"Before I left for work today…on this very phone. She wasn't too pleased to hear a woman at the other end of the line. So, will you answer a few questions for me or not? I promise never to call you again if you do. I'm sure that'll make Gwen a very happy woman."

"I don't even know you." Brian stated, now sounding frazzled.

Now, I do believe that honesty is the best policy. But when attempting to ferret out a killer, perhaps not so much. "Your wife doesn't know that." I pointed out in the most menacing voice I could muster up. Apparently with great success, as he caved and agreed to meet me at lunch time the following day. Oh Merciful Monkeys! What had I gotten myself into?

## CHAPTER SEVENTEEN

The next day, I pulled into a McDonald's about ten minutes from school, wondering if Brian would show or not. Part of me kind of hoped that he wouldn't. I really had no clue what could be gained from a face to face meeting that couldn't be found out over the phone. What had I been thinking when I intimidated him into seeing me in person? Clearly I *hadn't* been thinking.

Too late to worry about that, I realized when I heard my name. "Diana?" asked a tall guy with thick auburn hair and an athletic build. Damn, Carrie had good taste in men! Physically speaking at least.

"Yes. I assume you're Brian."

"Correct." he confirmed, giving me the once over. "Let's make this quick. I need to get back to work." As did I. Looking around the crowded restaurant, it dawned on me that this was a terrible place to conduct my discreet inquiries. I'd chosen a place I knew would be packed to avoid being alone with him, which was good. But, it also meant that there were a large amount of prying eyes- many accompanied by gossipy mouths- surrounding us. In the town where I worked no less.

How many of these observant eyes belonged to Redmond School parents? And did any of them know Brian? Or that he was a cheating husband? I prayed not as we slid into one of the only empty booths left, foregoing food altogether.

"So, what do you want?" my less than thrilled lunch date asked, still checking me out.

That was a very good question. A seasoned investigator like Detective Donovan, probably even that loose lipped cutie pie, Deputy Miller, would surely have come prepared with a list of questions. Heck, even one of my students would be able to whip off a good ten queries faster than my lame ass was taking to come up with just one.

Finally, I kicked my jitters to the curb and asked the handsome stranger outright if Carrie had known he was married or not. He claimed that she was completely unaware of his marital status and that, in fact, they communicated chiefly via text. "I designated times that she could and couldn't call me," the adulterous Adonis explained. "Told her it was due to my work schedule and obligations, but mainly it was just so my wife wouldn't find out."

For a duplicitous louse, Brian seemed to be answering quite candidly. His story had the ring of truth to it. Obviously any guy who pursued other women behind his wife's back would only take calls from his lady friends when it was convenient for him. I gave him points for being frank with me at least. Of course, carrying on with anyone other than his wife held a point value of negative ten so he was still "in the red" with me."

After hearing that they'd only been out three times, it looked like another dead end. So I thanked Brian for his time, vowed not to contact him again or sic the cops on him without due cause, and we headed out of the fast food joint. We parted ways, and I hurried back to my car to avoid the chill in the air.

Once inside, I cranked the heat up and popped my seatbelt into place. I wasn't surprised at all to learn that my friend had been in the dark about her date's marital ties because Carrie had been way too good of a person to screw around with somebody else's man. But, it was a relief to confirm my own somewhat biased assumption. Unfortunately, that was *all* I'd gotten out of this virtually wasteful meeting.

Back at school, I was anxious to let Dale know that Carrie hadn't willingly entered into a relationship with someone already spoken for. But, Tuesdays were the days that Mr. Badger was stuck doing the ever delightful lunch duty in the cafeteria. What teacher *wouldn't* want to spend thirty minutes of their work day reminding a hundred little chatterboxes to eat instead of socialize, cleaning up yogurt that had been squeezed too hard and shot three feet in the air, and trying to jam straws into juice box holes that were entirely too small while inhaling the questionable aromas emanating from the "delicious and nutritious" hot lunches? Any teacher in their right mind, of course! Trust me, by the end of that hellish half hour, Dale Badger would be in serious need of some happy news. And seeing as I'd been a total dunce a day earlier, dropping the adultery bomb into his lap without taking his own spousal discord into account, I absolutely owed it to him to lift his spirits.

To my immense relief, the tidbit I shared with Mr. B. *did* seem to improve his mood, and by the time bell rang at three o'clock and twenty five little bodies had been sent packing, his annoyance with me had apparently subsided. I was pleased to hear his, "Hey," in my classroom doorway a few minutes later. Naturally, he'd come to find out how I had obtained the facts that exonerated Carrie, so I spilled each and every detail, starting with the startling discovery that Brian was married while wedged between a television and a decades old listening center in the closet and concluding with the less than informative "lunch" at Mickey D's.

Dale remained as silent as one of my classroom Phantom's invisible assaults during my animated tell all, simply shaking his head in disbelief at my escapades. "Okay," he finally uttered once my tale was told, "First off, I can't believe that you refuse to give up against the one in a million odds that Carrie's fall wasn't merely an accident."

"What about the note left in my box? Clearly there's something to find out."

"I've been thinking about that, too. Just because somebody doesn't want you to uncover information of some sort, doesn't necessarily mean it's linked to Carrie's death.

"But, back to today, I must comment on you **blackmailing** some random dude to force him into lunching with you. Your love life must be in worse shape than I thought." said he whose wife had jumped ship three months ago, I reminded myself as he chuckled at his weak attempt at humor. "How in the world did you muster up the gonads to attempt that? You're hardly a shrinking violet, but that takes some audacity."

"I'm just determined to find out the truth, I guess."

"Even if it means eating crow in the end?"

"I'll **gladly** eat crow once I'm a hundred percent certain that what happened was purely accidental. In fact, I'll be thrilled beyond belief if my crazy ass notions are only figments of my T.V. infused imagination. But, don't we owe it to Carrie, our *friend,* to ensure that nothing else played out that night and somebody's getting away with something?"

My powers of persuasion were clearly in fine form that day because, miraculously, my nay saying colleague actually conceded at that point. Maybe hearing that I **hoped** to be proven incorrect helped change his mind. He wouldn't be egging me on by any means. Of that I was a hundred percent certain. But having him semi- on board was good enough.

But, of course, once that discussion came to its end, another equally serious one began. Dale was insistent that I apologize to Mrs. Holier Than Thou, who'd reported my late arrival to Mr. Welkey. "She's only kissing his ass because she wants a job, you realize." I impressed upon him.

"Whatever her motives may be, kissing *her* ass may be in *your* best interest."

"Meaning?"

"Meaning that it's important to keep peace in the workplace. You don't have to become bosom buddies with her, but...."

Yeah, Blessed Bunting's BFF was a role I *so* would not be filling any time soon.

"But saying you're sorry won't kill you, Diana. Preferably before she says anything to George....or the superintendent....about it."

That four lettered friend nearly escaped my lips again as the realization hit me. If Annette had reported me for arriving *on the dot* to get into our administrator's good graces, she'd sure as sh...sure as *sugar* have no qualms about crying to him about me cussing her out...in an elementary school classroom, no less. Dale was dead on the money this time. "I'm gonna go talk to her right this minute!"

But as I turned to leave, I stopped in my tracks, having spotted the lanky frame of our eavesdropping custodian just outside the door. "How long has Creepy Jim been standing out there?" I inquired in a whisper, nodding my head ever so slightly that Dale might not have even picked up on the subtle gesture.

"No clue. I didn't notice him until you pointed him out." Not too surprising since Callahan was purposely lingering in the shadows. Obviously he'd been listening in on our conversation for some indeterminate amount of time. Otherwise he would have waltzed right into the classroom like he did every other day. Whatever. My mission was to catch Annette before she left school. Striding quickly and confidently across the well- worn carpet, I paused just long enough to alert the creepy custodian that I was aware he'd been out there lurking. "Hi Jim, did you need me? Looks like you've been waiting out here for me."

"Oh, no. No. I was going to dump your trash but I didn't want to disturb you two." That was bull. But since I'd been poking my own nose into other peoples' business too, calling him out would not only have been embarrassing to him, but hypocritical of me. Still, I wasn't particularly thrilled to have him spying on us like that. I understood then how my bullied lunch guest must have felt. Perhaps an apology to him was also in order?

The lights were off in Joan's classroom, meaning the loose lipped substitute had already gone. Damn. I'd have to make it a point to get up early and speak with her before school the next morning. Hopefully my partially sincere words of contrition would pacify Little Miss Sin Buster and my boss would never hear a word about my outburst. *If* he hadn't caught wind of it as of yet in the day and a half that had passed.

"I'm going to head out." Dale told me after Jim had emptied my trash barrels and sauntered down the hall towards the front of the building. "Are you coming?"

"No, I need to stay for a few minutes to run off some worksheets for the *Parker's New Pet* reading group tomorrow. You don't need to wait though."

As always, "a few minutes" turned into forty five, so I didn't wind up leaving until just after four. Exiting through the side door of the building, I noticed a pretty young woman with gorgeous long brown hair standing by the few parked cars left in the lot at that hour. Presumably she was a parent coming to meet with her child's teacher or retrieve her offspring's forgotten homework. But, why was she over here instead of ringing the bell at the front door, the protocol for Redmond's after school visitors?

"Hi there," I smiled, wondering if she was lost or needed assistance.

"Hello, *Diana*." she replied icily, taking several steps towards me. Caught off guard, my mind attempted to place her…without any luck. An angry mom? Or possibly a stepmom I'd never met? Whoever she was, the grimace on her beautifully made up face concerned me.

"Are you here to see me?" I asked her, completely baffled by this time.

"I am," she declared firmly. "Don't worry. You shouldn't recognize me. But, I recognize *you*. You're the slut who had lunch with my husband this afternoon."

O……M…..G !

CHAPTER EIGHTEEN

I'd love to say that I told this chick off as fiercely as I'd laid into Annette Bunting the day before, but truth be told, I simply stood there in silence for at least a full minute. I had absolutely no idea what to say or do in that frozen moment in time. Fortunately, I'd never been confronted by a jealous significant other or spurned ex in my twenty seven years. Probably because I didn't get involved with married men or unfaithful losers! Alas, Brian's wife didn't know that about me and, boy, did she look pissed!

"You're speechless, I see. Let me spell it out for you. I'm Gwen Fox, Brian's wife." Aha! *Fox* was his last name. That "BF" on Carrie's phone was for Brian Fox, not 'boyfriend' as I'd initially assumed. Not that that really mattered right now. "You *did* know he was married, seeing as we spoke on the phone yesterday." How the heck did she know it was me who'd called? Evidently she recognized the quizzical look on my face because she went on to explain. "You really should block your number when you call to set up a booty call with someone else's man, honey."

"No. You've got it all wrong, Gwen. Honestly. I…"

"I do *not* have it *wrong*, honey! 'Redmond Elementary' was displayed right there on his caller ID." Good point. But how did one block a phone number from a public building? If it could be accomplished, I surely had no idea how to do it. But, admitting to be a technology invalid would be awkward at a moment like this so I kept my trap shut.

"It wasn't a booty call or even a *date.*" I insisted.

"Really? Then what was that clandestine rendezvous at McDonald's today? A fast food health inspection? A coupon swapping party? Don't take me for a fool. I overheard my wannabe player

146

making plans to meet your skanky ass last night, and he was oblivious as always. My hubby is mighty fine to look at, even better in bed, but he's not very bright." That was how she knew my name, too, she went on to reveal.

Earlier today, she'd quite cleverly arrived at the restaurant's parking lot incognito at eleven forty five to scope out the situation, then followed me back to work upon my departure. "I would've dealt with you right then and there, but you got into the building before I was able to park. That's why I'm here now instead."

"What is it that you want from me?"

"Well, duh. I want you to keep away from Brian, you stupid ho. You aren't the first bimbo he's tried to corral and you most certainly won't be the last. But, I find out *every* time and I *always* put a stop to his shenanigans."

By throwing his "bimbo" down the stairs? Thus far, the irate woman had attacked me only verbally, but was she capable of a physical assault as well? I glanced nervously around the area, hoping that someone else was in the vicinity in case she became violent. Realizing the potential danger, I needed to make her understand that in no way, shape, or form did I want nor desire her cheating scumbag of a husband. "Honestly, Mrs. Fox, we were just discussing a mutual friend. There's nothing more to…"

"Little girl, don't play games with me."

"I'm not. Really."

"Just stay the hell away from my husband. Little girls who try to play big girl games *never* win in the end." she snarled, moving in way too close for my comfort. "You listen to me," she demanded, looking me straight in the eye. My stomach felt hollow and I instinctively took a step back. "Karma's a bitch, and so am I."

"No kidding." I muttered without thinking. Wham! In a flash, the palm of her hand made contact with the side of my face, causing me to stagger backwards. Regaining my balance, I put my gloved hand against my stinging cheek as Gwen Fox strutted off victoriously and hopped into her silver Ford Focus.

I half stumbled and half ran to my own car and fell inside, the contents of my school bag tumbling out as I did so. My heart raced nonstop and my face stung as I slammed and locked the door. Breathing out a few short breaths, I leaned my head back against the freezing cold headrest. Shock overcame me and I began to laugh uncontrollably like an inmate at an insane asylum. Better laughter than tears, I supposed, as I reflected on my unexpected and peculiar reaction to the confrontation I'd just endured.

"I just got bitch- slapped." I said aloud, flabbergasted, yet strangely amused at the same time. That was a scene that belonged on *General Hospital* or some other trashy over the top nighttime drama, not in *my* life. Me, Miss Diana Fallon, lovable law abiding first grade teacher, bitch - slapped! I guess there *is* a first time for everything. Though hopefully that was the first and *last* time for that type of experience.

Once I regained my composure and glanced down to where Gwen's vehicle had been parked, I saw that, mercifully, the silver Focus was no longer there. Although I wanted to hate her, or at least be infuriated by her actions, I actually felt kind of bad for Gwen Fox. Obviously, Brian was a bozo whose attempts at infidelity had forced his wife to fight to keep her rocky marriage intact. Granted, I never wanted to see her hateful face again, but I couldn't really blame her for jumping to the wrong conclusion. Had I not strong-armed Carrie's date into seeing me face to face, this entire episode could have been avoided altogether.

The question was what to do next. Text Erica, of course! That girl was going to *die* when she heard this one! *Just had my face slapped.* I typed.

*WTF?* was her first response. *By who?* was the next.

*LOL Brian's wife*

*Brian Who?*

*Carrie's Brian*

*OMFG Call me NOW!!!*

So I did. Call her, that is, which of course delayed my departure even longer since I wasn't about to talk and drive. Only a fool does that….and unfortunately the world is full of them.

I waved to Barbara Barrett, a second grade teacher, as she loaded her bag and a large heap of papers into her car, which was parked beside mine, all the while relaying the story of being confronted by Gwen Fox to Erica. Gradually, the remnants of daylight faded away and the inferior lights that were supposed to adequately light up the parking lot came on. The faculty had been complaining about those foolish lights for ages, but, unsurprisingly, the town budget could never find enough money to replace them.

Honestly, though, I didn't give a hoot about the lack of sufficient illumination while I was filling in my curly haired friend about "the showdown" as I'd decided to refer to the incident. I was just about to finish up my call when a sudden banging on my window caused me to let out a bloodcurdling scream and drop my phone. "Diana? Diana!" I could faintly hear Erica shrieking from somewhere beneath me.

"Dear God Almighty!" I panted, recognizing Jim Callahan's pale face just inches away from mine on the other side of the glass. Clutching my chest with one hand, I used the other to lower the driver's side window a bit.

"Are you all right?" inquired my unexpected visitor, whose arrival I'd presumably missed due to the sucky lighting. Where the hell had he been when I was about to get my ass kicked a half hour before?

"No thanks to you!" I snapped very nastily. "You almost gave me a friggin' heart attack pounding on my window like that!"

Jim looked guiltier than OJ Simpson and Richard Nixon combined. "I am so sorry, Diana. I didn't mean to startle you. Are you okay? You left quite a while ago, and when I came out to put the trash into the dumpster I saw your car still here. You having car trouble? I can call Triple A for you."

"No, I'm all set." I answered, feeling badly about my abrupt and rude reply. Here he was looking out for me and I'd nearly bitten his head off, being scared out of my pants and all. "Thanks for checking on me. I've just been chatting on my cell to…oh my God! Erica!" Frantically, my hand swept every which way underneath and beside my seat. "Hold on, Jim. I've still got Erica…Talbot…on the line. Well, I hope she's still there." And that she hadn't hung up to call the police to report another Redmond School teacher being killed!

Finally, my wrist brushed against the buttons of my phone and I was able to snatch it. "Erica? Are you there?"

"Of course I'm here you idiot! Haven't you heard me screaming your name at the top of my lungs? What in holy hell is going on? Is that Gwen woman back?"

"No, it's only Cree...um, Jim....Callahan. I'll call you back when I get home. I need to get outta here." Thanking the guy who had inadvertently scared the crap out of me one last time, I was off. His intent had been very sweet...but, damn, he was still creepy! Especially popping up in the darkness like that. What a day!

That night I slept like a baby. My crazy day of interrogating one Fox, being attacked by another, and repeating both stories multiple times (to Erica, Joan, *and* Dale) had worn me out for sure. Throw into the mix correcting a set of phonics papers, three stacks of math worksheets, and deciphering the kids' "My Favorite Thing to Eat" sentences and I was out like a light before nine thirty!

After that lengthy stretch of sleep that I was unaccustomed to, arriving at school early to make amends with Big Mouth Bunting was way easier than it would've been after a normal night's sleep and having to duke it out with my snooze alarm. As I approached the classroom door, I paused to read the nameplate beside it. *Mrs. Petrillo*. Oh how I wished she was inside instead of the woman who would likely make me beg for her forgiveness. Without a doubt, it was completely unprofessional and superbly inappropriate to toss out an F-bomb at a colleague, especially one whose faith was so important to her. But, it wasn't like it was capable of exploding, sending her to meet her Maker prematurely for Heaven's sake (no pun intended....really)!

Well the angels above (perhaps my sweet granny, who'd passed away just under a year earlier, or maybe even that weird little red haired boy with one eye from my own first grade class at Van Vort Elementary who'd choked on a seashell many years back) were looking down upon me that morning for sure. Not only did Mrs. Bunting graciously accept my apology, she actually smiled at me when she did. That was a rarity.

Naturally, my suspicious mind then began pondering what *else* might be behind that supposedly friendly facial movement. Had she already reported me to George Welkey or, far worse, the superintendent of schools? Was she awaiting my impending forced resignation so she could swoop in and snatch my position? Or had she very un-Christianly rigged a booby trap on my desk that would shoot paint all over me when I opened it?

*Stop!* I mentally chided the irrational part of my brain, which was on extreme overload these days. "Have a good day." I told her.

"I will." was her reply. And with that, her gaze returned to the Bible she'd been reading when I'd entered. One had to assume that by now the woman could locate *any* verse in the Good Book in ten seconds flat. I wondered if she might actually propose that as a Field Day activity later in the year as I journeyed across the hall to my own classroom. Whew! That was much easier than anticipated.

Not so easy was explaining to Jackson Maloney why bringing an electric drill to school was neither necessary nor safe. A drill! Confiscating the device, I buzzed the office to send someone down to retrieve it. Power tools aren't exactly something you can send your daily messenger upstairs with to give Mrs. Wise with a post-it note attached.

Immediately after the art teacher had departed with the wildly inappropriate share and tell item, the bell rang and students scurried this way and that to get to their seats before I started them off on the Pledge of Allegiance. I'd only gotten two words of it out when Kendall Varney screeched, "Miss Fallon, there's a coat on the coat room floor!!!!!" Had Kendall been around during the Revolutionary War, there'd have been no need for Paul Revere's famous Midnight Ride. Little Kendall and her mega mouth right here in Arwell could simply have shrieked that the British were on their way, and those soldiers in Lexington and Concord would've gotten the message loud and clear.

Despite the urgency in Kendall's voice, a coat on the floor was *not* a reason to interrupt the Pledge. Child abduction, yes! Pee dribbling down one's leg, absolutely! But the coat would still be there when we were done reciting the mandated ode to our country, so I ignored her cries for the time being and continued onward. Once finished, I replied, quite demurely, "There's a coat on the coat room floor? Hmmm….let me guess. Is it white with brown teddy bears on it?"

"Yessss!" Kendall responded, clearly amazed by my magical powers of deduction.

"Go hang it up, Georgette." If only predicting winning lottery numbers was as easy as predicting which disorganized child's outerwear was on the floor. I'd win that million hands down!

Forty minutes later, when I returned from dropping the kids off for art, the coat was back on the floor. "What a shocker," I mumbled, sticking it back onto its owner's hook.

Surveying all of the other multi colored winter wear and backpacks tidily hung up made me think of Carrie's tan coat hanging on the coatrack in the kitchen. Cassie had been confused about it being there. So why was the coat on the rack if Carrie didn't typically hang it there? Why, on that particular day, when she was planning to come meet us at Santino's, would she change her habit of dropping it over a chair? Obviously she would be putting the coat back on when she left for the restaurant.

Was there a reason she decided to tidy up the kitchen that afternoon, and, if so, what would have prompted her to do so? We were similar in that respect. I, too, tend to plunk down my stuff wherever it lands, unconcerned about everything being in its perfect spot. The only time I worried about my house being in order was when company was coming. Unless…what if she *was* expecting company? Someone that she wanted to impress maybe? That might explain it. But, who would be important enough for that to matter?

Then it hit me. A man! A man she was interested in. Perhaps the very man I'd sat across from in a booth less than twenty four hours earlier…Brian Fox!

## CHAPTER NINETEEN

Needless to say, some lobe of my brain worked fast and furious, shooting out scenarios starring Bad Boy Brian and Good Girl Carrie, all of which concluded with the same ghastly finale: Carrie dead at the bottom of the stairs.

*Carrie invites her new beau in, they giggle and flirt a bit, and then the happy times come to a screeching halt when Mr. Fox coldly tells her that he can't see her anymore. "I'm married." he reveals, sending a heartbroken Carrie running upstairs. Brian follows her, slimily trying to apologize, caressing his latest conquest. "Don't touch me!" she screams, losing her footing at the top of the stairs and tumbling to her death.*

*Carrie invites her new beau inside, they chat happily, and Brian excuses himself to the second floor bathroom. Having gone upstairs for some other unknown reason, she overhears him talking to Gwen on his cell and confronts him. "Does she know about us?" Carrie demands.*

*"Of course not!"*

*"She will soon enough." the pretty blonde sneers. Brian isn't about to let that happen. He grabs Carrie and slams her against the wall. The pair struggles, and he shoves her down the staircase.*

*Cassie invites Brian inside for a quick visit before she has to leave to meet her coworkers for dinner. They spend some quality time together, maybe even share a smooch, and Brian makes his departure. The doorbell rings just moments later. Carrie answers the door, only to find a furious*

*Gwen on the steps. Gwen, who'd followed her husband on a hunch, rants and raves about Carrie being a homewrecker and slaps her. Frightened, Carrie bolts up the stairs to escape, threatening to call the cops. But, Gwen doesn't stop with a mere slap. She darts up the staircase, reaching "the other woman" at the very top. Yanking on her with all of her might, the fuming wife flings Carrie downward.*

Having run through six or seven possible ways Carrie's fatal fall may have been caused, I wanted to call Detective Donovan and explore each one of them with him. But, how plausible were these quickly generated theories? I needed to run them by somebody else to hear their opinion before I could comfortably suggest them to the police, who could very well laugh me right out of the station and tell me to butt out. That would be more embarrassing than the day I came back to class after lunch with a soup stain on the crotch of my beige slacks. Given their own propensity for wetting themselves, I'm pretty certain a few of my cherubs continue to believe that I peed myself that day, despite my extensive explanation.

Lunchtime rolled around fairly quickly. Rushing to fit three reading groups in on mornings when your class had a special subject always made the first half of the day fly right by. Thankfully, keeping busy kept my mind off of the mental images I'd conjured up earlier.

Erica was my top pick to test out the bushel of murder scenarios, however I remembered that she had to take baby Savannah into Children's Hospital in Boston for some bloodwork that day. With Option Number One unavailable, I tried my second choice, but wound up talking to the Petrillo's answering machine instead. "Hi Joan. It's Diana. I feel like I haven't seen you in ages. Maybe I'll pop by after school for a bit if that's okay. If not, call my cell and let me know. Bye!"

Granted, I had seen Joan probably a week prior and spoken to her just about every day since, but when there's gossip to spread or a murder to solve, just one day can seem like an eternity!

That left Dale to act as my sounding board. I knew that Mr. Badger would be less enthusiastic than either woman, but he also wouldn't mince words if my ideas were flawed or just plain preposterous. As expected, when I nabbed him eating a lemon yogurt at his desk, I was pretty sure his eyes rolled, but at least he let me babble on for the next five minutes without belittling, mocking, or vetoing the bevy of stories I tossed out. "You never know," was his casual reaction when I was done presenting my thoughts. I didn't know how to interpret his comment. Was he finally coming around to the possibility of something more than just a tragic accident? More likely, my kind friend was simply trying to placate me. With any luck, Joan and/or Erica would be a tad more supportive….or shoot me down straight away.

I'd read aloud to my class a childhood favorite, *The Little Red Hen*, a few days back and, man, could I relate to her! The industrious little farm bird repeatedly asked her friends Dog, Cat, and Goose for help planting her wheat, harvesting it, even taking it to the miller's to be ground. But, each time, her animal pals declined to assist her and the poor hard working hen had to do it all on her own. I was starting to feel a bit like that little red hen myself. "Who will help me look into Miss Landry's 'accident'?" I asked sweetly.

"Not I." said Mr. Badger.

"Not I." said Mrs. Petrillo.

"Not I." said Mrs. Talbot.

But in the end, her hard work paid off, and when her greedy friends all wanted to help her *eat* the bread she'd baked, that feisty feathered female told them all to screw themselves and ate the entire loaf herself. Right on, hen! Wouldn't *my* friends feel foolish if I turned up some solid evidence that Carrie Landry's demise had not been the result of a simple slip and fall!

Once my workday concluded, I stopped at the Landry's to change into something more comfortable and was pleased to find that it was uncharacteristically mild outside. What a nice break from the cold and snow that Mother Nature typically brought to Arwell on most January days.

"Where are you off to?" Cassie inquired when I came downstairs wearing jeans and a visibly well -worn Old Navy tee shirt that I was in love with.

"Over to Joan's for a visit. By the way, I've been thinking about Carrie's coat a lot." More like obsessing over it. Whatever. You say "tomato", I say "Why the hell isn't anyone else in this town skeptical about this first grade fatality?"

"About it being on the coat rack, you mean?"

"Yes. I've come up with a few ways that things might have happened leading up to Carrie's fall *if* it wasn't just a simple accident."

"Really? I'd love to hear them. I haven't said anything to my parents, but there could definitely be a chance something else went down." Finally, another sane individual wasn't dismissing the *possibility*. This Little Red Hen was gaining ground. "I feel bad saying this," Cassie continued, "but they're driving me crazy. Thank God we're leaving for New Jersey tomorrow morning."

"The funeral is on Friday, right?"

"Yes, this has been terrible for them, especially my mom. I'm hoping once that's over with and we go back to our normal everyday lives, it'll be easier on her." As "easy" as it could be for any parent who'd lost their twenty four year old daughter so suddenly.

"Why don't you come to the Petrillo's with me? I was going to share my ideas with Joan. It's so nice out, I think I may even walk over. I want to take advantage of this weather while it's here. I'm sure it'll be back to Arctic like weather tomorrow."

"That sounds good. I'd love to get out of the house for a bit. Let me just pull on a fleece."

As we left a minute or two later, I very purposely locked the front door behind us. No need to make it easier for a maniacal killer to break in and wait for us in the shadows if, in fact, such a perpetrator existed and felt the urge to attack another young teacher. We were only a few steps away from the end of the driveway when a dark colored car pulled up to us. "What the…?"

"Hi girls,"

"Oh, it's *you*." Cassie replied rather rudely.

"It is," smiled Miles Kendrick, the hot neighbor from across the street that I'd invited in and thrown out in less than sixty seconds. Apparently he wasn't holding it against me. "Can I give you ladies a lift somewhere?" he asked, even though he was heading in the opposite direction than us.

"No, we're good." my companion assured him hastily.

"Thanks anyway." I added with a friendly smile. "We need the exercise after being cooped up indoors so much recently."

"Ah, gotcha. Doesn't look like either of *you* need much exercise though." Was that a compliment he'd tossed at us with a flirtatious wink?

"Sorry, we're in a rush, Miles." Cassie tartly answered before I could speak. "Come on, Diana." she motioned, continuing down the sidewalk towards Perth Street.

"Bye!" I said politely, to make up for the lack of manners she'd demonstrated.

"For now," Miles cooed, raising the car window.

"What was that all about?" I asked.

"What do you mean?"

"You didn't seem very sociable."

"With him? No, thanks. That egomaniac thinks he's God's Gift to women."

"He is kind of hunky," I blushed.

"Physically appealing, yes. But, he's a pig. Ever since he moved in, he's hit on both Carrie *and* me. He's got *one* thing on his mind."

"Maybe he thought you were the same person." was my defense, albeit lame.

"Oh he knew all right. First off, we both had our own cars and he saw us together more than once. His penis said 'Pretty blonde!' and that's all he saw. It didn't matter that we were both independent college educated women with brains and careers."

Clearly the Landry sisters had written off Miles Kendrick and that was that. What a shame, if that truly was his mindset. Because Miles with his moustache and dazzling green eyes was quite the hottie.

By the time I'd gotten the lowdown on their handsome neighbor, we'd reached Joan and Warren's. Max's car was in the driveway next to theirs. Maybe he'd be able to occupy his brother's time to allow Joan some "girl time" with us.

Apparently not, I realized when the muscular man let us in. The three of them had been sitting at the kitchen table together, with one empty chair awaiting me. "Hi, Diana. How's it going?" he greeted us. "Cassie, so sorry to hear about your sister." What a nice guy he was. I just hoped she wouldn't brush him off like she'd just done with Miles.

"Oh, hi Cassie. I didn't know you were coming. Nice to see you." Joan said, "Let me grab that wooden chair from the bedroom for you."

"Don't go to any trouble," I insisted. "I can stand." Not that I truly had any great desire to remain on my feet the entire time, mind you. I was hoping Max would prove himself chivalrous by offering me his seat, then leading Warren elsewhere so we gals could have some privacy.

But, as most women of my generation can attest to, chivalry is pretty much dead. Much like the good friend I'd come to talk about with my other good friend, unaware that her brother-in-law and mentally afflicted husband would be weighing in on my conjectures. Awkward. It's one thing to have your friends think you're crazier than a loon, but I was reluctant to let anyone else in on that special privilege. Warren wasn't an issue so much since he, sadly, would be unlikely to recall anything we discussed today or offer up any usable feedback. Max, on the other hand, was fully coherent and might just take it all in silently, then have a grand laugh at my expense some night while he was out drinking with his buddies. Worse yet, he might shoot down every hypothesis I put forth here and now to my face. I wasn't sure which was worse.

If I was going to persuade Detective Donovan, or anyone in a position of authority, to take my concerns seriously, though, I needed to look past my own potential personal humiliation. Time to yank on those big girl panties and just say what I wanted to say. Consequences be damned.

I was grateful to Cassie for jumping in as I explained about the coat being hung up instead of tossed over a chair. "She *never* hung it up." Carrie's sister verified.

"So, I thought that perhaps Carrie had tried to tidy up a little because she was expecting someone, more specifically the guy she was seeing, Brian Fox."

"How is Carrie?" Warren asked. "I haven't seen her in quite some time." Uh oh. Things were not off to a great start.

Adept, by now, at handling his unintentionally inappropriate interjections, Joan jumped right in to remind him of Carrie's passing. "Remember, I told you about it right after it happened."

"Yes, yes. That's right. I'm so sorry," the mistaken man expressed, looking straight at Cassie. "Sometimes I forget things." he stated.

"It's no problem," she told him with a dismissive wave of her hand. "I forget things all the time too." It was an uncomfortable moment, but even more so it was sad. I thought that Warren's comment might be a cue for Max to excuse himself and his brother from this already disconcerting discussion, but no dice.

"I apologize," Joan whispered discreetly, wringing her hands together.

"There's no need." I told her softly. "It isn't his fault. We all understand the situation."

At that point, I flung the risk of embarrassing myself right out the window and plunged full force ahead with my abundance of ideas as the group listened patiently and politely. After babbling on and on and on, my eyes scanned the four faces staring at me. "So what do you think?"

CHAPTER TWENTY

Joan took her time answering, formulating her reply so as not to offend me I assumed. "Diana, your mind works in a wonderful and creative way." she declared, starting off with something positive, as every good teacher tries to do at parent conferences…before dropping the bomb that the child was dumber than a slug or more hyper than a puppy on speed or behaved more like an eight *month* old instead of an eight *year* old. "But, this is all just speculation. You have no evidence whatsoever that this Brian or his wife were anywhere near the girls' house the night that Carrie…well, you know."

"It *is* pure speculation," I admitted, "And I'm not saying that it *did* happen in one of these ways. Just that it *could* have. And, it's frustrating to know that I'm the only one thinking this way."

"I'm not discounting anything." Joan explained, "But if the police are satisfied enough to release the body, they must have collected adequate information to help them conclude that her fall was simply an accident."

"That doesn't necessarily mean that they're correct."

"No, it doesn't." Cassie agreed, giving me some halfhearted support which I readily accepted.

Then it was Max's turn to get in on the action. "It seems as though you're basing your disbelief on one minute detail, that the coat was on the coat rack." Did I even want to hear his opinion? Not really. But, being the person I knew least well probably also made him the most objective so I kept my mouth shut and heard him out.

"Isn't it possible that one of the police officers hung it up when they were there the next morning?" he reasoned. "Or maybe Cassie absentmindedly picked it up while processing her grief just to keep her hands busy." Cassie shrugged, not denying his idea as a possibility. Traitor.

"Maybe I'm a fool then." I gave in dejectedly. "Maybe my mind keeps coming up with these outrageous alternatives to keep me from facing the fact that sometimes life is unfair, that it sucks that my friend died because she took a misstep or because her shoe was untied."

"Honey, you're not a fool." Joan consoled me. Just shy of being old enough to be my mother, she often fell into that role when the need arose. "I just don't think you should drag people into this that almost positively had nothing to do with this tragedy."

It was at that precise moment that Warren vociferously announced that he had to use the bathroom. "I need to go pee. I need to go right now!" I used the opportunity to lighten up the mood. "It's just like you're at work, Joan. Instead of little Titus or not so little Marlene letting you know they've gotta go, you've got Warren here to help keep you from missing out."

"I'll take him." Max stated, moving behind Warren to lift him up from his seat. I tried not to stare, but was surprised and saddened by the lack of mobility he had. Slumping against his brother, Warren made an attempt to walk, although his movement was clearly being facilitated by Max. Poor Joan. "I think it's a good time for a nap anyway," said Max. "I'll put him in bed after he goes." he told Joan.

Not wanting to be rude, I wondered if I should ignore the decline in her husband, but pretending wasn't really my style. "He was walking fine when I was here last week." I observed aloud. "Did he just start having trouble getting around on his own?"

"No," Joan said with great pain in her voice. "He has good days and bad days and days that can go from one extreme to the other too" she explained. "Some days he's able to walk pretty

165

well by himself, other days he shuffles and just moves at a slower pace, and then there are days that he requires more assistance, like today." Likewise, his brain functioning followed a similar unpredictable pattern she informed us.

"I'm so sorry, Joan." Cassie offered.

"Me too. But, at least I'm able to use up all of those sick days I've accrued over the years to be here with him. I'm thankful for that."

"So sad." I lamented, remembering meeting my colleague's husband several years earlier at my first Redmond holiday party. "The poor guy."

"Yup, there's nothing we can do to change his prognosis, but we'll do anything else we can to help him maintain his quality of life."

We stuck around for some idle, more pleasant, chit chat until suppertime. Cassie needed to finish packing for her trip to New Jersey, and I wanted to give Erica a call before I started in on my schoolwork so we bade Joan goodnight and headed out the door. "Will you two be alright walking home? It's dark out." For those of you unfamiliar with winter in Massachusetts, let's just say that the sun is *not* our friend during those months. It shows up as late as possible and disappears as soon as it can each and every day. Kind of like the second grade teacher whose classroom is right above mine.

"We'll be fine." I guaranteed her.

"I can drive you if you want."

"Don't be silly," Cassie agreed, "The streetlights are on." And the temperature had fallen quite a few degrees, too, the chill in the air let us know when we opened the door to make our exit.

"I'll talk to you soon." I promised as the two of us sped up to get ourselves home and out of the frosty evening as quickly as we could.

After heating up some soup in the microwave, I phoned Erica to get her take on things. Were the Petrillo clan and Dale and Mr. Welkey and any other naysayers right? Was I making a mountain out of a molehill?

The baby was cranky so our conversation was rather one sided. I jabbered while Erica took care of her mommy duties and threw back a monosyllabic reply here and there. "Does Savannah want some peaches?" she cooed as I laid out my final death scenario to her. "Does Savannah want Mr. Blue Bear to play with?" Where was my mouthy, sarcastic, no BS girlfriend when I needed her most?

I am *never* having children, I mentally resolved as Erica hollered for her husband to retrieve Mr. Blue Bear from under the dining room table, where the irritable infant had flung him. The only solid piece of wisdom my frazzled pal was able to give me was that she believed Brian Fox's statement about Carrie not knowing that he was married prior to the day she died. "Obviously if she'd learned that her new man was two timing his wife, she wouldn't have bothered tidying up the house just to invite him in and tell him to piss off and lose her number pronto." This, I took as official backing for my theories that involved Carrie finding out that crucial detail while Brian was in the house. *If* he ever was in her house.

"My money's on that wenchbag wife of his." Erica bluntly declared. "It's evident that she's got a temper, given that she struck you. Right out in public, no less. Did you file a complaint against her with the police like I advised you to do by the way?"

I hadn't, nor did I plan to. "First off, it was only a slap." Hardly enjoyable, but it wasn't like she hurled me onto the pavement and repeatedly stomped on my face with her UGGs. The more prevalent reason, however, was that I wasn't keen on the cops finding out about my inquiries. "What if they charge me with obstruction of justice or something?"

"You've watched one too many reruns of *Law and Order*, girl. The worst that…oh, honey, no!" she suddenly shrieked (quite loudly- thanks so much!) into my ear. "Diana, I've gotta go. My husband is absolutely *useless*. But, you need to let the police know about Gwen Fox even if you don't file an actual complaint against her."

"Okay, but…" A dial tone was the only reply I got. Maybe Erica was right, though. Did Detective Donovan and his cohorts even know that Brian Fox and his ill-tempered wife were linked to the first grade teacher whose death they'd ruled accidental? Would he…or anybody at the Arwell Police Department…even care if I filled them in about this lopsided love triangle?

Cops, rightfully so, are taught to be suspicious. But, surely they wouldn't dismiss the idea that a well-liked mild mannered elementary school teacher could be embroiled in a romantic entanglement that could possibly have led to her murder. Would they? Granted, most of the "bad teacher" stories featured on the news involved high school teachers and their inappropriate relationships with their teenaged pupils, but not *every* primary school teacher led a squeaky clean private life. Most of us, yes. We were right in there with the millions of other Americans who led less than exciting lives. But, having only been privy to behind the scenes gossip in Arwell for just a few years, I already knew a couple of supremely juicy stories about very un-teacherly behavior outside of the classroom. Undoubtedly, a seasoned veteran like Leticia Devane had oodles of secrets she could spill. Not that she ever would.

Having let my nerves deter me a good fifteen minutes, I had finally begun dialing the non-emergency number for the police department when Cassie entered the room. "There's a scarf missing too." She informed me.

"Carrie's you mean?"

"No, mine. But, she wore it a lot with her tan coat. It's plaid with mostly tan and green, which goes well with her coat and that god awful green knit hat. Damn. I wanted to take it with me down to my parents'."

"The scarf? Let's look for them then." I suggested. Searching the house from top to bottom could very well turn up the missing winter accessories, but what else might it turn up? I hadn't been brazen enough to snoop around the house, even when Cassie wasn't home. It felt too much like an invasion of the sisters' privacy. But as long as one sister was down for it, I was all in.

The pair of us checked the entire ground floor, room by room, and came up empty handed. Upstairs, in Carrie's bedroom, the room I was now occupying, we hoped for better luck. "If they aren't in the kitchen, which they're not, this is where I'd expect to find them." Cassie said. Had she not looked in here yet? To the best of my knowledge, she hadn't come in while I'd been staying with her, though she certainly had every right to. It was her house.

I, myself, hadn't felt comfortable moving my deceased friend's things about or removing her clothes or belonging from the beautiful maple dresser in the room. Though I did hang some of my work clothes on hangers in her closet and set some of my health and beauty products on the chair by the door, most of my stuff remained in the boxes pushed up against the wall.

"I'll take the closet." Carrie stated, sliding one of the mirrored doors open. "I just grabbed the first decent looking dress I saw when I was in here to get clothes for her...burial." she expounded as I opened the dresser's top drawer. Nothing but jeans and sweatshirts. "As a matter of fact," she continued, "I never even thought to look up here for the hat. What a fool I am!" More like in shock or overwhelmed with grief. But what an immense fool *I'd* look like if the "missing" hat that played a key role in making me consider foul play had been inside this very house all along! "I will kill you if it's up here!" I almost said aloud, immediately regretting my choice of words and thankful I'd had plenty of practice biting my tongue in the presence of children.

But, neither the knit hat nor the plaid scarf turned up. In fact, it wasn't until I was just about to close the bottom drawer that something did. "What's this?" A yellow pom-pom? "Oh, it's a key chain," An inexpensive metal loop with a fuzzy yellow Pac Man, a small tagboard card, and (duh!) a key attached to it. And on the card was the owner's name. Miles Kendrick!

"What's *that* doing in there? Hidden away in her dresser drawer like that?" Carrie's sister wanted to know. "Why does she even have *his* key?" she asked rather angrily.

"Don't look at me."

"Give it to me! I should waltz right across the street and shove this right up..."

"Simmer down, girl." Dang. Mr. Kendrick sure did make her blood boil. "Why don't you let me return it to him." was my suggestion. Otherwise, I was afraid that Tremaine Street might just become the scene of another crime (or *a* crime if those who disagreed with my ideas turned out to be correct).

# A FIRST GRADE FATALITY

I sent Cassie back to her room to keep packing and dropped the key on top of the dresser. Seeing it sure had put Carrie's sis into a foul mood. Was there more behind Cassie's intense dislike of her neighbor or had being in her dead sibling's bedroom for the first extended period of time simply put her on edge? Either way, there was no use beating a dead horse. And, more importantly, we hadn't turned up the hat or scarf.

Glancing at the digital clock on Carrie's nightstand sent me into a momentary panic. I had yet to correct any of the days' seatwork papers, cut out a hundred construction paper circles for the next day's math lesson, or fulfill my duty as a police informant. Checking over a first grade student's classwork was fairly easy compared to independent assignments done in the upper grades so that wouldn't be difficult to get done, but cutting the circles out would take some time. Simple, just time consuming, as so many teacher's tasks are. If it were feasible, I'd have had the kids cut out their own shapes, but that would literally take up the entire hour of math. And I was already feeling like I'd been going at too slow a pace to get to all of the concepts I was expected to fit in.

Putting off my phone call to the police was prudent, I convinced myself, then admitted it was merely outright procrastination. After killing a few more minutes trying to mentally come up with synonyms and slang terms for "police" (cops, pigs, the boys in blue...), I bit the proverbial bullet and punched in the numbers on my cell and gulped a few times while waiting for someone- hopefully someone nice and kind who encouraged assistance from non- law enforcement personnel- to pick up. "Could I please speak to Detective Paul?" I politely requested, only to be informed that there was no detective by that name on staff. Huh?

Then it dawned on me! I'd neglected to include the detective's *last* name in my request. Wonderful! Now I'd be labelled as a bubble-brained idiot in addition to an intrusive pain in the ass! Instantly, I clarified my embarrassing error in a long winded ramble that the answerer would most likely relay and mock with her workmates as soon as she hung up.

"I'm sorry, Detective Donovan isn't on duty. Could I take a message?" *A message, a message. Should I just leave a message?* That might work out nicely. Just name Brian and Gwen Fox as person of interest in the Landry case and be done with it. Of course, there was no official Landry case as far as I knew. Plus, he'd probably want more info from me than just their names, and I'd wind up having to deal with him directly anyhow. What if she showed up in the middle of my science lesson on birds' nests the following day? Every child in my class would go home and spread the word that Miss Fallon had been taken out of the room by a police officer. Do you know how many emails from frantic moms, dads, and other guardians that would garner? Ugh! *And* I'd have to reply to them all. No way! "No message," I decided.

But before the woman could hang up, I exclaimed, "Wait!" Oh, My Pretty Pony! She must *really* be thinking I was some delusional crackhead at this point. "Is Deputy Miller there by any chance? Deputy *Frank* Miller." I clarified, in case there was more than one. Miller is a fairly common surname after all, and I sure as heck didn't want to wind up being connected to some random deputy and humiliate myself even further!

Mercifully, Frank Miller was there and I was connected to him without being asked for my name. I'd have assumed one would be asked for their identity before being transferred to the appropriate party. She was probably just thankful to get rid of me! I was mighty thankful myself. The last thing I wanted was for this law enforcement professional to know it was fellow town employee, Miss Diana "Fool" Fallon, who'd made such a jackass of herself.

As with my previous two interactions with the deputy, whose cute smile I envisioned the moment he came on the line, he was super friendly and assured me that I was not being a nuisance by calling to report something I felt could be relevant to any case, current or closed. Unfortunately, sharing Carrie's ties to Mr. and Mrs. Fox was a day late and a dollar short. Not only had Arwell's top notch team uncovered Brian's and Gwen's connection to the deceased Miss Landry, Deputy Miller very politely informed me, but they had taken it a step further than little ole me and confirmed that both husband and wife had alibis for the span of time estimated to include the time of Carrie's death.

Marvelous! My two most likely suspects…well, actually, my *only* suspects…were in the clear. Oops. My bad. I hadn't been served up a mere *slice* of humble pie. I'd wolfed down the whole extra large pie faster than one of those ferociously fat folks who can't even get out of their bed would have!

Not wanting to awaken either Warren or baby Savannah, I resorted to texting my two friends to fill them in on both the Fox's alibi and the scarf that had disappeared along with Carrie's hat. Then, at long last, I settled down onto the couch downstairs and dove into the pile of schoolwork I'd ignored since getting home. Two hours later, all of the work was done and I was tucked away in my bed. I was beat and apparently fell asleep right away.

In what seemed like a very short time, the alarm clock shrilled at me to get up. Pounding the snooze button, for some reason, did nothing to mute the annoying sound. Wait! The red digits I spotted through squinted eyes read 2:17. "What the…?" The phone! It was my cell phone ringing, I realized, fumbling blindly around to locate it. "Hello!" I answered frantically. Why on Earth was somebody calling me at this ungodly hour? "Hello?" I repeated.

"Back off, bitch…or else." Click.

CHAPTER TWENTY ONE

Even groggy and half asleep, I couldn't help but be shaken by the menace in the caller's voice…nor the meaning of his words. If I didn't "back off", he'd make me sorry for not following his late night advice. It was a man, wasn't it? Possibly a woman disguising her voice, but it had sounded more male to me.

And what exactly had I been ordered to back off from? Asking questions about Carrie's tumble down the stairs? Brainstorming different ways her fall could have occurred? Feeding tidbits of info to the police? All of the above was the most likely answer. Which meant that there *was* more to the story, as I'd been attempting to convince everyone under the sun for days now!

This alarming phone call in the middle of the night brought back to mind the note that had been left in my mailbox at school. What had it said? "Don't get involved or you could get hurt too"? Something along those lines. Honestly, after handing it over to the cops, I had kind of forgotten about it, believe it or not. Perhaps because the wording of it had not been quite as vicious, and dropping it into my box wasn't quite so confrontational. It was more like a friendly warning to bring an end to my queries for my own well -being. Naturally, when I'd first read it, panic mode had set it at once. But becoming so focused on dredging up details about the night Carrie died, I'd put my own personal safety on the back burner apparently.

This time, the anonymous source wanted to be crystal clear about the imminent danger I'd be placing myself in if his (or her?) words were not heeded. There was **nothing** friendly about this! The question was, would I let my mystery caller intimidate me into giving up on my quest for truth and justice? Or would my stubbornness get the best of me, especially when I now knew *for* *sure* that there was information about her fatal fall that somebody didn't want me to uncover? A very good question, one that kept me awake in my bed for the next four hours.

There was no way in the world that slumber would come my way after receiving such an unwelcome wake up call. I was frightened, plain and simple. Around five forty five, I heard Cassie leave to go meet her parents for an early breakfast before they traveled back to their home state. Being alone in the house only increased my fear. I wished that staying in bed, wrapped up in blankets, all day was an option. Getting out of it meant that I would have to face the January cold and, possibly, the person who'd been keeping tabs on me for the last week.

Summoning up the courage I needed to get myself to work that Thursday morning was almost as hard as figuring out which of the people I'd spoken to, or spent time with, recently was willing to inflict retribution on me for snooping around too much. But, somehow I managed, double checking that Cassie had locked the front door behind her before going through my regular a.m. routine.

Once I was inside the Redmond School, I felt a bit more at ease, hopeful that harm was less likely to come my way in such a public place. Even if my unknown foe was willing to hurt me, or worse, a classroom with twenty four tiny eyewitnesses was a less than ideal setting to carry out such a plan.

The demands of the school day distracted me from the scare I'd endured hours earlier. Midmorning, I conducted a lesson on long vowel sounds with a small group of students who'd had difficulty sounding out words when they read. Holding up a card that depicted a sheep, I asked, "What is the vowel sound you hear in the middle of this word?"

"I need to take a dump." chubby little Terrence Watson announced to the group.

"Excuse me?" I replied, my voice raising an octave as I sent him a stern look.

"I need to take a dump!" he informed us a second time, in a much louder voice.

"Terrence, my reply to you was not because I'm hard of hearing and needed you to repeat yourself. I was hoping that you might rephrase what you'd said in a more polite manner." No such luck. "Perhaps you could have said, 'Miss Fallon, I need to use the restroom.' instead."

"Yeah, okay." But, I knew that the chances of that actually happening were slim to none. Sadly, Terrence's home life was not as stable as a good percentage of the students who attended Redmond Elementary. Mom was no longer in the picture so he currently resided with his father. Dad was a gruff burly biker, hardly the best role model for a young boy. I wasn't aware if Papa Watson was a member of the Hell's Angels or not, but he most certainly could have been conceived in and/or raised in Hell based on the crude remarks he'd made to me at parent conferences in the fall about my physical appearance. Most notably my buttocks, lips, and cleavage. Horrified does not come close to fully describing how I felt as I ushered him out to the hallway at the end of our ten minute session.

During my lunch break, I phoned the Arwell P.D. for the second time in less than twenty four hours. This time, to file a report about the unsettling call I'd gotten. Thus far, I had kept this threat under my hat, worried that if I brought it up to Dale or anyone else at work, the chance of me not breaking down into tears was less than the chance of Lindsay Lohan staying vice free for an entire year.

Still, informing the police was necessary for two reasons. First off, I wanted them to be aware that I'd been straight out threatened. Whoever had made that call had stepped it up a notch from an anonymous note the first time around. They weren't playing games now. That ominous message in the dead of night was meant to terrify me and had done the trick. Also, the fact that somebody felt the need to scare me off spoke volumes. If Carrie Landry had simply tripped and fallen to her death, there would be absolutely no reason for anyone to terrorize me. Someone out there was hiding something, and I wanted the police to find out what it was.

All afternoon, I was on edge. When I'd called to let the police know about the previous night's scare tactics, the officer I spoke to asked me to come down to the station after work to discuss the matter in person. While I was glad they were taking me seriously, a face to face interrogation about the newest threat with one or more officers made it that much more real to me that my life could really be in danger.

Normally being bogged down with bus duty on a blustery cold afternoon would have been something I would complain about, particularly since I was covering for another teacher who was out sick. But, this time I didn't mind it so much. Anything to put off my trip to the police station a little longer. Yeah, I'd hightailed it down there with Cassie to extract information from them and had voluntarily gotten in touch with them again the prior evening. But, this time was different. I had been summoned, which somehow made it more nerve wracking.

Outside, I patrolled the bus lines, but my mind was elsewhere. Masses of diminutive bus riders could have trampled poor Leticia Devane without me realizing it. A taller looking boy with jet black hair yanking a smaller one, a student of Dale's I thought, by his backpack snapped me back to attention. "Hey! Hey!" I shouted to attract the bigger one. "Let go of him! You can't drag him around like that."

The offender looked up at me with wide eyes and an annoyed expression. "It's okay. He's my *brother*." As if that made a difference!

"No, it is *not* okay. Just because he's related to you doesn't give you the right to hurt him that way. Would you enjoy being pulled around that way?" I attempted to reason. Just then, Leticia called for Bus 6, so the siblings marched off before I thought to get their names for Mr. Welkey. Not long after that, the final two buses arrived for pick up and Miss Devane and I headed back inside. "Where are your gloves?" the elderly woman inquired briskly, as if I were one of her first grade charges.

"Must've left them in my room." I answered. My hands were red and stiff, yet I'd not even noticed until that moment.

"Are you all right, Diana? You're looking a little peaked today. Perhaps you're coming down with something." Apparently my lack of sleep was taking its toll on my appearance. Splendid.

"Have a good night," I smiled as we walked by her classroom and she turned in.

"You too. Be sure to take some aspirin when you get home." Aspirin? If only that could make things right in my world again. Stepping into my own room, a sudden sound off to my left startled me and I let out a scream and backed up against the nearby wall.

"Hey, sorry. Didn't mean to surprise you like that." Dale Badger said, closing my closet door. "I was just looking for that box of yellow cubes." was his explanation. Of course. I mean why else would he be in there? "What's up with you today? You're not quite yourself. Is anything wrong?"

"You might say that." was my cryptic reply. 'Sit down and I'll tell you." I directed him, pulling out a child sized orange chair at my reading table to park my exhausted behind in. Then, forgetting that a waterworks display might follow, I spilled my guts.

"I'm coming with you then, and I'm not taking 'no' for an answer." Mr. B. told me when I'd finished filling him in. Without a teardrop in sight, I'd like to add.

Normally Miss Independent, I was frankly too tired and anxious to argue about it. "Get your coat and things, and I'll meet you in the hallway in a minute." Presumably shocked by my lack of resistance, my self-appointed companion scrambled to his feet and rushed off. If only my class followed directions that well!

Our meeting with the cops was unexpectedly short and sweet. I reported what I had told the officer at lunch, remembered to tell them that hitting *69 had told me that the caller's number was blocked, and lied about my level of involvement in the investigation. "I've been voicing concerns about Carrie's fall ever since it happened." I told them, "And coming up with ways it could have happened, but that's it."

"But, she's *very* vocal about it." Dale added, prepared to say more till I gave him the evil eye, a move every teacher masters within the first year of his or her career. I was then officially asked to keep my theories to myself, stop asking questions, and pretend that everything in the world was hunky dory.

"Will do." I promised, though in all honesty I wasn't one hundred percent certain it was a promise I could fully keep. My curiosity had been subdued to an extent, yet there was no way I could stop my mind from thinking about what had been done to my friend. However, I *would* keep these thoughts to myself as best I could, fearful of what might happen to me if I didn't. Fear is a pretty good motivator. "Thanks for coming with me," I gratefully told Dale once we had exited the building.

"No problem. I didn't want you going in alone. Just make sure you listen to what they said.

Stop snooping. Stop detecting. Stop sticking your nose where it doesn't belong. Now that they have reason to believe there's more to Carrie's death than they thought, you no longer need to solve this mystery single handedly. Let them do their jobs. It's what they get paid to do."

"I know!" I insisted, a little nastier than intended. "Well, thanks again. I'm going to get going. I want to stop at Joan's on my way home. Warren wasn't doing very well yesterday, and she was clearly stressed out about him."

"Do you mind if I tag along? I haven't talked to her in a while. Maybe there's something I can help her out with around the house. Lifting or moving something." So off we went.

While driving, my mind began to wander. Something I had seen or heard today was bothering me. What was it? Switching the radio to a Taylor Swift song, I tried to forget about it in the hopes that it would come to me. And, that it did, as I sang along with Taylor about her silly ex who thought they had a chance of reuniting.

It was the boys in the bus line, the littler one being dragged around by his brother. What had the older sibling quipped when I tried to discipline him? Something about his behavior being acceptable because they were related. That triggered another similar memory of the boy who'd been pushed down the steps of the bus the week before. Had those boys been brothers too? If so, what was up with all these physical altercations between brothers?

Oh no! *That's* what had been tucked away in my subconscious. Siblings acting violently toward one another. Could that be the case with another set of relatives I was acquainted with, only with more permanent repercussions? "Could she be responsible?" I mumbled to myself. Could Cassie Landry be the one who'd caused her sister's fatal fall?

No. That was crazy. Right? Thinking back to the forceful hug she'd given me the day Carrie's body was found, I knew that she possessed the physical strength to overpower her little sis. But, had she any motive? None that I could come up with. As the only living offspring, one would assume she was now the sole heir to whatever her parents owned. But, Arthur and Judy Landry weren't billionaires with homes in Miami, London, and New York City. They were a typical New Jersey couple as far as I knew. And both were in good health. Knocking off Carrie would be useless with both of her parents still alive.

If there was another potential motive, it was unbeknownst to me. Still, Cassie had been extremely adamant that she, herself, had not been the intended target when I brought up that line of thinking some days ago. Had she convinced herself that wasn't the case in order to alleviate her own worries or because she was positive that her sister was the correct mark?

I was grasping at straws again, wasn't I? Why on Earth was I so obsessed with this? But, as unlikely as it seemed, the fact of the matter was that I could be living with Carrie's killer!

## CHAPTER TWENTY TWO

Understanding that my overly suspicious mind was working overtime and that pointing a finger at Cassie was a tad premature, I spoke not a word of my latest theory, just as the police had directed me, when Dale and I arrived at Joan's house. She and Warren were sitting at the table in the kitchen again today, this time looking through an album of family photos. "Come on in," Joan motioned to us without getting up.

"Hi, hope you don't mind us showing up unannounced." I said as Dale and I came inside.

"Not at all. Take a seat. I'm just showing Warren some pictures of relatives we haven't seen in quite some time."

"Oh, cool. How's it going, Warren?"

"Good, Diana." Ah, he recognized me! This must be one of the good days. "Hey! Who's this intruder?" he continued, his index finger pointing straight at Dale. Uh oh. Maybe not such a good day after all. "Who are you? I don't know you." Warren's "intruder" looked like a deer in headlights, unsure of how to react.

"Warren, it's Dale." Joan told him quickly.

"Dale? I've never seen him before. He's an intruder. Where did he come from? Is he from Canada?"

"No, not Canada. He works at my school. Remember? He's a teacher."

"Oh? A teacher. Okay. My mind is a little mixed up these days." he said by way of explanation. "Don't mind me."

A FIRST GRADE FATALITY

"No worries," Mr. B. replied very carefully, "It's been awhile since you've seen me. Joan, is there anything you need done while we're here by the way?"

"No, I think we're good. But, thank you for the offer."

"We aren't planning to stay long." I told her, realizing that she may not want unexpected visitors on top of taking care of Warren. "We just wanted to pop in and say hello and see how you guys were doing and if you needed anything." But, maybe our visit had paid off in an unexpected way also, I thought. Warren's inquiry brought up yet another option for my brain cells to consider. Had a random intruder invaded the Landry sisters' home and killed Carrie? Could she have stumbled onto a robbery in progress and been knocked down the stairs when the burglar took off?

"You've got that Nancy Drew look in your eyes again." Dale noticed. "Didn't we just put a kibosh on all that at the police station?"

"The police station!" Joan cried out. Dammit, Dale! My plan had been to keep that disturbing tidbit from her. The last thing she needed was somebody else to worry over. Too bad Jabberjaws couldn't read minds.

"It was nothing," I reassured her.

"Oh yeah, she wasn't arrested or anything like that. They only wanted to talk to her about..." *No*, I silently commanded him. "You **did** tell her about the call, Diana. Yes?"

"Uh, actually no." I sneered through clenched teeth. But I couldn't really be too angry with him for spilling the beans. Granted, I had believed that common sense would prevail and he would refrain from mentioning my late night scare to her, but I hadn't come right out and

184

instructed him to keep mum. "It was nothing. Really. Some clown made a prank call to me last night. That's it."

Dale wasn't catching my drift, however. "Clowns wear rubber noses and juggle." he stated, "The dude on the phone called you a bitch and warned you to stop asking questions about Carrie's accident. Or non -accident as the case may be. Who knows at this point?"

Joan's eyes widened in horror. "Oh, Diana! Are you all right? What happened? What did he say?" At that point, there was nothing to be gained by not telling her. So, I did. "Are you positive it was a man?" she asked. 'Couldn't it have been that psychotic Gwen Fox telling you to back off. From her man, that is."

Gwen? "Back off, bitch…" the caller had demanded. "Or else." Although I was almost certain that the threatening voice belonged to a man, that didn't mean that the scare tactics hadn't been orchestrated by someone else, even a woman. And Gwen Fox was definitely nasty enough to pull a stunt like that. "I suppose," I admitted.

That did fit in quite nicely with my newest notion that some person, unknown by any of us, had broken into Carrie's house and, somehow, caused her to fall down the stairs. It was possible that my late night warning and Carrie's death weren't related whatsoever. Menacing Monkeys! I didn't have a clue what to think any more. As it was, I was basing my latest theory on the words of an Alzheimer's patient…and most of the other leads I had pursued came from six and seven year olds! Not exactly the most efficient way to go about solving a crime.

As I pulled my car into the driveway at the Landry house a few minutes later, red brake lights glowed in the driveway across the street. Miles Kendrick must just have pulled in too, which was handy because I wanted to ask him about that key of his in Carrie's drawer.

Thankfully the street lights came on earlier during this time of the year. Questioning him in the dark, unable to watch his every move and the expression on his face, wasn't something I was prepared to do. "Hello!" I called out as I crossed the street. Miles greeted me in similar fashion, making his way toward me, looking quite stylish in his dark suit and tie. "I just have a quick question for you."

"Am I free for dinner? As a matter of fact, I am." he grinned. His ultra white teeth glistened under the rays of light coming down upon us. "Good to know," I replied, though my night would hardly have been ruined without that useless piece of knowledge. "I came across a key with your name attached to it in Carrie's room last night. When we spoke about spare keys before, you never mentioned that she had a copy of yours so I was surprised when I found it."

Miles shifted his position slightly. "If I recall correctly, you only inquired about a spare key to the sisters' house, not mine." True. But, I still found it odd that he hadn't brought up the fact that Carrie had a key to his house during our previous conversation.

"I suppose you're right," I agreed, hoping to keep him talking.

"I frequently am," he smiled. What was up with the constant smirking? Was he trying to charm his way into my heart…or my pants? Either way, it wasn't working. Yes, he was easy on the eyes, but his pompous attitude and pushy flirtation made him look conceited and unappealing. I was beginning to understand why Cassie wasn't a fan.

"Anyhow, I wanted to check with you to see if you wanted your key back. After all, I am a virtual stranger."

"I'm not worried. I'd forgotten about it, in fact. I asked her to keep it for me after my cleaning lady forgot hers one time. Who knows, maybe you'll see fit to come pay me a visit some night."

186

What a pig. "That won't be happening, but I'm happy to hold onto it for your cleaning lady should she ever need it again. Interesting how Carrie had it tucked away in a bureau drawer, don't you think?" I pressed.

"Just making sure it wouldn't get misplaced, I guess."

"Yeah, or maybe she was trying to keep it from Cassie. She didn't know it was there until I found it."

"Just as well. Cassie doesn't seem to like me much. She'd probably throw it in the trash."

"Why is that?"

"Why isn't she fond of me? No idea. Most women are."

There didn't seem to be anything more he could shed light on so it was time to break up this little festival of self praising. "Tell your cleaning lady to give us a shout if she's locked out." I told the attractive yet annoying lothario as I walked back across the street.

"I will. Have a good night."

"Thank you." I replied, fiddling with my keys to get inside and away from my narcissistic neighbor ASAP.

Once I was settled, I threw a Lean Cuisine entrée in the microwave and pulled out my laptop. Warren Petrillo's comment about an intruder was stuck in my head. Since Brian and Gwen were out of the running and nobody else had a negative word to say about Carrie, never mind a motive to harm her, an intruder seemed a logical option. I quickly typed a message to Joan:

*You know how Warren thought Dale was an intruder today? I'm thinking maybe that's what happened the night Carrie fell. Some lowlife thief broke into her house and either she stumbled across him in the act and fell running away, or the punk tried to assault her, causing her to tumble. Yes? No? What do you think?*

If jumping to conclusions was an Olympic event, I was pretty sure I'd win the gold. Two hours ago, I was dabbling with the idea of Cassie Landry being a murderess. Maybe I could get two medals for jumping from one idea to the other with such immense speed too!

Before my nuked nutrition was done warming, I heard back from her:

*Yes, that makes a lot of sense. An intruder. Hope the cops catch him breaking into another house and bust him!*

That would be the optimal conclusion to this unhappy story. Then I could stop spending all of my time plotting out "what if" scenarios.

I had just peeled the hot layer of plastic protecting my tasty meal and sat down to eat when the doorbell rang. Who could be at the door at this hour? Unexpected guests during the evening were not common in my world. I prayed it wasn't Miles.

I flipped on the outdoor light and cautiously peered out the small pane of glass beside the door to find out who my uninvited visitor was. Standing on the doorstep, bundled up in a huge red parka, was the older woman I'd spoken to when I had canvassed the neighborhood for information, Dorothy Charm. Hesitantly, I opened the door.

"Hello. I hope I'm not disturbing you." She was, but Miss Manners would surely disapprove if I told her so. "Not at all," I lied. "What can I do for you? Would you like to come inside?"

"Oh no, I won't keep you but a minute. It's just that…well, I saw that car again last night, that same car that stopped in front of your house before." That was unsettling. Was somebody spying on me and, if so, for what purpose? Were they planning to break in during the night and murder me in my sleep? "It slowed down as it did the other time. Then it came to a stop for a minute or so out front and drove off."

"When was this? What time?" I wanted to know. It had to be the person who had called me. Had he driven by to make sure I was home? That'd be a waste of his time. Why not just call and hang up if by some chance I was having a late night rendezvous and someone else answered? Or had he come by afterwards to see if his warning had spooked me into sleeping with all the lights on? Neither way made sense to me, but this mystery man may not be the most rational fellow in town.

"About three thirty. A little after, I think."

"Well, thank you so much for letting me know, Mrs. Charm. I appreciate it very much." Now I felt obligated to pay her back for keeping me abreast of my secretive visitor's nocturnal movements. "Won't you come in for some coffee or something?"

"No, no. I need to go watch *Jeopardy*. I just wanted to let you know. Next time, I'll try to get the license plate number. I would have last night, but I'm not as quick as I once was."

Personally, I hoped there wouldn't be a next time. "You've done more than enough, really. Don't worry about the license number. But, if you do see the vehicle again, would you please call me. Here, I'll jot down my number for you."

"Thanks, again!" I called out as she waved back at me from the sidewalk soon thereafter. I stood on the steps, watching to make sure the elderly watchwoman got safely inside. The fence between the two properties prevented me from seeing her go in, but once I heard her front door close, I hurried inside myself.

I was damned near frozen solid, having been outdoors in only my lightweight blouse and knee high skirt for a few minutes. Before tossing my dinner back into the microwave, I grabbed a heavy looking navy blue cardigan off of the coat rack under Carrie's coat and flung it on. Eating my-not-so-delicious-after-all chicken and rice in silence, my mind was racing faster than Wilma Rudolph and FloJo combined.

How had Carrie's fall happened? Had it been accidental or deliberate? Someone out there had the answer, but who? Whomever it was knew that I was a blatant disbeliever of the official verdict and also of my propensity to toss out new potential explanations on a daily basis. But, how?

Chances were that this individual was very likely somebody that I had regular contact with. *Or*, they were getting their information from someone I was well acquainted with. Did that make things better or worse? Having a complete stranger as an adversary was terrifying because not only did they lack a personal connection to me that might make them wary of going too far, but they could also be emotionally unbalanced and set off by the least little thing. Anyone I passed on the street or in the supermarket could be the culprit. But, if a person that I had a relationship with or had met or chatted with in a social or professional setting was my unknown foe, I would be angered as well as frightened. Whatever the case, the chance of me getting any sleep that night was about as probable as Big Bird selling weed in the back alleys on *Sesame Street*.

Trash T.V. was able to distract me for a while, but eventually my weary eyes started to flutter, and going to bed was my best option. However, being safely tucked under the covers didn't equate to a trip to the Land of Nod. In the blink of an eye, it was three fifteen and I'd done nothing but toss and turn for the past two and a half hours.

# A FIRST GRADE FATALITY

Somebody in the normally normal town of Arwell, Massachusetts was nervous that I would uncover the truth about their involvement in Carrie's death. How far would he…or she…go to thwart my plans to just that? Leaving me a note, threatening me over the telephone, and driving by the place I was staying were distressing enough. But, it seemed like this person was getting more and more desperate with each day that passed. Would a Molotov cocktail come crashing through a window some night as I slept, or *attempted* to sleep?

Mrs. Charm had seen the mysterious automobile around three thirty, roughly twenty four hours earlier. The previous time she'd caught sight of it was about that same time, if I recalled correctly. Since falling asleep didn't seem to be in the cards, I decided that I may as well use my time productively. Throwing the covers off, I ambled out of the bedroom, down the hall, and, very carefully, down the stairs in the dark. Setting up a chair from the kitchen in front of the small window beside the front door of the house, I wrapped myself up in the pink afghan on the couch and began my stakeout.

For a long while (or at least what felt like a long while since the hands of the clock were obscured by the blackness of night), I sat there doing nothing but staring straight ahead. Closer to falling asleep than I had been in bed, I was jolted awake by the sudden appearance of what looked like headlights coming from the direction of Perth Street. I shifted my body to get a better view.

Exactly as Dorothy Charm had described, the car approached very slowly and came to a stop in front of Carrie and Cassie's house. My muscles tensed, awaiting the driver's next move. I ducked further into the shadows and tilted my head in order to identify at least some of the numbers and letters on the long dark vehicle's plate. The first two symbols were faintly visible as I strained my eyes to read them.

Just then, the driver accelerated a tiny bit, bringing the automobile quite close to the streetlight on the opposite side of the road. "That car looks familiar," I heard myself whisper. As it moved along a little bit more, my body froze and my breathing seemed to screech to a halt. I *did* recognize that beat up Buick *and* the man behind the wheel. It was "Creepy Jim" Callahan!

CHAPTER TWENTY THREE

After the custodian drove off, I returned to the bed I should already have been in at that hour. Although I now knew that it was "Creepy Jim" who'd been making sneaky late night visits to the neighborhood, I still didn't know why. Nor could I come to a decision about what to do next.

Callahan wasn't breaking any laws driving by during the wee hours so the police couldn't do much, if anything, about it, I assumed. Should I tell my principal about it? He was Jim's boss also, but he had no control over what his employees did after hours off school grounds. Yet, I felt that telling somebody was definitely the best course of action. If I turned up missing or, God forbid, dead like Carrie, at least he would be the number one suspect.

Erica, as much as I loved her, had too big of a mouth. I didn't want all sorts of people getting involved in this weirdness or forming a lynch mob to go after the janitor. Dale was a decent option, but being a *man*, he'd probably confront Jim head on, and I wasn't sure that a showdown was the wisest route to take either. Joan could be trusted to be discreet, but adding one more thing to her already full plate seemed unfair. Until I figured out how I wanted to use my newfound knowledge, keeping quiet about Jim's drive-bys might be my best bet, my sleep deprived mind concluded. But, I did need to share what I'd learned with someone soon.

The exhausted body that went with that sleepless brain was none too happy about having to crawl out of bed a few hours later that morning. Calling in sick was an option, but as a teacher, being out sick was more work than actually being there, even when you were sick as a dog. I'd have to write copious notes to accompany my lesson plans for a sub and email them to Sylvia if I was to stay home and not feel completely guilty about it. Frankly, I couldn't even remember what I had planned for most of the day or what materials the substitute would need, so I'd need to go into school to check my plan book to do that anyway. Screw that. "At least it's Friday." I reminded myself numerous times as I pulled myself together and got my tired self to school on time. Big girl panties on, my goal was to appear far more composed than I truly was and make it through the following seven hours without crumpling to the floor with fatigue and/or anxiety issues.

"Look what the cat dragged in," dear Annette remarked as I passed her in the corridor. Wench.

"Difficulty sleeping," I explained succinctly, overcoming my catlike urge to scratch her eyes out and leave her in a heap on the floor for "Creepy Jim" to deposit in the dumpster.

Next up was Dale. "What's up with you? Did you get another call?" he asked, throwing in a comment about how I looked like a pile of the odiferous substance squeezed out of dog's back end.

"Gee, thanks. You're obviously in a mood."

"You can blame that on my whore of a wife."

"At this hour? Why? Did she make you an early morning call?"

"No!" he snapped back, as if the answer should be crystal clear. In the state I was in, even the sum of two plus two wasn't crystal clear. "On my way home last night, after we left Joan's, I stopped at that place by my house to get a sub. I'll give you three guesses as to who was there. Yes, *her*!" he declared irately, never giving me a chance to take a stab at it. Even on zero sleep, I would've gotten that one right!

"Follow me," I wearily instructed Mr. B. as I made my way down the hall to my classroom.

Yup, I confirmed with a quick look behind me, he was still behind me as I plunked down my book bag and took my coat off. I felt like Mary with her little lamb. Badger babbled on about how Jodi was there with the idiot she'd left him for, whom she was pawing like a horned up teenager. "Well, that sucks." Not the best way to cheer him up admittedly, but it was all I had at the moment.

"No kidding! What is it with people? Jodi all over that jerk, Carrie running around with that Brian guy…"

"*Totally* different situation." I conveyed with a glare.

"Whatever," he shrugged, "I'll see you at lunch."

"Buh bye," I replied less than lovingly, unzipping my bag to get prepared for the onslaught of tiny noise makers who would invade my personal space within minutes. Ugh.

As it turned out, Dale wound up having a last minute meeting regarding one of his learning disabled students during our lunch break. So, even if I'd wanted to take him into my confidences about Jim Callahan's early morning *I Spy* routine, it wasn't possible. Instead, I sat at my desk attempting to come up with a list of partners for the afternoon's math lesson, too distracted to accomplish much more than that.

In the same spot, just before the first graders would start filing up the stairs from the cafeteria, I heard an irritating "Knock, knock" from the doorway. Annette. Hooray.

Why in blazes was she in here instead of perusing her Bible for the sixty thousandth time? Apparently just to annoy me, I realized, when she gleefully announced that George Welkey had agreed to have her take over Carrie's class if Joan returned to work before the end of the school year in June.

"Joan probably won't be back," I informed her, aware of the progression of Warren's Alzheimer's.

"Either way," she smiled smugly, "At least I'm certain that I'll be here at Redmond for the remainder of the year.

"Yahoo!" I cried out with joy. Slapping on a party hat, I spun around the room like an intoxicated sorority girl. Yeah, right! As if. "Good for you," is all I actually said, with little enthusiasm.

"I hate to sound so cold and selfish, but I have to admit that I'm thrilled to have steady employment for the next several months. Praise the Lord!" the annoying one raved.

I understood that solid income, even as a long term sub (whose daily take was hardly comparable to the work done each day), would benefit her family. For her happiness about that, I couldn't fault Mrs. Bunting. But, did she have to act so heartlessly about it? Her stroke of good luck had come about by the bad circumstances of two other women. That was just plain wrong of her. Fortunately, the Lord Above blessed me as well at that very moment, as Annette was nearly trampled by my troops as they returned from lunch. "Come on in, guys!" I welcomed them with a small laugh.

Following a lesson on shapes, I led my class down to the cafeteria for their weekly Phys. Ed. period and headed back to my room in the hopes of working on my plan book. But, of course, that didn't quite work out the way I'd planned. The instant I sat down, my thoughts of reading and math left almost immediately when my mind wandered back to the unpleasant realization I had come to at suppertime the prior night. The person who'd been trying to scare me into letting sleeping dogs lie was very aware of most everything I said and did on a daily basis.

Since Jim was the one making secretive nightly visits to the Landry house, did that mean that he was also behind the note and phone call? Very likely, yes. He was in a perfect position to listen in on staff members engaging in conversations throughout the school day as he stealthily moved about the building taking care of his various duties. In fact, I'd busted the creeper for eavesdropping on Dale and myself that week!

He'd definitely been keeping abreast of my suspicions about Carrie's so-called accident. The question was *why*. Was it simple curiosity or something more sinister? Was it possible that Jim Callahan was staying well informed to protect himself? Could *he* be the one who'd killed Carrie? That was tough to swallow, but not altogether impossible. Though he seemed to have no motive, neither did anyone else. With less than an hour of the school day left, I made up my mind right then and there to find out what the hell our mysterious custodian was up to as soon as the kids were gone that afternoon.

My bravado diminished with each tick of the minute hand, but while my class colored and cut out their jungle animals for the first grade bulletin board in our hallway, I worked out a plan that would hopefully keep me from becoming the second Redmond School casualty if "Creepy Jim" *was* looking to put an immediate end to my speculations and sleuthing.

Seconds after every little Sammy and Sandy had made their escape for the weekend, I darted across to Dale's classroom to confirm that he wasn't leaving for at least a half an hour, which would give me plenty of time to conduct a little Q and A session with the mysterious custodian. With Mr. Badger close by to serve as my security guard, my nerves lessened a wee bit. "Don't leave without me." I had commanded. *And, if by some chance you hear me screaming bloody murder or spot me running for my life from a demented custodial employee, please haul ass to save me,* I added mentally. Keeping my friend in the dark a little longer was a necessity if I wanted to get to the bottom of things without his interference. I'd get way more out of Jim by questioning him privately.

A few minutes later, as expected, Mr. Callahan entered my classroom with the intent of emptying the trash. "Hi, Jim!" I waved, knowing that would reel him in for a chat. "Could I talk to you for a sec?"

"Sure," replied the fly about to be snagged in my web, a tad too excitedly for my liking. So...how exactly would one phrase an inquiry to determine whether or not someone had threatened her life and/or caused the death of her close friend in addition to staking out her residence? Hmm...

"Do you need me to do something for you?"

Well, yeah.

"Heavy box to put on top of your cabinet?" the dutiful worker asked oh-so-innocently.

"Oh, uh...no. I actually wanted to ask you something." Time to dive in. Make that **cannonball** in. "Did you drive by Carrie's house this morning at, say, three thirty or so?" Blindsided like a Survivor contestant at Tribal Council by my direct and unexpected question, a look of sheer panic spread across the older man's face.

"I...um...well...Miss Fallon, Diana...you see...uh..."

*Please don't faint or be rendered catatonic or die on me now*, I pleaded silently. "Creepy

Jim's" always pale face seemed extra pale, and he looked as though his legs might buckle at any moment. "Spit it out!" I wanted to shout at him, but withheld the demand in favor of remaining in the role of "good cop"…or sympathetic victim, whatever worked best! "Why don't you sit down," I encouraged him, tugging a child sized chair over to him. Wordlessly, he collapsed onto it with a thump. "Well?" I prompted him impatiently.

"I'm so sorry." *Sorry about what, fool? Driving by my house like a freak? Flinging my friend down the stairs to her death?* Just what was "Creepy Jim" Callahan sorry for?

"Go on. You **did** drive by the house then? More than once*." Don't deny it, sucker. I saw you with my own eyes!*

"Yes, I've driven past it quite a few times. I have trouble sleeping." he said, as if that explained it all.

"**Why**?" I demanded, abandoning the "good cop" persona for "impatient, annoyed, anxiety ridden, overtired cop" instead.

"To make sure you were all right over there at her house." he revealed. "I know that you've been trying to find out what happened to Miss Landry. I wanted to make sure that nothing bad happened to you too." Sweet gesture, but a bizarre way to go about it. *If* he was telling me the truth. For all I knew, he was a wannabe peeping tom who had yet to escalate to the next stage of perversion.

"I thought you might stop looking into her accident when I left that note in your mailbox. But, it didn't seem to work so I decided to keep an eye on her house in case anyone tried to attack you or harm you." *Or stalk me?* Oh, wait a minute, he already had that base covered!

If my self-appointed bodyguard was being honest, then maybe I had been wrong this whole time. Maybe Carrie hadn't been murdered and I had been acting like a crazy woman for nothing. His note was one of the first things that convinced me that there was something amiss. A sense of relief washed over me. "So, I assume you were the one who called me in the middle of the night too?"

"Huh?" he replied with a dumb look on his face. What a freakin' weirdo he was, spying on me and making me believe that some mysterious menace was out to get me! "The *call*." I emphasized. "Wednesday night. Telling me to 'back off, bitch'." The custodian's frog eyes bulged at my use of the "b" word.

"I'd never call you that word, Diana. You're always very nice. *Everyone* likes you." That was a nice compliment. I liked to think he was right about that much at least. I'm far from perfect, but I do try my best to treat people properly. Even spooky ass coworkers who obsess over my personal safety and occasionally scare the crap out of me *and* a certain snotty substitute that worked my last nerve on a daily basis.

"So you're telling me that you wrote the note warning me to stop snooping and watched the house to protect me, but you *weren't* the guy on the phone? "

"Nope."

It actually made sense in a way. The note had been phrased a lot more nicely than the nasty caller's venomous words. Wasn't that just Piss Purple Perfect! I had my very own "safety stalker" lurking about *and* some other unknown fiend on my case too! Marvelous.

## CHAPTER TWENTY FOUR

"He's been doing *what*?" a wide eyed Dale replied in a semi-shout when I filled him in on the activities of the overly involved janitor. "And you're just getting around to telling me this *now*!"

"Keep it calm. It is what it is, and hopefully it's over and done with. I let him know in no uncertain terms that I did *not* want any more drive bys in the dark of night. I told him that although I appreciated him having my back, he needs to back off starting *now*. Well, technically *then*, like ten minutes ago when I actually said it. Ha ha ha!"

"Have you lost your mind? How is it that you are laughing about this? You are going to tell Welkey about it, aren't you?"

Well…"Not necessarily. If the Creepy Creeper keeps creepin', I will. Otherwise, no harm's been done. At least now I know that whoever made the phone call hasn't been watching me at home. That makes me feel a lot safer."

"Yeah, unless it's *him* who made the call and he's a pathological liar in addition to being a 'watcher'." Okay, so he had a point there.

"Don't worry. I'll be fine. Trust me." I reassured him, which didn't really seem to do the trick. "I'll see you on Monday or talk to you over the weekend."

"All right," he finally gave in, climbing into his car as I hopped into mine and let the heat get going. Dale beeped his horn at me and drove off, leaving me alone with my thoughts. Padding by Carrie's darkened classroom on our way out, it had dawned on me that, like all "big" news items in Arwell, the buzz surrounding "the untimely death of a local elementary school teacher" had died down after only a couple of weeks. Some other O.M.G. event would soon take over as the "it" topic of local discussions and gossip.

Typically I was indifferent to the grapevine and the news it carried. This time, though, it made me sad. At least when the Richmond School parents and other residents of the town were speculating about her cause of death, accidental vs. intentional, they'd been thinking about her. Talking about her. Worrying about her. Now, half a month later, Carrie Landry had been forgotten. No more talk. No more concern. No more Carrie. That sucked. Wiping tears from my eyes, I backed out of my parking space, more than ready to get home.

My presumption that Jim Callahan had been forthcoming with the truth and nothing but the truth could be a mistake, I reasoned. But, truly, his explanations had the ring of sincerity. He'd seemed embarrassed at being found out and was legitimately taken aback when I brought up the threat I'd received earlier in the week. "Crap," I muttered to myself as I pulled up to a stoplight, realizing that the identity of the caller was still a mystery, as was his or her "source". Who in my small relatively boring first grade world was working against me?

For the five hundredth time in a fortnight, I began mentally pondering if someone at school could be involved, either directly or unwittingly.

*Dale? My mind flashed back to the comment he had made that same morning, comparing his own unfaithful ex to Carrie, who was seeing a married man. Unknowingly, I reminded myself.*

*Annette? A prissy preachy pain in my butt. With a bible as her Siamese twin, she'd spouted off about sinning when I'd foolishly put Carrie's personal business out there for her to overhear. And she was pretty desperate for a full time teaching position.*

# A FIRST GRADE FATALITY

*Leticia Devane? Oh please! She was like a hundred and twelve and "old school" when it came to professional confidentiality. Gossip for her Century Plus Club probably consisted of Stella's constipation woes or Mr. Fletcher's missing dentures. There was no way in the world that the old schoolmarm had a featured role in this mystery!*

*Likewise was Joan. Yes, she was aware of my strong objections to the "accident" ruling and my subsequent accusations of foul play. But, who would she pass it along to? Her husband who'd forget what she'd told him ten minutes later? Then again, the Petrillos were Arwell residents, like Carrie, so gabbing to a neighbor was certainly a possibility. One that hadn't entered my addled brain until now.*

*Mama Erica, too, was constantly kept in the loop via my many emails, texts, and calls. And Erica Talbot did love to talk! Her loose lips and the local Mommy Network could easily have spread my suspicions far and wide. In which case, my theory that someone close to me was involved flew right out the window.* A four letter word oozed slowly from my lips at that realization.

Of course, there was also the possibility that another of my colleagues had heard about my carrying on about a mystery culprit having a hand in my friend's fatal fall too. George Welkey was quite well known in the community. Who was to say that he hadn't spilled some info after imbibing a tad too much with his old fogey cronies? He'd let me off the hook pretty easily that day I'd been called into his office, but I could just imagine him complaining about his fruit loop first grade teacher trying to make drama out of nothing. Even Fran Vespa, the librarian, had checked with her police connection for me. Ugh! I was going to drive myself batty if some jaw dropping tidbit didn't drop onto my lap soon.

Decidedly close to ripping off my face in annoyance, however, did not slow this girl down. The term "glutton for punishment" was synonymous with the name Diana Marie Fallon these days. So, I shifted my thoughts to who on my ever growing list might possibly have caused Carrie to fall without malicious intent, as that prospect seemed a lot more logical than a motiveless murder.

Much as I hated it, the fact that Carrie had gone out with Brian Fox popped up as the one remote bone of contention that someone may have had against her. If that person went to her home to broach the subject with her and an argument had ensued, perhaps her visitor had absent mindedly shoved her out of frustration, sending her down the stairs. If that was the case, two suspects came to mind rather quickly, one of whom I dared not even consider as the guilty party. Annette Bunting or Dale Badger.

In my heart, I was unable to believe that my sole male teaching colleague could be responsible for the loss of my other dear friend. He'd have been overwhelmed with guilt and horror stricken. No way would he be able to hide that from me.

But, would the sin busting substitute be ballsy enough to show up at Carrie's house to lecture her on the consequences of engaging in a relationship with someone who'd pledged fidelity before her best bud, God? That, arguably, was easier for me to envision, and from what I could recall, Mrs. Bunting had supposedly gone grocery shopping after her shift at the after school program was over. As an alibi, that wasn't the strongest. The meddlesome mother could totally have made a pit stop on her way to Market Basket or Shaws or whichever supermarket she blessed with her purchases.

But, did we even know the time of death? Merciful Marionettes! My memory was about as reliable as poor Warren Petrillo's lately. Too many facts and even more suppositions will clog your brain eventually. Had Deputy Miller slipped that info to Cassie or me? I had zero recollection of it. Fuming at my failure to remember had me yearning to call Cassie. But, that was out of the question. I may be nosy as heck or dredging up drama where there was none, but I was neither tacky nor insensitive. And calling a woman to attain such a fact on the day that her only sibling had been buried was both.

As I turned into the driveway of the Landry's house, a sudden mind blip mocked me for neglecting some pertinent piece of data floating around in my head. Shifting into the "park" position, I closed my eyes in the hopes of figuring out exactly what it was.

Well, hold your horses, cowgirl, and lasso those accusations you just dealt out! There was no way Annette or Dale (duh!) could have come to this house to face off with Carrie about her involvement with Brian Fox. Clearly my ten gallon hat was on too tightly and was cutting off circulation to my befuddled brain. Neither of that pair was even aware that Carrie's guy was married until days *after* Cassie had found her sister's crumpled body at the base of the staircase. Guess it had slipped my mind that yours truly and her big mouth had let them in on that bit of information following my own surprise discovery of it. Good thing the Arwell citizens' tax dollars were paying me to mold the minds of little ones and not to assist Arwell's finest in their crime fighting endeavors.

"You are a moron." I told myself in the mirror as I wiped my face clear of makeup. Ignoring my grumbling stomach, I opted to dedicate myself to some brainless fun instead. Facebook! After a solid hour and a half of commenting on random posts, watching videos of a fat guy falling into a manhole and a raccoon playing checkers, and way too many rounds of Candy Crush, I made oatmeal and texted Joan to avoid waking Warren if he was in bed.

# A FIRST GRADE FATALITY

*Call me for a Phantom Farter update when you can* I typed between spoonfuls of Quaker Oats. Before I'd finished the bowl, my trusty cell phone rang, displaying Joan's number in light green digits. "Phantom Farter Hotline," I answered like a silly fool. "How may I help you?"

"Oh, Diana! You are too much!" Joan chuckled. "You've lost it, girl." After the massive brain overload and major mental blunders I'd committed on my way home, I was inclined to agree.

"I've narrowed it down to seven kids because somebody let out a brutal blast of silent but deadly air while I was doing a guided reading lesson with the Owls group at the back table this morning. Actually, make that six! Matthew was absent the other day when the Phantom let one rip." Fingering the perpetrator of multiple gas attacks was nearly as difficult as fingering the person or persons in the know about Carrie's final moments.

"Oh no! That back table is a tight squeeze. How did they react?

"Half of them didn't even notice. I have no idea how! Thankfully the ones who did were all quiet nice kids who were too polite to point it out."

"Was that little Jones girl there?"

"Tameka. She was. I think you could be right about her."

"I told you. Have you ever seen what that child eats at lunch?" Needless to say, I had not. On the increasing chance that Joan's suspicions were correct, I wisely avoided the adorable suspect when she ate.

"Like what? Prunes?"

"No! She's always got…" Noise in the background caused her to stop abruptly. "Hold on a second. I think Warren's awake. Warren? Is that you? What the…"

"Joan? Are you all right? Joan?" No verbal reply, just a muffled conversation and the sound of the phone being dropped. What was going on? Trying to decipher what was being said, it sounded like Warren had asked about his suit being ironed. "For Bill Clinton's party." he claimed. That poor couple.

"Diana, are you still there?"

"Holy crap!" I screamed, startled by Joan's sudden return and loud inquiry.

"I'll have to give you a call tomorrow. He's trying to get out of bed again."

"No problem. I'll talk to you then. Good luck." Holy moly! She certainly had her hands full. Caring for just one adult who lacked the mental capacity to adhere to logical reasoning was as tough as trying to keep twenty four first grade bums in their seats at the same time, if not tougher.

Having eaten the remainder of my "meal", I washed the bowl, then snatched a bag of Doritos out of the cupboard and settled in on the couch with my snack and twenty something handwriting papers that were in dire need of some red ink. Mindlessly flipping channels, I was in ecstasy when an episode of *Catfish* filled my screen.

"Yes!" Watching Nev and Max solve some bizarre online lover's mystery would take my mind off of the mysteries closer to home. Those boys were hot! Even hotter now that I'd learned that they were not only *not* a couple, but were both straight!

Midway through the stack of handwriting assignments, I came to Cody Burnette's paper. He was a bright boy, but his fine motor skills were quite weak, as evidenced by his penmanship. Today, it had been Cody who had alerted me that Georgette's coat was on the floor yet again.

Because she'd been out of the room at the time, I'd had him hang it up for her, which caused an uproar at dismissal. The helpful boy had mistakenly hung the garment on the wrong hook, so the coat's owner had flown into a panic, believing that her precious teddy bear coat had been stolen. I'd wanted to say, "Girlfriend, with the number of times that you've left it on the damned floor, that thing is dirtier than a chinchilla after its dust bath. If someone was going to steal a coat, don't you think they'd at least go for a *clean* one?" But, since the sarcasm would have flown right over her irresponsible little head, I refrained.

Kickboxing kangaroos! I quickly hit the pause button so that I wouldn't miss the big reveal of the online imposter while I pondered my latest and greatest connection. Carrie's coat had been found in the wrong spot after her body was found. Didn't it make sense, then, that somebody other than Carrie could have put it there, unaware that she never used the coat rack? How had it taken me this long to figure that out? It made perfect sense. What a birdbrain I was!

Taking into consideration this new hunch could be an indication that Carrie had gone out some time between arriving home from school and the time she died. Why else would the coat not be in its usual place? Nobody would have reason to move it from the back of the chair to the rack across the room.

Proceeding logically, one could then assume that upon Carrie's return (from wherever she'd gone), she was accompanied by another person. That person, accordingly, hung up her coat in the place where it would appear to go- the coat rack. But, why wouldn't Carrie have put away her own coat? It was her house, after all. Unless she wasn't able to.

Perhaps the teacher hadn't even fallen down the stairs. Maybe she had died elsewhere!

CHAPTER TWENTY FIVE

Whoa! If that was the case, so many of the ideas I had bandied about would have to be tossed out of the equation altogether! Carrie dying at another location meant that her corpse- what a horrifying word to use when talking about my friend- had been moved back to her own house, probably to hide the fact that she had gone somewhere…and died there. That "somewhere" would be the *true* scene of the crime. To keep from being incriminated, the person she'd been with when she'd been fatally injured had then brought Miss Landry home to divert suspicion from himself or herself.

This was falling right into place. Finally. I vaguely recalled Deputy Miller mentioning something about the amount of blood under Carrie. The medical examiner had noted it in his report too. What exactly had his observation been though? Lack of blood from her head wound? That, too, could easily be attributed to her being killed elsewhere. There'd have been blood where she died for sure.

But, what about her green knit hat and the plaid scarf? Where were they? Were they inadvertently left behind when her body was moved?

None of her neighbors, at least the few I'd been able to talk to, remembered seeing Carrie leave her house that afternoon. But, now, I felt that she'd almost certainly gone out. Most of my previous suppositions had been off the mark, though, I reminded myself. I could be going gangbusters for nothing.

Keeping in mind that her keys and phone were locked up in her car left only two possibilities as to how she'd gotten anywhere. Either someone had picked Carrie up and driven her or she had been on foot. If she had gone off with someone in their vehicle, she could have gone anyplace, but if she'd left on foot, it must have been to use the phone at a nearby house.

Miles Kendrick claimed that he was out of town at the time, but obviously if he was involved in Carrie's death, he'd lie through his teeth. What if the arrogant hunk was home and Carrie had shown up unexpectedly, having let herself in with his key to use his phone? Might she have witnessed him doing something? Maybe Miles had been engaging in criminal behavior even! His pretty neighbor arrives, spots him, he attempts to coerce her into remaining quiet about what's she's seen, a struggle ensues, and BOOM, he slams Carrie's head against the wall or countertop or floor. Not knowing if the police had verified Kendrick's whereabouts for that night was killing me. He could be a murderer!

On the other hand, it was possible that Carrie didn't even realize that her things were locked in her vehicle, in which case she wouldn't have needed to use his telephone or anyone else's.

I refused to believe that anybody who knew and cared about Carrie would blatantly hide the truth about how my friend had died, particularly if it had been accidental. So what other viable suspects, besides Miles, would be devious enough to plant her body back at her own house after watching Carrie take her final breath? Only one person came to mind .The possessive and potentially vindictive Gwen Fox.

I could totally see her doing that. She was a woman scorned, and she was certainly willing to get physical. My cheek was proof of that. Though she may not have intended to land a deadly blow, her temper could have gotten the best of her. Carrie could have been knocked to the ground, smashing her head. Panic may have set in at first, but Mrs. Fox was one cool customer. Once she overcame the initial shock and realized the repercussions her actions could bring, I had no doubt that she would start scurrying to cover her ass. She and Brian had alibis. But, were they each other's? Had they claimed to have been together that night? If so, Mr. Fox could have lied to protect his wife.

As a matter of fact, Brian could have helped her out in more ways than one. Moving Carrie's body to another location, a place that would make the young woman's death look like a simple tragedy, would probably have been possible with adrenaline pumping through the unintentional killer's body. But, it would've been far easier if she had assistance with the unpleasant task. And Brian Fox was in good shape. Maybe the cheating hubby felt that he owed her that much, and the pair had transported the dead teacher back to the Landry's house and staged it to look like she'd tumbled down the stairs.

If only there was a way for me to find out if both spouses had been proven to be in the clear by less dubious sources than one another. Finding out whether Miles Kendrick was actually out of town on that date would also be mighty helpful. But, how? Would the police tell me if I asked? I doubted that. At this late hour on a Friday night, I was drawing a blank on how I could confirm or refute their claims. So, reluctantly, and perhaps foolishly, I decided to reach out to my merry band of doubters for suggestions.

Given the lengthiness of what I wanted to relay and the fact that one or more of them could be in bed already, email was my best option. So, I tapped away on my keyboard, attempting to provide a concise version of my newly developed premises: Carrie being killed elsewhere. Her lifeless body being moved home to conceal the actual place she'd died and/or the involvement of the guilty party. The coat being mistakenly hung up in the wrong place by someone other than Carrie. My desire to get the lowdown on the true whereabouts of Miles, Brian, and Gwen that night. Forty minutes later I hit "send", and my somewhat succinct (okay, not so much!) summary was on its way to the trio of Badger, Talbot, and Petrillo.

Returning to the sofa for what turned out to be a *Catfish* marathon, I had high hopes (well, maybe hopes of medium size would be more accurate) that at least one of them would respond positively to my latest ideas. Another one or two, I was pretty sure, would inevitably bite my head off for ignoring the Arwell P.D.'s directive to cease digging into this matter. Oh well. What can I say? Apparently I'm better at giving directions than following them. My bad.

The next morning brought the weekend. Praise the Lord! Or not. Surely Annette Bunting had praised Him enough for the entire town. If not, she'd probably flogged herself for neglecting to do so. Yikes! I was in Bitch Mode 3000 even after a full ten hours of sleep. No menacing phone calls. No night long worries about being murdered in Carrie's bed. And, with luck, no overnight visit by a certain creepazoid custodian! That one I can't vouch for though.

At noon, I checked my email to find out who, if anyone had weighed in on my latest theory. Only Dale had, and his words were minimal, though his tone was quite clear. *Didn't you give this up? Call me.* And I would. But, first I'd phone Joan. She was a lot less likely to berate me for my continual efforts to uncover the truth, even if she wasn't gung ho about it.

"Hi! Did you see the email I sent you last night?" I inquired impatiently before she had the opportunity to get in a word.

"I can't talk right now. Bad day for Warren. I'll try to call you later." she tersely told me. Uh oh. That wasn't good. So, I moved on to the next call.

"You!" Dale answered, having seen my number on the caller ID screen. "*What* are you doing? Were you not right beside me at the police station the other day being told to butt out?" Clearly a rhetorical question.

"Oh, come on, Dale. Don't you think it makes perfect sense? Carrie must have died some other place and was brought back to her house to confuse everyone!"

"Listen. I'm not going to argue about this with you. Could it have happened? Yes. Would it explain the coat on the rack? Yes. Even though I personally don't think the stupid coat has one iota to with this. However, *you* should not be the one worrying about this. Leave it to the people who get paid to do this kind of thinking for a living. Have you forgotten about the call in the middle of the night? Because apparently it did nothing to dissuade you."

"Are you done ranting?" I calmly asked when he finally let me speak.

"I am."

"Good. Because I'm not in the mood to hear you chide me for caring about my friend. *Our* friend."

"You're missing my point, Diana. For whatever reason, someone wants you to stop poking your nose into this and we don't know what steps they might take if you don't cooperate."

I appreciated his concern for my well-being and told him as much. I just couldn't let it go. I needed to find out about the circumstances that ended Carrie's life, despite the potential consequences. Part of me wanted to slap some sense into myself, but another, stronger, part kept cheering me on, convinced I was close to figuring it all out. "So, I assume you think it would be a waste of time for me to turn this information over to the cops?"

"It's not information. It's speculation. There's a big difference. So, no, I see no need to tell them what you're thinking. Currently thinking, that is. It changes daily. *But*, if the alternative is you running around town like the Big Bad Wolf on the trail of a tasty pig, then by all means, tell them."

"First off, the wolf was a bad guy. I'm not. Secondly, I took that warning seriously the other night. I didn't go sneaking around Arwell peering in the windows of the three people highest on my list of suspects." Though, if I thought it would get me closer to a final answer, I might have.

"Enough on this topic." my oppositional colleague decided. "Wait till you hear what I stumbled across this morning!" Hopefully not another dead body.

"Okay, I'm waiting."

"You're such a wiseass, Fallon! Anyway, I went online to see if I could find any fun lessons we could use during *The Little Red Hen* unit..." The Little Red Hen. Remember her? The busy bird that nobody would help out. These days, I was considering legally changing my name to Little Red Fallon or maybe getting a tattoo of the red hen on one of my butt cheeks.

"So, there I am, clicking onto various links, and guess what popped up on the screen!"

"A mental institution you want to commit me to due to my nonstop obsession with murder plots and dear friends?" What? He asked me to guess!

"No! A strip joint! Named, of all things, The Little Red Hen. Isn't that whacked?"

"Um, yeah! Why the hell would you name a strip club after a chicken that bakes bread?" I agreed, stopping momentarily to perversely wonder if there was an adjoining club for the ladies called The Little Red Cock. Then again, not many women would be all that excited to see ones that were *little*…or red!

"No kidding! I laughed my ass off for like ten minutes after the website appeared. The Little Red Hen? Wouldn't a better name be The Little Red Pus…"

"Ewww! Stop!" That word was not a word I cared to hear when discussing female anatomy or any other topic, thank you very much. Nor did the image of a red one do anything but remind me to add maxi pads to my grocery list.

"You have to google it." he insisted. Consenting to do so when I returned from running some errands, we ended our call after a few final disciplinary words from Mr. Badger regarding my enquiring mind.

For the next couple of hours, I pretended to be a normal human being living a ho-hum life with no aspirations of solving the mystery surrounding her coworker's unpleasant expiration. I bought tasty fresh veggies and oodles of other edibles at Stop and Shop. I treated myself to some new lipstick and eye liner at Walgreens. I filled my tank at the cheapest gas station around, pleased that the weather was once again reasonably mild for wintertime. A very nice uneventful afternoon.

My cell phone rang from inside the pocket of my coat when I was roughly halfway back to Cassie's house. But, unlike too many brainless Massachusetts drivers, I waited until I was stopped at the next set of lights to fish it out. No matter what a good number of people say, talking on the telephone and driving a car are *not* compatible activities. Waiting three minutes to find out who had called wouldn't kill me. Taking the call just might. As much as I missed my recently departed friend, I hoped it would be many many years before we'd reunite.

Erica's number showed up on the list of missed calls so I returned her call after putting away all of my produce, frozen entrees, and the scrumptious Brigham's peppermint ice cream I planned to dive into that night. Thankfully, *this* friend felt the idea of Carrie's body being relocated, while gruesome to imagine, quite plausible. "You should really share this with that detective who was at her house the morning Cassie found her." Ha! So there, Dale Badger! Although if I did take Erica's advice, it would be with some trepidation. Detective Donovan, et al weren't likely to accept my assistance or, as I had a feeling they would say, my interference.

Our talk didn't last long since Mrs. Talbot was expecting the original Mrs. Talbot, a.k.a. her monster-in-law, for an early dinner. Probably for the best because she and I had a penchant for hours long gab fests, and I needed to start the hunt for a new place to live. Leaving the bulk of my purchased goods, still in their bags, on the kitchen floor, I headed upstairs to fire up my laptop and begin searching for affordable apartments in nearby towns.

Alas, my good intentions vanished pretty quickly once I hit the worldwide web. Before I knew it, I'd been led astray…to the Little Red Hen website! I just had to see it with my own eyes. Then, I'd be able to focus on finding myself a new residence, preferably one close to, but not in, Arwell and that wouldn't break the bank, forcing me to teach summer school when I'd rather be perfecting my tan at Scusset Beach. And if it weren't for that social media genius, Mark Zuckerberg, hunting for homes *would* have been next on my agenda. But, realistically, who can be online and not feel compelled to take a gander at Facebook?

Truth be told, Twitter, Instagram, and a host of other newer forms of brain numbing venues were more popular with many people my age. But, Facebook was the preferred site of Arwell Public School employees. So, between my sorely lacking technology skills and my desire to keep up with everyone from my cousins to the receptionist at my dentist's office, off I went to check out what was new on FB that hour.

Navigating onto my own profile, I was surprised to see a photo of some dude in a cowboy hat alongside a beautiful African American girl that Cassie had apparently posted to my page a few days earlier. Reading the caption below the picture, I learned that he was the lead singer for the Branson Boys and that he'd proposed to his longtime girlfriend, a Nigerian supermodel. Nice for them, but I really didn't care. Although I had enjoyed their concert when I'd gone with Cassie, that didn't mean I wanted to be provided with details of their every move. But, following suit, I posted it to someone else's "wall" who had attended their concert a few days before we had seen their Providence show. *Thought you might like this since you saw them in Boston* I typed in. He was probably as uninterested about the engagement as I was, especially being a guy. But he could delete it if he wanted. I wouldn't take it personally…especially since I was deleting Cassie's post.

The rest of my afternoon and evening were more productive than most. A local realtor's website gave me a dozen or so places to check into further. My lesson plans for all subject areas except math got done in one sitting. And I even spent an hour and a half reading a trashy romance before bed. It was no *Fifty Shades of Gray*, but it was still pretty steamy. As I lay in bed after switching the lamp beside Carrie's bed off, I debated the issue of bringing my theory about her body being moved to the police. I was still undecided when I nodded off.

But, my slumber was short lived. Several hours later, while my weary body was rejuvenating itself, I was jolted awake in the darkness by the deafening crash of glass shattering!

## CHAPTER TWENTY SIX

Terror rampaged through me as I lay there, frozen in a supine position. My breathing slowed as I groggily attempted to figure out what I should do. Lying perfectly still, deathly afraid that the slightest movement would alert an intruder to my whereabouts, my ears took in every bit of the silence. Was there somebody downstairs who planned to attack or kill me? As quietly as I could, I extended my arm toward the nightstand to my left. When my fingers landed on the cell phone, they instinctively curled around it and pulled it close to my chest. Should I call 911 immediately from bed or get myself into the bathroom, where I could lock the door first?

Lightly tossing back the covers, I slid over, barely allowing my feet to touch the floor. Fearing that the bed would squeak as I stood up, I positioned my shaky hands beside me, gently pushing myself upward. Fully erect, I dared not move, but had no choice in the matter. Listening intently, my ears didn't detect any further sound. But, that meant nothing. Someone could have stealthily crept up the stairs and be waiting to ambush me. Biting down on my quivering bottom lip, I moved tentatively in the direction of the door, one step at a time.

My eyes hadn't fully adjusted to the dark by the time I reached the doorway, but I'd be able to run my hands along the wall to guide myself to the bathroom several feet away. Unless there was somebody out in the hall, waiting for me to walk just a few steps closer before they pounced. The fear that was paralyzing me gave way and I made a mad dash into the hallway, ramming into the wall opposite Carrie's bedroom. Crying out, I fumbled along till I caught sight of a sliver of the moon through the bathroom window on the back side of the house. Lunging forward, I slammed the door behind me and clumsily got the lock turned.

Thank God, I was safe! Nobody had grabbed me, but that didn't necessarily mean there wasn't anyone on the first floor. Sliding my fingertips across the small screen, it took me two tries to accurately enter the three digit emergency number into my phone. Once connected, it was only seconds before I was able to explain my situation and give the address to the woman who had answered. "Officers are on their way. Somebody called just before you with the same report. You said that you *are* safe for now, correct?"

"I think so. Yes."

"Good. Stay right where you are until the officers arrive. I'll stay on the line until they do."

"Thank you," I panted, just as a loud banging sound came from below. "I think someone's down there!"

"Inside the house?"

"I'm not sure," I said softly, my ears peeled.

"Hello! Is anyone in there?" came a man's voice, followed by more banging. "It's the Arwell Police Department, responding to a call." Oh, Hallelujah!

"They're here!" I informed the woman at the other end of the line. As fast as I could, I undid the lock and flung the bathroom door open. Feeling my way to the second floor light switch, I flipped it on so I wouldn't wind up in a heap at the bottom of the stairs as my friend had. Lights on, I charged down to let the police in.

It wasn't until I had unlocked the door and the two officers were inside that I turned on the overhead lights in the living room and noticed the gaping hole in one of the front windows. Not even a hole, really. Just a few jagged pieces of glass poking out from the window frame.

Surveying the carpeted floor, I spotted a large grayish white rock beside the coffee table, the obvious cause of the destruction.

"Wait here," the thinner Hispanic looking officer commanded as the younger Caucasian one closed the front door. I wasn't sure if he was talking to me, his partner, or both of us. Evidently just me, I realized when the second officer roamed off to check the rest of the rooms on the first floor.

Who had done this? And why tonight? Even if I was dead on with my assumption that Carrie had been moved back to the house after she was dead, and I felt confident about this idea, the only people I'd told were my friends. There was no way in the world that I would ever believe that Joan or Dale or Erica was responsible for this latest scare tactic or the previous attempt to frighten me on Wednesday night.

Then a disturbing thought came to me. Yesterday I had confronted Jim Callahan and told him to stop keeping tabs on me at the house. Was he furious with me for telling him to back off so bluntly? His reasoning was that he was trying to protect me from harm. He could have been lying, though I didn't think he'd have been able to come up with a believable story on the spot like he had. Maybe he was mad because I hadn't thrown myself at his feet in gratitude. Or my exaggerated notion that he was a stalker wasn't far off the mark. Perhaps he had some ulterior motive for watching the house each night.

If he was simply a good guy with a good heart who happened to make me feel uncomfortable, I'd hate to throw him under the bus for naught. Chances were that whoever threw the rock through the window, scaring the crap out of me (figuratively speaking, thank goodness!), was also the one who'd made the threatening phone call. Likewise, he or she was the person who had messed up by hanging Carrie's coat in the wrong spot when they came here to the house to set up her body for Cassie to find the next morning.

Vacillating between "Creepy Jim" and the mystery person who was up to their neck in this Carrie situation, I laid it all out for officers Garcia and Clarkson. When those fellows asked if I had any ideas about who might have committed this vandalistic act, they had *no* idea what they were getting themselves into. Surely, they'd never believed that my answer to such a simple question would be anything but simple. Or that they'd be stuck listening to me rant and rattle on for over thirty five minutes. Never mind coffee, this pair would need a stiff drink after I finally concluded my long winded tales of death, deception, unending vexing, and harassment.

Panic set in as the slender Officer Garcia stared silently at me while his other half made a call. Did they think I was a paranoid schizophrenic or a delusional head case who'd tossed the rock through the window to grab some time in their spotlight? Thankfully not, since they offered me a ride to a friend's house instead of to the mental ward.

I hadn't even thought about where I would spend the remainder of the night until they mentioned it. The Petrillos were just around the corner and Joan *had* invited me to stay with them before I'd accepted Cassie's offer. But, calling in the middle of the night and disturbing Warren's sleep didn't sit well with me. The Talbots also weren't too far away, but Savannah had been sleeping for longer periods of time overnight recently, and I didn't want to screw that up either. Dale lived a greater distance away, but since he was now living alone, I wouldn't disrupt anyone but him. How would it look, though, if I spent the night at his house? It would be perfectly innocent, of course, but the rumor mill was sure to get word out that Miss Fallon was seen leaving the home of her recently separated male colleague early the next morning. No, thank you.

A nearby Holiday Inn seemed like my best bet. But, the more I thought about it, the less I was in favor of going there. Yes, it would definitely be nice to spend some worry free time in a pristine hotel room, but why should I shell out my hard earned cash because some bully had launched a rock through the window? Despite earning a piddly teacher's salary, I could certainly afford a night's stay, but I also wanted to show the rock throwing jerk that I wasn't so easily intimidated.

After hearing that I planned to remain in the house in spite of the nasty scare I'd had, Officer Garcia left, leaving Clarkson to help me cover up the broken window. Using a sturdy piece of cardboard, some heavy duty tape, and a few thick beach towels to lessen the draft, the two of us managed to shroud the opening relatively well in no time at all.

As I stood in the outer doorway, ready to close and lock the door behind the police officer as he departed, lights from across the street caught my eye. Miles Kendrick was peering out one of the windows on the first floor of his house. Perhaps he'd glimpsed the flashing blue lights from his bed and come down to take a look. But, the patrol cars had arrived quite some time ago. Was he waiting until the second cruiser drove off to make an appearance as my knight in shining armor? Or simply checking out his handiwork and its after-effects?

Either way, he was bound to be disappointed when I shut the door, padded back upstairs and turned off the lights. Was I certifiable for staying here rather than going elsewhere for the rest of the night? That was the question I debated in my head for the next three hours as I lay in Carrie's bed, tucked in well, with eyes wide open.

At some point, I fell asleep, and the next thing I knew it was closing in on eight thirty Sunday morning. After slipping downstairs to ensure that the window was secure, crawling back into bed was my next course of action. Mentally and physically, I just wasn't ready to face anyone or anything yet. Like an ostrich with her head in the sand, I stayed there until almost noon.

When I finally came out of hiding to rejoin the real world, I took baby steps, heading back to the computer's version of the "real world" first. When Facebook popped up on my screen, I scrolled down to see if anyone else's Saturday night had been as dramatic as mine. Somehow I doubted it. Munching on a bowl of Rice Krispies, I scanned the dozens of new posts, confirming my hunch that I was the only gal who'd been lucky enough to have two gentlemen callers show up at my door in the wee hours of the morning. Posting such a teasing comment would have been kind of fun, but it occurred to me that I might want to inform the house's owner about the damage done to her property before I filled in the rest of the free world.

The tiny red icon at the top of the page indicated I had two unread messages so I clicked onto it to see who they were from. The first was from Cassie: *coming home Tuesday, I think- see you then.* Yeah, to a house with all windows intact hopefully. Did homeowner's insurance cover vandalism? Having never owned a home, I was clueless. I'd make some calls later to find out. If not, the cost of the replacement window and its installation would take a good chunk of my next paycheck. There was no way I would allow Cassie to pay one red cent for an act that my stubbornness had inadvertently invited.

The second message, however, puzzled me. In response to the engagement pic I'd shared with Max Petrillo, his reply read: *I've never seen the Branson Boys live.* Really? Did my memory suck that badly? I could've sworn Joan had said that he went to their Boston show the day that Dale and I had been looking for information about the memorial service for Carrie in the newspaper. And I was almost positive there had been a photo that he or someone he'd gone with had put up on FB too, hadn't there? To satisfy my curiosity (yet again…but on a non-death related topic, I'd like to point out!), I typed his name into the search bar to bring up his page, then dragged the mouse down, scanning dates and pictures. Nope, no Branson Boys concert photo or blurb appeared anywhere within his posts from the last couple of months. Weird. I remember thinking that he looked really good in a cowboy hat.

Intent on proving to myself that my memory wasn't *completely* shot due to my overthinking and fixation on deadly doings, I googled "Branson Brothers tour dates" to affirm that the rising country group *had* played in Boston recently. "Okay, that's what I thought!" I told the computer screen. The computer, happily, did not reply, verifying that I wasn't as "out of it" as school secretary non- extraordinaire, Sylvia Wise! Yet.

The band had played at the Orpheum Theatre in the city, gone up to Manchester, New Hampshire to do a show, then concluded their area dates in Providence, where Cassie and I were members of their audience. At least my mind was properly functioning to some degree. But, why was the image of Max and some guy flashing a peace sign ingrained in my brain then? And why would Warren's brother deny attending the concert when I was ninety nine percent certain that he had? That made no sense. Then again, a number of things weren't making sense to me these days.

My eyes zoned in on the date of their Boston show. For some reason, that date rang a bell. Zipping over to the Arwell Public Schools' website, I checked to see if it had some sort of relevance on the Redmond School's online calendar of events. It didn't.

"Wait a minute…" A sharp intake of breath followed. Now it made *perfect* sense, and I knew exactly why that son of a bitch was lying about not being at that concert.

## CHAPTER TWENTY SEVEN

The Wednesday night that the Branson Boys had played at the Orpheum in Boston was the night that Carrie had died. The night that the Redmond School's first grade teachers had met for dinner at Santino's. The night that Max Petrillo was taking care of his brother…or was supposed to be at any rate! Unless he was magician Criss Angel in disguise, Joan's brother-in-law couldn't have been in two places at the same time. If he'd been watching the Branson Boys in person in Boston, an hour or so north of Arwell, he sure as hell wasn't keeping an eye on Warren as Joan believed. What a selfish jerk!

He must have come to Joan and Warren's house as arranged, waited for his sister-in-law to leave, then hightailed it up Route 93 to see the concert, at least some of it, and made it back to the Petrillo's house by the time Joan returned home. Warren had probably been asleep the whole time so Max's absence would have gone unnoticed. How many other times had he pulled this type of stunt with Joan being none the wiser? She would be *livid* when she found out.

Interfering in a family's personal business was always tricky when that family wasn't your own. Granted, I'd stuck my nose a few places lately that perhaps it needn't have been while trying to find out about Carrie's "accident". But, my inquiries hadn't turned family member against family member, which would surely happen if I told Joan about what Max had seemingly done that night. I didn't want to create another Hatfields vs McCoys situation, but there was no way I could keep this from her. She was one of my best friends and her husband's well-being could be at stake. God only knew what might have happened if, by some chance, Warren had woken up and wandered away from their house into the woods or onto a busy street with lots of traffic!

Putting my concerns about our friend's death on the backburner, my focus now shifted to how I was going to deliver this jarring news to my other, live, friend. Joan was going to fume when she learned of Max's deception. This needed to be done face to face without a doubt.

Forgetting that I'd rolled out of bed no more than an hour ago and pretty much looked like Medusa having a bad hair day, I donned a pair of jeans and a bright green turtleneck and flung my unruly hair under a ratty looking Red Sox cap from the Landry's coatrack. Adding my pink ski jacket and a pair of gray leather gloves to the stunning ensemble, I grabbed my keys off the counter and walked out the back door, nervous at having to upset Joan this way. The typical January cold nipped at the exposed skin of my face immediately, but the bitter chill I'd complained about so many times in the past barely registered with me today.

As an attempt to put off the unpleasant task ahead of me, I opted to walk to the Petrillo's instead of hopping in the car as I'd planned to do. Stepping onto the sidewalk, I mentally rehearsed how I could best present what I'd learned to Joan. Even the sight of Miles Kendrick's eagle eyes watching me from inside his house didn't bother me. This was *not* going to be fun or easy.

As I walked down Perth Street, nearing the Petrillo's mailbox, my nervousness quadrupled. How was Joan going to react? Would she fly off the handle and claw Max's eyes out or would she be rendered speechless after finding out that her husband had been left unattended one or more times by the man she so often praised for his willingness to help her out?

I was about to find out, I knew, as I rapped softly on the door. Joan looked wary as she opened it. "Hey, Diana. Come on in. Where's your car? Don't tell me you walked over here in the freezing cold!"

"I did."

"Girl, you are crazy. Get inside before you freeze to death out there."

"We need to talk." I blurted out.

She looked at me anxiously. "What's wrong?"

"I discovered something…by accident…about Max and Warren. About the night that Carrie was killed." Mrs. Petrillo froze where she was, her face now full of fear.

With a teardrop developing in each eye, she stared at me in silence. When she finally spoke, her voice was barely a whisper. "I knew you'd find out." she said, wiping away the tears that now ran down her cheeks. "But it wasn't his fault. Really. He didn't know what he was doing."

Why was she defending Max? And why was she crying about it? "He *knew* what he was doing." I declared firmly. No way should he be let off the hook for behaving so irresponsibly.

"He didn't!" Joan shouted loudly at me. "You *know* he didn't!" What in the world was she talking about?

"He was all alone with no one to remind him who she was. He thought she'd broken into the house. He never would have harmed her if…"

The last few words that she uttered, I missed altogether as a light went off in my head. Then another and another. At long last, the dim bulbs in my brain were glowing like a neon sign advertising a Broadway show. Oh. My. God.

"I didn't understand why she was here until after you told me about her keys being locked in her car. Then it all made sense."

It made sense all right. Finally. Carrie **had** walked someplace that night, following the exact route I'd just taken. Of course! She'd gone to the Petrillo's when she'd discovered where her keys and purse were. But, neither Joan nor Max had been there to assist her. Only Warren.

Warren, who was in and out of reality on a daily basis due to his illness. Warren, who sometimes recognized people he knew and sometimes didn't. Warren, who, like others who suffered from Alzheimer's, could get physical or even violent at times.

Why hadn't that possibility come to me sooner? Then again, Joan hadn't spoken up when I mentioned that I wondered if one of Carrie's neighbors had a key. Maybe that's why my mind hadn't gone there. I'd taken for granted that my friends were always one hundred percent honest with me. What a naïve fool I was.

Carrie had a key to Miles's house and could have gone inside to use his phone, or even Dorothy Charm's if she was home. If only she had. But, why bother making a call if she could get what she needed just as easily? "**You** had her spare key."

"Yes," Joan admitted. Carrie had given her a copy of her house and car keys prior to Cassie moving in. "She must have come over to get the keys after I'd already left and woken up Warren when she knocked. When nobody came to the door, she used the key I keep under the swan statue to let herself in like I told her to do if she ever needed to. It's my fault she's dead, Diana."

"No, it isn't." If anyone was to blame for what had happened to Carrie, it was Max Petrillo. No wonder he lied about not being at the Branson Boys concert. He must have assumed that I'd put two and two together. Which I eventually did, **after** he lied to me. That reckless jackass should have stuck to the truth because now his dishonesty had come back to bite him in the butt big time.

"I only wanted to get out of the house for a little while." Joan sobbed. "If I'd just stayed home, Warren wouldn't have been woken up or..."

Or what? I dreaded hearing the exact details, but... "He didn't recognize Carrie." was the extent of my prodding.

"No, he didn't know who she was even by the time I got home. When I came in, he was...sitting on top of her. Straddling her. She was dead. I knew even before I felt for a pulse or a heartbeat." Warren had mistaken our colleague for a stranger who had broken into his home. "I stopped the intruder." he'd proudly announced to his wife upon her return.

Words escaped me as I envisioned what might have taken place when the two came face to face in the kitchen. Had Carrie assumed nobody was home and been blindsided by Warren? Or had he simply startled her, and she had tried to identify herself and explain her presence, to no avail?

"He must have pushed her or knocked her to the floor somehow, causing her to hit the back of her head."

Or might he have taken Carrie's head in his hands and slammed it against the floor once she was down? It had to have been a forceful blow to kill her. A hollowness in my stomach accompanied that grisly thought, but I tried to remain objective. Neither of us had been there to see it so it was anyone's guess. How must poor Joan have felt stepping into such a tragic scene?

My heart went out to her. "I can't imagine coming home and finding them like that."

"I didn't know what to do, Diana. I went into panic mode. As soon as I regained my wits a little, I called Max. He didn't answer the first time." Of course not, the irresponsible jerk was movin' and groovin' to the Branson Boys in his cowboy hat, leaving his sister-in-law to clean up the mess he'd caused! "So I texted him a minute later and he came down right away. In under an hour. God only knows how fast he must have driven. He's much better than me in a crisis so I asked him what we should do."

"Calling the police would've been a good start!" As badly as I felt for Joan, she'd clearly not used sound judgment that night.

"I didn't want Warren to go to jail!" she elucidated emphatically. "So, when Max suggested that we keep them out of it, I agreed right away." Naturally. He didn't want the authorities to know that he was at fault for his brother being unsupervised at the time of Carrie's assault. Knowing nothing about criminal law, I wondered if he could be charged with criminal negligence. If so, my voice would be the loudest one cheering in the courtroom when he was convicted.

"Then we had to figure out what to do with the…with Carrie. She couldn't be found in our house if we were going to keep Warren's involvement a secret so Max decided…"

Max! "Where is *Max* right now?" I demanded. "Call him and tell him to get his sorry ass down here so I can give him a piece of my mind!"

"Oh no, Diana. He'll be furious with me for telling you all this."

"Well, too bad for him!" I was furious, myself, and intended to hear what he had to say about his thoughtless and despicable actions. "In fact, let me have your cell for a minute. Set it up for me to text him." I instructed her, unwilling to let my technological ineptness get in the way of having it out with him ASAP.

"Let's leave him out of this. He doesn't even need to know that you know."

"Oh, he's **going to know**! I want him to. I also want him to know that I didn't appreciate his little scare tactics."

"I am *so* sorry about that, Diana. I *promise* you that I had no idea he would call you like that. You must have been scared out of your mind. When you told me what he had said to you over the phone, I was absolutely *livid* with him."

"I believe you, Joan." And I did. Despite being mixed up in this terrible situation, she was only guilty of making some poor choices in the interest of her husband. "But, trust me, the rock was a thousand times more frightening."

"The *rock*? What are you talking about?"

It didn't surprise me that she wasn't aware of the prior night's incident. If she had been ticked off about his call to me, then she would be horrified and infuriated by the shattered window. "Give me the phone." I repeated. *TROUBLE. GET TO MY HOUSE NOW.* I quickly typed, in all caps to express the urgency of the request. Next up, giving my friend a recount of Max's latest attempt to terrify me.

The overwhelming remorse Joan displayed almost made me regret telling her. But, things needed to be out in the open. So, as we awaited the arrival of the younger Petrillo brother, I pumped her for more details about what had transpired once Max had shown up at her house that fateful night.

Because she lived so close by, the decision to move Carrie to her own home was a simple one for Max. Wrapping her body in a blanket, he would carry it to her house in the dead of night and stage the scene to make it appear as though she had fallen down the stairs. Making it look like she'd never left her house was also Max's doing. Eliminating that train of thought was imperative in order to protect his brother.

And himself, I reminded myself, even if Joan was willing to overlook that important factor. That explained why Carrie's coat had been hung on the coatrack. Someone who had never been to the sisters' home would not have known about Carrie's tendency to toss it over a chair at the kitchen table. "But, the coat was clean." I said, puzzled by this portion of the story. "Why wasn't there blood all over it?" Rather a gruesome question, but a necessary one. The lack of blood on it just didn't seem possible.

"Honestly, I have no idea. There really wasn't a lot of blood, given that she died from a head wound. But, her green knit cap and her scarf soaked up most of what there was." Joan explained as best she could. "Max lifted her head and I slid a towel underneath her so the coat never made contact with the back of her head, I don't think. The way my hands were trembling, I'm surprised that she didn't wind up with blood all over her."

Deputy Miller had told us that every head injury was different, as was the amount of blood that escaped from each one. The severity of the injury wasn't necessarily reflected by how much blood had seeped out.

The bloodied winter accessories wouldn't have fit the story of Carrie being home all night. I supposed that was why they'd needed to be disposed of. Under the sad circumstances, a missing scarf and hat were likely to be overlooked. But, thankfully, they hadn't been. Otherwise I might never have come to find out the truth. Although, I wasn't quite sure if that was a good thing or a bad thing yet.

"We need to have the police here before Max arrives." I impressed upon Joan. Uncertain about his location when I'd sent the text on her phone, there was no way of telling when he'd show up since there had been no reply from his end. It was possible that he hadn't read the message yet, but I wasn't taking any chances.

"It might be better if you called them." was my advice. Although she wasn't directly involved in Carrie's death, Joan had knowledge of it and had assisted in tampering with the scene in an attempt to throw off law enforcement, which was bound to have consequences. Confessing to these acts would probably be in her best interest, I felt.

Stubbornly, she refused to make the call. Protecting her husband, I completely understood. But, in doing so, Max Petrillo would never be held accountable for his actions. "Then I'll call," I decided, taking out my cell. "Max left Warren here alone that night, Joan. It's *his* fault that Carrie is dead and I want him punished!"

Joan's anxiety level rose. "You can't." she replied meekly.

"I *am*." I declared.

"Please don't!" she begged, visibly distraught now. "Max didn't leave Warren home by himself that night, Diana. *I* did."

## CHAPTER TWENTY EIGHT

What? It took a minute for her words to register. "*You* left Warren alone? I thought Max was here watching him when you left."

"No. Initially, he was supposed to be. But, that afternoon, he called to tell me that his friend had won free tickets to that Branson Boys concert. He wanted to go, so he was unable to stay with Warren."

"Why didn't you just call one of us to cancel then? We would have understood."

"I was going to. But, I'd *really* been looking forward to getting together with you guys. I just wanted to have a normal life again for a few hours. A few laughs, a little fun. And Warren almost never gets out of bed when I put him down for the night."

I wasn't quite sure what to say. Here I'd been placing the blame on her brother-in-law when in reality, it wasn't his fault at all. "So, Max didn't know you were going to leave Warren unattended?"

"No, he had no idea about it. Not until after I came home and found them on the floor. You can imagine how enraged he was when I told him what had happened. But, honestly, I thought Warren would sleep the whole time I was gone like he does almost every other night. He isn't prone to violence either. Carrie coming in unexpectedly must have thrown him off."

I hoped that what Joan was telling me was true. "Hasn't he pushed you around before?" I asked, recalling some comment she had made in the past.

"Yes, he'll struggle with me, or Max, from time to time if he's in an uncooperative mood.

But, he's *never* struck us or done anything remotely harmful. He just didn't know what was going on that night."

I was torn. I had to believe that my good friend, who had even left her job of many years to care for her spouse, wouldn't have allowed him to be alone in the house if she truly felt that he was a danger to himself or others. Nonetheless, had she not made that decision, Carrie Landry would still be alive.

Pondering this complex moral dilemma, my mind was elsewhere when Max arrived. I'd not even heard his car pull in, yet, suddenly, there he was walking in the door. "What's *she* doing here?" he demanded angrily as he glared in my direction.

"She knows. Everything."

The younger Petrillo was clearly annoyed. I was nervous about what he might do. "You do realize that this entire mess is *her* fault, don't you?" he snarled, pointing an accusatory finger at his brother's wife. I suddenly recalled the day Joan had come to help clean my apartment, just a few days after Carrie's purported fall. "*I'm* here now. There won't be any problems." he had snarled at her as we were leaving her house. That comment took on a whole new meaning now.

Friend or not, I couldn't deny Joan's culpability. But, Max also played an active role in everything that had followed. He was no innocent angel. "Joan may be guilty of leaving Warren home alone, but your interference and scheme to cover things up only complicated matters." I reminded him in an angry tone.

"Interference? I don't think so. She called *me* to fix the problem that *she* caused. Whatever I've done has been to make sure that my brother doesn't suffer because of *her* stupidity. I was only trying to protect Warren and cover Joan's ass too. Why else would I have told her to call

Carrie after she found the body? To make it seem like she thought Carrie was still alive at that late hour. How does that help *me*? It doesn't. It helped her and only her."

What he said made sense. But, that didn't mean that his plot to hide the truth was a good idea. "If the two of you had been honest and called the cops that night to explain what had happened, we wouldn't be in this predicament right now." Damn, I was pissed at the two of them! "You've put me in a very difficult position here."

"*We* did?" Max roared, "Try again. You put *yourself* in this position with your nonstop questions and conjectures. If you had kept your nose out of it, you wouldn't even know about any of this." Much as I hated it, he was right on that count too. If I had left things alone, I had to concede, my nosy self wouldn't currently be jammed between a rock and a hard place. What in Holy Hell should I do?

Joan prattled on for several minutes about Warren being an innocent victim and promised that her often confused mate would never again be left home alone or put into a situation where he could do anybody physical harm. "He's already on the waiting list for several nursing facilities with staff that have experience in caring for Alzheimer's patients. *Please* don't make Warren pay for my foolish mistake." she pleaded, with guilt in her heart and tears in her eyes.

For the time being, I was inclined to keep my mouth shut and keep what I'd learned to myself, at least until I had more time to think about the gobs of new information that had come my way. "I won't say anything...for now. But, I can't make any promises."

"Thank you, Diana!" Joan sobbed, grasping me in a tight embrace. Had I not been so overwhelmed with shock and nerves and astonishment at what had gone down, I would likely have been sobbing too. "I do think the two of you should think about coming clean to the police." I encouraged the pair, even though I knew that the chance of them taking my advice was slimmer than a supermodel the month before New York Fashion Week.

"I've gotta go." I said, sauntering over to the door. "By the way," I directed my gaze towards Max. "I didn't appreciate your late night threat Wednesday night. It interrupted my beauty sleep."

"Listen, I did what I had to do." he shrugged casually. "When Joan told me that you had noticed that the scarf was missing, I hoped the call would scare you off."

"And the rock?"

"Isn't it obvious? You'd figured out that Carrie didn't die at home and that her body had been moved. Clearly, I needed to step it up a notch to get my message across to someone so thick. "

"Message received, loud and clear. But, do expect a call from me soon. To let you know the cost of replacing the window. It's Cassie's, not mine. She's already been robbed of her sister. It's the least you can do." With that, I turned my back on the dirty look he shot me and walked out of the house.

I spent the remainder of the day slumped on the couch and pacing around the house absentmindedly. I talked to no one, for fear of what might slip out of my mouth once I began to speak. Finally, around nine thirty, I changed into my nightgown and plunked myself onto Carrie's bed. An important decision needed to be made, one that would affect many lives and perhaps even alter the course of some. Understanding that what I opted to do would have such an impact was not a feeling I relished whatsoever. I closed my eyes in the hopes that the perfect solution would come to me in my dreams.

A FIRST GRADE FATALITY

When my Monday morning began, much too soon for a sleepyhead like me, who had barely slept a wink, I went through the usual motions and readied myself for the work week ahead. Regardless of whether or not the facts about how Carrie had really been killed came to light or not, by my own doing or in some other way, I had a job to do and a life to lead. I intended to do both, comfortable with the choices I had made overnight.

Dale was out sick that day, so I spent my lunch hour in solitude, happily munching on a Granny Smith apple. Although I spent much of the previous day wishing I'd never found out what really transpired the night Carrie left us forever, the truth had brought closure to me. Tomorrow is never a guarantee, my friend's death had helped me realize. I needed to make the most of each new day, in her memory.

Were it possible to bring forth only *some* of what I had learned and dictate suitable consequences to each individual, I would have had very little difficulty. But the Petrillos were a package deal. To incriminate one would incriminate all three.

Joan had lied to me, by omission, time after time. But, the remorse I had seen as she pled for me to stay silent had been genuine. In my heart, I knew that Joan had been tortured internally from the moment she had stepped through the door and found her husband atop her dead friend. "How can I face her parents?" Joan had asked at the memorial service, wondering how *she* could have let this happen to their daughter. She would forever be haunted by that night and the part that she had played in bringing Carrie's life to its end.

Warren had killed Carrie Landry, but the tragic results were unintentional. Would Joan's ailing husband ever have assaulted the sweet young teacher if his memory had not been affected by the wicked disease that would eventually claim his own life? Never. Poor Warren had been unnecessarily and unfairly punished long before he'd made that terrible mistake and taken a life. I prayed that he would soon be someplace where trained professionals could keep watch over his actions and health.

As for Max Petrillo, the fury I'd originally felt towards him had subsided once Joan had admitted that she, not her brother-in-law, was the one responsible for Warren being home alone when Carrie arrived. However, the "solution" he had come up with still did not sit well with me. The thought of the muscleman hauling Carrie's body around, devoid of emotion for the lifeless girl, made me angry. Faulting him for wanting to keep his brother and sister-in-law safe would be wrong, as well as hypocritical. But, I couldn't help but wonder how things may have played out if he'd simply reported the tragic incident to the authorities. Would Warren have been taken from his home and/or sent to prison? Could Joan have been implicated as an accessory and faced equally dire consequences? I really had no idea and hoped that we would never find out those answers.

I'd probably never find out how or why the Redmond School rumor mill had begun spinning the tale that the young first grade teacher had been *murdered* either, but it is what it is. Sometimes those parents on the ball fields right on point with the "information" they spread, and other times they're dead wrong. But, if it hadn't been for that inaccurate gossip, I might not have been so determined to find out what had happened that night.

I'd left a Dunkin Donuts gift card on "Creepy Jim's" desk in his dreary office on my way in that morning to thank him for "watching out for me" as well, since he, too, had played a part in my obsessive quest for the truth. Had he not written that note, unwittingly reinforcing my belief that something fishy was going on, I might very well have given up on my search.

Oh, who I am I kidding? My one track mind would surely have found some other reason to rationalize my sleuthing and suspicions! Either way, I would now have to "eat crow" because my investigating had turned up "nothing". Dale was going to *love* rubbing that in my face. Oh well.

If I truly believed that it would help the Landry family to know the truth, my decision to keep mum or not would have been even more difficult. Yes, it had ended the nagging suspicions that had plagued me, and I could now put it behind me and move on. But, would hearing that their daughter or sister or cousin had spent her final moments face to face with an attacker, most likely terrified, make it *easier* for them to accept their loss? Certainly not. It was gut wrenching enough to know that Carrie would never marry or have children of her own or experience countless other joys.

Letting Carrie Landry's family and friends believe that her "fall down the stairs" was a simple accident was best for everyone involved. Because, in reality, this "first grade fatality" *was* just an accident after all.

www.ingramcontent.com/pod-product-compliance
Lightning Source LLC
Chambersburg PA
CBHW070606130626
46556CB00001B/284